bookmark

noun (place in book,

a strip of leather, ca.
one's place in a book.

Bookmark

© 2025 by Blair Grant. All rights reserved, including the right to reproduce this work in any form.

ISBN: 9798265728685

This is a work of fiction. Names, characters, places, and incidents are either products of the author's imagination or are used fictitiously. Any resemblance to actual persons, living or dead, events, or locales is entirely coincidental.

BOOKMARK

Blair Grant

Content warning

This novel explores themes of trauma, domestic abuse, and suicide, which may be distressing for some readers. If you or someone you know is affected by these issues, please seek support from a qualified professional or a trusted helpline in your area.

Chapter one

The pages of a book have the capacity to stifle and satisfy in equal measure. The reader, if they allow it, may be taken away from racing thoughts or responsibility, even for the briefest of moments. Or, as the pages are turned, the tip of a finger licked for traction, the words may provide the fuel for the narrative in their head to gallop onwards. The reins have fallen from my hands, thinks the reader, and the horse steams further ahead.

Then the page is turned. The horse slows. The heart stops racing. More words are read and the breathing calms, no longer audible, until the reader is once again taken in by the story. Or the opposite is true. For who has not felt that it is only when a book is opened and read, that the uncontrollable horses of life settle to graze? If only until the page is folded over, or a bookmark placed within, before it finds itself once again on the dusty shelf, bedside floor or table.

The only books that Ellis saw that morning remained unopened, at least to him, protected from the morning dew within their forced shelter of white recycling bags. The driver had only just turned the radio on, but the music was still too faint to hear for those stood outside the cab. Ellis hoped it would still be playing on the way back to base; anything to avoid the forced conversation. The jovial voice of the presenter allowed all who sat on the dusty seats to dull their thoughts as the lorry made its way through the nondescript villages and towns. The drive gave each of them time to contemplate. Each man, all of whom would be tired and most of them hungry, would have purposefully spent another day sorting through pavement side bins full of discarded waste. Empty cans of beans lay beside the structural remains of used jam jars and condiment bottles, most of which lay in shards at the bottom of each box. Beside the boxes lay sacks full of paper and cardboard.

  The tip of his finger turned pale before the blood came. It was not of the deep kind regularly seen by those whose hands were cast into buckets of tin and glass, yet even the smallest of grazes could bleed. The loose flap of skin that now hung over the gash gave the wound a route for the droplets to gather, then fall, onto the pavement. Pushing the finger against the inside of his trouser pocket, Ellis watched as the blood soaked into the fabric and left a mottled crimson mark that grew slowly around the edges. The jeans, though on their fourth or fifth outing of the week, were still relatively clean. Most importantly they were dry, a rarity that summer.

  On a good day, the contents would be washed and intact, ready to be sorted into the various bin compartments of the truck. That summer rarely provided good days. The wispy, paintbrush stroke clouds of the morning had turned into a mass of greying darkness, brooding and heavy with rain. Its promise soon followed, soaking the workers as they walked through the cul-de-sacs, well-kept gardens, and the occasional tree-lined street.

The pebble-dashed houses showed little sign of life from their respective inhabitants. At that time in the morning it was already too late for some, yet too early for others. Hours before, cars would have left the various driveways destined for jobs, some loved, most disliked. The office small talk would follow, then onto the new timesheets and meetings with bosses, or the school lessons, appointments and weekly food shops. The items of sixteen B had been scrawled quickly in what was now smudged black ink onto the back of a ripped envelope: Toilet roll. Oranges. Milk. Bread. Bleach. Onions. Toothpaste. Midweek life in note form. Ellis held it before stuffing it into one of the compartments alongside a bundle of newspapers. On top of the bundle lay a book, in good condition with its cover intact. Ellis lifted it up and inspected the nondescript picture on the front. 'Watching the Door,' read the title. He turned it in his hands and without thinking walked towards the cab. He opened his bag and cast the book into it. Once done, he returned his attention back to his duties.

Others in the lane still slept, for reasons known only to them. It did not concern anyone else. If they were to wake up now and peer out their windows at the summer morning outside, they would see an empty street, but for the three refuse collectors. They would look down to observe the men picking up blue and white boxes with netting over them to keep the birds and the wind out, each as destructive a force as the other. Nothing to see, they would think, and as good a signal to go back to bed as any other.

Then they would pull the still warm covers over their bodies, hoping for sleep, or perhaps a different outcome the next time they woke. They would hear the various glass bottles and jars clinking and smashing as they were cast into the truck. A good ear would recognise the difference between the sizes and contents. It would know if one was empty or filled with the plentiful rain of that week.

There were no plasters in the truck's cab, but a cigarette paper, rolled over several times then folded to form an elongated triangle, stopped the bleeding that the jeans could not. Gloves were of course available, yellow and bright, but they soon filled with water, and when mixed with the humidity of the summer, made working – and smoking – increasingly difficult as the day progressed. On most days the bins of the town would be emptied by mid-afternoon and the men would huddle together in the cab. The drive allowed each to savour in the respite that comes after a period of activity, made greater from the enjoyment of not having to work, but still getting paid for the time. Ellis knew that this day would be like all the others.

'What are you learning Italian for?' sneered the driver.

'I wanted to do something different,' said Ellis, forcing down his desire to ask in return what business it was of his.

The book was out of sight, but he knew that it had been seen some days ago when he emptied his bag. The answer was a well-rehearsed one. Simple and non-committal - something to kill any follow up question.

A grunt and upwards nod of the driver's head signalled the end of the conversation. To Ellis' left sat Jordan. Between his feet lay a plastic bag containing what would by now have been cans of warm lager. Without any breakfast it hits one more strongly. There's a different effect of the alcohol when sitting in a pub with friends, sipping over-priced beer or cider and watching whatever football happens to be on. One still gets the warm feeling of something better, whatever better means, being just round the corner, and the knowledge that whatever it was, is, had been or could have been, was not as bad as it was before the drink had been swallowed. No, it's not a new aftershave. Yes, we are still in touch. They are well thanks. Not bad. And you? Glad to hear it. Pub conversation is not mirrored in the cab of a bin lorry first thing in the morning. This was an unwritten rule, and one followed by all.

While others lay in their beds, warm and dozing, Jordan's third can was already empty and placed back in the plastic bag. The rest would be spaced in neat intervals until the drive back to base. But at that time in the morning, the thought remained a distant one. Ellis looked over at his fellow workers and watched as Jordan rubbed a dirty sleeve over his runny nose. The movement made Ellis sniff involuntarily and the smell of the driver's breath, heavy and strong with the staleness of coffee, met his nostrils. Shaking his head at the offer of a can, eyebrows were raised, and a slight smile came across Jordan's face. At this time there's a dullness that comes from the beer. It's a warming dullness, filled with some positivity, but a dullness all the same.

'I'll see to it then,' said the sleep-deprived, raspy voice.

Ellis looked on as the can was sunk in four gulps. The tin was then crushed between Jordan's long fingers, before the sleeve, speckled with white paint and the now dried dirt of whatever had sat inside the last row of sodden recycling boxes, was once again brought up to his running nose. The host of the radio show read the headlines of the morning and cigarettes were rolled.

Now, some hours later, the cans are long finished, and they give a dull rattle as the lorry turns a corner, their sound a reminder of the morning. The cigarette paper has done its job, but a proper scab will take some days to form. Ellis looked in his bag and rooted around between used sandwich bags and a half-drunk bottle of water. He retrieved an ochre, yellowing pair of waterproof gloves, slightly older than the ones that were now being handed out at the base, then placed them on the dashboard ready for tomorrow's shift. As with today, yesterday, and the days that came before, they would not be used.

He looked ahead and watched as the driver weaved the lorry through the bends and corners of small country roads. The rain came down in sheets now, heavier than before, hitting the windscreen of the truck, before being cast aside by the heavy-duty black windscreen wipers. The radio had been turned off and the drive back was silent, all but for a snoring passenger who had rested his head unintentionally on Ellis' shoulder. The smell of rolling tobacco and stale beer met his nose as he shook his left shoulder upwards, forcing Jordan to wake with a grunt. Looking briefly with anger and confusion at the two men beside him, he turned to face the passenger side window, placed a head, damp with sweat, on the headrest, and fell back asleep.

Approaching his flat later that afternoon, Ellis noticed a smashed bottle outside the main door, the broken glass on this occasion not being caused by himself or his colleagues. The intercom remained out of use, its blue and orange wires pushing out from the casing to form bow-shapes that sat against the door. Paint flaked around the rim of the safety glass, and Ellis rubbed his thumb along its rim and watched as a brown patch fell silently to the cold, concrete floor. Reaching for his keys, the cut on his finger rubbed against the seam of his jean pocket and he inhaled sharply, swearing under his breath. The stairwell light was broken but the June summer evening lit his path to the top floor. From outside the communal window on the second floor, he heard the noise of car stereos and faint voices from the street below. The rota for cleaning the stairs lay on the floor outside flat four, the drying Sellotape that had held it up over the weekend now gathering dust.

Once inside, he looked at the scattered pizza and chip shop takeaway menus on the floor and scanned the other letters between the food offerings. He guessed two of them to be a council tax bill and a bank statement and this proved to be correct. Without a need to keep either and with no shredder available, he tore both letters evenly into strips and pushed them inside the remnants of a litre bottle of Pepsi Max. Watching as they settled into the now flat, black liquid, he shook the bottle until it formed a semi-solid grey lump of paper. This efficient – if unconventional – approach to personal finance safety was a regular pastime.

In the kitchen, Ellis took two onions from the bottom of his fridge and removed the outer brown skin. Taking a blunt knife from the drawer, he strained upwards and lifted a worn wooden chopping board down from its hook. Slicing the onion as finely as he could, his mind wandered to that day at work and what was to come tomorrow. There was nothing to come tomorrow, he reasoned, before placing a carrot on the chopping board and dicing it with the same blunt knife.

He pictured how he would spend his Thursday. He'd rub the sleep from his eyes as he stared outside of the curtained window, the phone alarm still ringing from its place on the seat by the bed. A hastily eaten breakfast of toast and coffee would follow. Perhaps a shower, perhaps not. The same clothes from today would be folded over on one arm of the living room sofa. Seven more payments left, and it was his. Clothes on. Out the door. Wait for the twenty-two bus. Sit down and enjoy the twenty minutes of relative calm before the bus dropped him off at the base. After six months, the routine now showed little variation. Sometimes the toast was brown, but not often.

The TV accompanied him at dinner. Eating mince with vegetables from a chipped off-white bowl, Ellis sat at his table and looked at the summer drinkers in the bar opposite. The late evening sun still shone brightly, and it bathed those standing with their pints, glasses of wine and cocktails, with a barley-coloured, pastel glow. Ellis watched as the owner of an art gallery pulled the shutters down, counting down the seconds from thirty in his head. After twenty two seconds, two seconds later than usual, the owner was pulling the front door behind him and locking it for the day. He too joined the gathered drinkers, and his deep red leather satchel shone warmly in the sun. Ellis chewed on his food, passing an undercooked piece of carrot between his teeth. He wondered how the owner had spent his day. He thought whether or not he had toast and coffee for his breakfast, or if he fell asleep each night with a sense of emptiness. No stress about the day to come, just the knowledge that it would be the same as any other.

Perhaps he busied himself taking calls and speaking to potential customers, before sourcing the very best art that he could afford, thought Ellis. After lunch, he may walk among his acquired paintings and take the time to appreciate them, whatever that meant to him. He could sit and write about how each piece of art made him feel, perhaps fearful that a steady stream of customers could swarm the shop at any minute to take them from him. Ellis wondered if the owner had a picture of a boat at sea. A boat that seemed to dip and rise in the swell on its canvas, and one that made those who saw it feel a growing anxiety; the kind that begins in the lower stomach and builds from there. He looked at the owner as he sipped his bottle of beer and asked himself if perhaps, he had a watercolour of a woman in the field, like the one Ellis had seen on the school trip. The one with the brown eyes. The one that made him involuntarily rub a calming finger over the bridge of his nose and focus on his breath as it steadily slowed.

It was then that he remembered the book that he had taken from the pile of newspapers that morning. Opening his bag, he removed it and was pleased to see that not only was it dry, but it was in far better condition than his initial inspection had pointed to. In fact, Ellis could have sworn that the book was brand new. He thought it strange how it had found its way onto the cold street where its next stop would have been turned to pulp, or burned, or whatever it was they did with the rubbish. He did not know, nor did he care. Had the book landed on the pile by some accident or misunderstanding? He considered the possibility. A heavy hand when rushed, or a tired set of eyes, could have seen the book move from what Ellis imagined to be its rightful place. Yes, he thought, a book could easily find itself cast aside in such wearied circumstances.

But no, he told himself. That was not the reason. This book was more likely to be an unwanted gift. Flicked through once then disposed of. 'Watching the door,' Ellis whispered. He thumbed the ivory pages and stopped on page 178 where at once his eyes were drawn to a scrap of orange and pale blue card. Taking it between his fingers he could see that it had once been a part of something bigger. A postcard perhaps, or a small print that someone had once kept on a desk or mantelpiece. He inspected the back for further clues and in the corner, in barely legible ink, scratched in what looked like haste, some letters smudged by a clumsy hand, he noticed the words. Redacted now by crease and by tear, he read what he believed to be the author's closing message. It read: '*I know this will not be enough, but I cannot in good conscience not give you something for the pain I have caused. Tell her,*' then where the next word should have been there was nothing. The paper canvas on which it had been written had long since been crumpled, torn and hidden, or washed away, never to be seen again down a swirling toilet. Yet the words that were read would remain, thought Ellis.

Chapter two

'Ho preso l'autobus per venire qui,' whispered Ellis to himself.

'Ho preso. L'autobus.'

'Per venire qui.'

'Ho preso.'

'Qui. Qui. Qui.'

Ellis slowly broke up the words then read the phrase over and over in his head, whispering the phonetic 'kwee' to himself. His right thumb held down page thirty-eight of the battered, second-hand Italian phrasebook. The scab on his finger had now formed and sat right below the knuckle.

'He was a journalist,' said a faint voice that travelled from across the room.

Ellis looked up, unsure if the statement was directed at him. 'Sorry?' he asked, scanning the room to see who had spoken.

'Mazzini,' said the voice, with an unwavering tone of confidence. 'Giuseppe Mazzini. Architect of Italian unification. I said he was a journalist,' came the voice of a man who sat towards the back of the canteen. 'Slumber not in the tents of your fathers. The world is advancing. Advance with it,' said the voice again. 'An interesting way of thinking, wouldn't you say? He wrote that. Have you heard it before?' asked the man. Ellis gave a faint smile and nodded. He was unaccustomed to hearing any conversation in the staff canteen this early in the morning, let alone anything directed at him. Even if it was a topic he had taken an interest in or been aware of, this hour of the day would have stifled his ability for any meaningful response.

'Eh, yeah... thanks for,' but before he could finish his sentence, the voice rose again.

'Mussolini too,' now louder than before. 'He used to be an editor. And a Marxist. Used to be, mind. But you know all that,' he added. 'He never saw Switzerland in the end,' laughed the man, smiling to himself with pleasure. 'Her name escapes me, but the mistress went the same way as he did. Clara, I think it was. Left in a pile with the rest of them on Piazzale Loreto,' he bellowed.

The four black metal legs of a green plastic chair were pushed back, causing a harsh, shrill and prolonged noise to echo across the room. Some others looked up from their flasks and newspapers at the impromptu movement.

'I noticed the book. Why Italian?' asked the man, who now stood unthreateningly over Ellis with his arm outstretched awaiting a reciprocal hand.

Ellis knew the man to be Andy. Before a day filled with lining up rubbish bins on the pavement, he was an auditor. Either that or a painter. Or an accountant. Ellis did not know; nobody quite knew, but he was something before this. At least that was what he heard other people in the canteen saying when Andy was out of earshot. He was something. Ellis had questioned what the something meant, then found himself getting annoyed by the implied meaning. What right did the men in the canteen have to place a label of something or someone onto another man? Was he himself something? He did not think so. The recognition of this made him retract further into himself and his thoughts that morning.

Everyone knew Andy around the base. Ellis and the others did not dislike him, but he was not someone that people sought the company of. Andy came with an atmosphere and a mood that Ellis found hard to place. It was not his demeanour or his mannerisms, nor had it anything to do with his personality as such, but a feeling of low-level disquiet could be sensed when he was near. Despite regularly striking up conversations with those who would listen, he was a quiet type, and far from imposing or brash. Andy looked at you with his clear blue eyes when he spoke. When he did, you listened, but you did not know why. Ellis wondered if that was what he found so unnerving.

Under his high-visibility yellow vest, Andy wore a threadbare long sleeved blue t-shirt. Ellis could just make out the white print of faded writing on the sleeve that read: Copenhagen. His boots looked new and had clearly been polished that morning. Ellis thought it noticeable given that this was far from common amongst the workers, not least of all because it was the end of another working week. A slightly sunburnt nose and cheekbones held up opaque, caramel-coloured glasses, and like most of the men in the canteen that morning, he was unshaven.

'I don't really know,' said Ellis, in response to the question. 'We studied a bit of French in school like most of us do, but I fancied something new,' he added, rubbing the short growth of his own two-day old stubble as he did so.

'Ellis!' called the driver, his head peering round the canteen door. 'That's us. Come on.' Ellis stood up and nodded in the direction of Andy.

'Cheers, Andy,' he said, as he made his way to the lorry and the start of that morning's shift. Andy smiled back and went back to the green chair by the window, watching as a steady procession of vans and lorries made their way out the yard and onto the main road. Someone had taken out the hose to clean one of the lorries and the smell of water on warm concrete still hung in the air. Andy inhaled deeply. Taking out a small notebook from his bag, he rooted around for a minute until he found a cracked, black biro between the detritus of orange peel, crumbs, plastic bags, two pairs of protective gloves and an unopened bottle of factor thirty sun cream. Looking across the now empty canteen, he licked the dry nib to stimulate the flow of ink. Writing something over a couple of lines, he paused, then put everything back in his bag before making his way out into the yard, kicking a loose stone as he did so.

Ellis thought the cab had a different atmosphere to it that morning. The first few hours passed by in the usual manner, which is to say that nothing of any note took place. Yet despite that, the mood of the trio was different to the previous days of the summer. The driver, a stout man in his fifties, whose control of the radio Ellis now realised was regularly used as a punishment for some perceived misdemeanour or unwelcome remark, had been left on that morning. Not only that, but the volume, which otherwise would be hovering above the faintly audible benchmark, was now at a normal level. The other passenger, Ellis' fellow curb side loader Jordan, was also in a strangely unfamiliar mood: one of happiness. He had initiated conversation from the moment the lorry left the depot.

'Andy's a good lad. The type of person who speaks a lot of sense and he knows what he's talking about most of the time,' said Jordan, his hand reaching into the plastic bag which was once again full of beer. 'I saw the pair of you talking earlier,' he added, hurriedly responding to Ellis' expression of shock at the unprompted conversation.

'Oh, yeah, yeah, you're right,' said Ellis, his voice wavering. 'How do you know him?' he asked, making eye contact with his colleague for what felt like the first time that week.

'We've known each other since we were kids, mate!' proclaimed Jordan. Ellis, taken aback by the jovial small talk looked across to the driver to gauge his reaction to their voices as they merged with the song playing on the radio. He kept his eyes on the road, but Ellis could distinctly make out that he was mouthing what looked to be the semi-correct lyrics of the song. Noticing Ellis was looking at him, he stopped, looked down at the radio, then took his eyes back on the road. The radio stayed on.

'We used to run about together at school,' added Jordan. 'I wasn't really interested in any of it, school, I mean, but he was. Didn't stop us getting on or anything like that, but he liked to learn, and I liked...well, I didn't!' Taking a sip from the can, he went on. 'One summer, I got a job working at the shop where the bookies is now. The one in town. Do you know it?' Ellis did not but nodded regardless.

'Right, well, it was just me and the owner, an old boy called Robert Prestwick. He used to be quite involved with the Church and unless you mentioned that or questioned him on anything, he usually treated you well. I had to come in and do the papers most mornings before someone else collected them for delivery. Anyway, when it was just me in the shop, I used to sneak a quarter bottle of whisky inside my sock, so it was hidden by my trouser leg. I'd make my way outside the back entrance and, making sure nobody was looking from the houses opposite, I'd hide it behind one of the big black bins on Melrose Street,' said Jordan. He smiled proudly to himself as he remembered the scene.

'Andy and I would take it down to the beach and get a fire going,' he added. 'We'd burn plastic, fish boxes, old netting and whatever driftwood we could find. When the sun went down, we would walk up and down the beach to find old cans. Beer, juice, anything would do. When you got a can, you'd give it a quick rinse in the sea, nothing fancy, but most of the time they needed a rinse. When you'd filled it up with sea water again you stuck the cans on some of the embers. After a minute or so, we'd pour the warm water over our hands. You ever poured warm water over your hands outside when you've drunk a quarter bottle of whisky, Ellis?' he asked.

Ellis had not, but he said yes regardless. He often did so. Jordan paused for a few seconds, looking down at the plastic bag between his feet. 'It's all ahead of you then,' he said quietly. Ellis did not know if he was supposed to hear what had just been said, so he kept quiet and pretended he had missed it. Jordan pointed outside at nothing in particular from the speeding lorry, the blur at the end of his finger fading as they drove on. After a couple of minutes, he continued with his story. Ellis recognised the same joviality and happiness in his tone and felt relieved. This had been the longest conversation he had had during work, and he now felt a genuine interest in hearing more about Andy, and, he hoped about Jordan.

'There was one day in English class he got up to read a poem he'd written. Well, you know what it's like, don't you? We all had to write something, but he was the first one up to read his. Anyway, nobody understood what he was talking about in the end! It was all about a tree that grew in the dark of the forest and how that related to our lives. Something about the movement of what we do, how we do it, and when, but like I say, we all just sat there,' laughed Jordan. 'I looked down at my own page and I've got all these sentences together that rhymed, then he went up and read something like that to everyone. I wasn't the only one who thought they didn't know what a poem was as you could see others making quick changes to their work when he was reading his,' Jordan said with a smile across his face. He took a sip from the can.

'Not by the time he'd finished though. When he finished, we were all listening,' said Jordan, pausing and looking across to the driver whose focus appeared to still be on the radio.

'Still though, you knew then he was different. Pretty sound lad. That's the same one he read at the funeral. Real shame what happened. A shame for him in a lot of ways, but he's still going. That's all you can do,' said Jordan, hesitating as he found the words. He opened another can, his fourth of the morning, and gave Ellis a faint smile. There was the briefest of silences as the radio cut to a second of static. Jordan pulled at a loose thread that hung from the base of his seatbelt. The driver broke the silence.

'That's lunchtime. We'll stop here then crack on after,' he said.

After they had eaten, there were only four or five more streets to do before they could all go home for the weekend. They all worked quickly on a Friday afternoon and before long, they were back at the base.

Ellis thought to himself that today had been one of the first days since late May without any rain. Now in the early afternoon, the sun stood proudly against a clear blue sky and bathed the workers in a bright, warming light. Ellis watched as nameless people, at least to him, left the base in cars, bicycles and on foot, impatient to get back to their lives and away from work for two days. Seven in the morning on Monday was a long way off and given greater distance by the bright sunshine forecast for the weekend. Ellis noticed that to a man, and they were all men, that each carried their own individual, well-worn smile. You could see it in the eyes of some, while others showed their joy – or was it relief, he wondered – across their lips. Lips that rose at the corners at the thought of spending time with family, or of walking, or meeting friends to talk and experience all that could be experienced in forty-eight hours. Smiles that came unintentionally from thoughts of companionship and live music, of cooking good food and reading the Sunday papers. He looked closely at the smiles and thought it unfair how his was the only face without one.

Chapter three

It is only when a found object is needed that it can truly be considered found. Ellis sat on his bedroom floor and watched as the wind blew at the tops of some far-off trees. His eye caught the flat roofs opposite his own; their tiles tarnished with soot and bird shit. Patches of moss and cream-white lichen grew towards the side closest to the eaves, then the colours changed, as did his gaze, now unfocused. Ellis looked ahead and felt the dry, dusty air touch the base of his nostrils and fill his stomach and chest, before he blew it out slowly through pursed lips. She had told him to do it. She had heard that someone had done it and recommended it to him. It mattered little now, he thought.

While cleaning that morning, he had come across a small box, hastily packed, from a previous visit to his parents' house. The office, he was told, would be important. No, that's not what his parents had said, he recalled. It would add market value, yes, that was it, and anything he could do to help them clear out some of his books would be appreciated.

Some of the contents sat in a broken cardboard box and one book in particular had piqued his interest. As such, 'The Early Universe,' a book for children, now sat open by his feet. He once again took it into his hands and felt the memory of youth flush over him. He could taste the strong orange flavoured cordial, not adequately diluted in the soft water, as it clung to, rasped at, then dried his throat. He could hear the TV theme songs and felt the dread of homework; the feeling of sketching paper and pencils on his skin. The drawings of stars that adorned his walls. The ripped pages. The paper cut. But what he saw then he did not remember. For in the back pages, a Christmas card had been placed. A robin redbreast sat atop the handle of a spade, as snow fell on the trees around it. He picked it up but nothing was written on it. He turned it over in his hands then smiled as a familiar scene came rushing back to him.

The winter in which the power went off then failed to come back for three days was one that Ellis remembered the clearest. Sometimes as he travelled to work on the bus, or walked alone with headphones in, a podcast for company, his thoughts took him to a place long embedded in his memory. When that happened, he had only to close his eyes, stilling his erratic thoughts, to hear the now jumbled and misremembered conversations from around the kitchen table. He could still see the shadows moving from wall to wall, cast from candle and torchlight; the jokes and stories told by his brother and parents, and the soup warmed on a blue-flamed camping gas stove. Mushroom was the best, he thought. Then chicken. Now sitting on his bedroom floor, he remembered clearly how he had taken this card, this Christmas card with its proud robin at its centre, to make a collage. To cut the paper and free it from within its cardboard frame.

The Penrice family had a fireplace in the middle of their living room wall, with two teal-green porcelain cats that sat at each end of the mantlepiece above the hearth. Gold and silver photo frames, crammed together to make the most of all available space - those at the back forced to lean against the textured wallpaper - housed some of the selected memories of Ellis' parents. An image of a family holiday to Greece, his mother and brother squinting through the sunshine and towards the camera, had been placed behind pictures of grandparents, cut-out school photos and the cake, clowns and assorted former classmates of selected birthday parties. A wedding picture was carefully placed in the centre of the otherwise jumbled scene, directly between the intricate cornicing that framed the fireplace. The faces of Ellis' parents, then in their early twenties, showed what Ellis always thought to be real happiness and joy. Smiling faces, that when captured at that exact moment by the wedding photographer and the simple push of a button, would be kept in place forever.

The faces showed no knowledge of the two boys that would follow, one year, then three years' later. Neither gave any indication of future successful job interviews and the subsequent job losses, or of bedroom discussions relating to wallpaper, money, and which bathroom suite they could afford. Discussions that would go on and take seed as winter passed to spring. The happy couple held hands, each looking and smiling beyond and behind the camera to something unseen, as confetti fell softly on them.

In those days, the days of set bedtimes, homework and family holidays, the house had been filled with plants of every kind imaginable. Green, drooping vines with tear-shaped leaves that sat within gravel, their white clay pots sandwiched between books, photo albums and lamps. Cacti in drying earth, grouped in threes and fours, lay in pastel-red ceramic pots, which changed colour and darkened when watered. Flowers in white, green and blue striped vases stood proudly on the kitchen windowsill, pollen falling in yellowing piles on the wood below. Scented candles and a selection of ornamental birds took up the rest of the space. Of this cluttered collection of family life over the years, it was the books and photo albums which Ellis thought of most often.

On days after school, these were regularly taken down to the floor by him and his brother, each sifting through the pictures and scanning the authors' names, related publishing information and synopses of dusty paper backs that neither had any intention of reading. 'What's an Aspidistra?' asked Ellis, safe in the knowledge that his brother did not know.

'Read it and see,' answered Cameron, the eldest of the two, who hesitated before kicking out and deftly landing the top of his foot on Ellis' thigh. Letting out a satisfied snort as he heard the groan of pain from his little brother, he took his focus back to the rural vista of Hemingway's 'The Sun Also Rises.'

That winter, when the power went down across the town, the ground froze, and the boys' father joked that the North Pole was warmer than their upstairs bathroom. They were one of the lucky families with access to a fire and each late afternoon, the sun having long set to fill windows with darkness, their mother would light the fire with long Cook's Matches and bundled up pieces of newspaper. Ellis and his brother would watch the match scratch across the textured surface at the side of the box, before bursting into flame with a crackle. The initial smell of smoke would fill the room before the fire took hold, casting the blaze high into the base of the chimney, and forcing what was often damp-smelling wood smoke upwards.

On any given year, as soon as the calendar on the corkboard in the kitchen was folded over to November, the fire would increasingly be used to warm the home. What started as a weekend tradition soon became a nightly affair following the power cut and the boys looked forward to it from the moment the winds grew, the nights got longer, and the first leaves began to fall from the trees.

Ellis' father, a good natured, erudite, and softly spoken man, never paid for any of the wood or coal that would be used over the autumn and winter. Instead, he would take long walks in August with the red sledge that Ellis had shared with his brother, dragging it behind him as he spent the long summer evenings walking through parks and along beaches. Horse chestnut and sycamore branches, which burned poorly when wet, would be bundled together with twine, then hauled along with whatever driftwood could be found.

The range of shapes, sizes, textures and condition of the varying tree species led to irregular seasoning. From October, one could tell which wood was still damp by the smell – an acrid scent that clung with purpose to any item of clothing or hair that it came into contact with. Of course, none of this mattered to his father. He would stand outside the shed as his woodpile grew with each passing evening, sweat pouring from his brow and soaking the back of his t-shirt. He gulped greedily from pints of cold tap water. Ellis now knew that it was a sense of pride and achievement that his father had felt in those moments. He would marvel and watch his father through the window as two minutes steadily passed to five, then five to ten. And still, his father's gaze would be set upon the contents of the shed. Occasionally he would look skywards, his stomach moving outwards as he took in the warm evening air through deep inhalations from his nose. Ellis did not understand why, but he welcomed the calming sensation as he watched the perennial scene each summer evening from inside the house.

Now an adult, and still sitting on his bedroom floor, Ellis again thought back to the power cut. He knew later that day he would go back to the family home, but for now, he simply sat and reminisced. The three days of going to the toilet with a torch and the memories of cold water, canned potatoes and tinned luncheon meat. The long evenings, each family member clad in a variety of woollen garments, were also spent listening to segments of the books that until then the brothers had only ever touched, tracing their fingers over the cover imagery and pronouncing the names of the authors. There was never anything read in full; Ellis and Cameron preferred it that way. A chapter of Kafka and some poetry by Updike. Eugene Onegin and Achebe's 'Things Fall Apart.' The communal reading stopped after the third night, when the sound of the TV and kitchen light signalled its end. But from that point on, Ellis no longer just looked at the covers of the books that nestled between the miniature owls and cranes, and those that lay piled in rows on the shelving. It was for these reasons that Ellis looked back warmly on that winter. But now, in what had been the rainiest summer he could remember, he sat on the bus on his way back to his parents' house.

The monthly visit was one that he did not dread, yet it was an experience that he had no longing for. The same questions would be asked and answered, with each response leading to a particular tone in his parents that assured Ellis of their disappointment, or sad frustration, without having to overtly raise or voice anything with him directly.

These days, the only sign of plants in the house were the flowers that had remained pressed between the pages of long-forgotten, untouched books. His parents both read on occasion, but the collected works, novels and poetry now played a predominantly decorative role. The cacti remained but were now as artificial as the pots that framed their plastic needles. The decorative birds stood resolute, a slight dust gathering on the branches they sat on.

Cameron was already sitting on the sofa drinking wine with his mother when Ellis walked in. There was a half-finished bottle nestled between two mallard duck replicas, each one flapping its clay wings outwards and away from the other. Ellis had not seen these particular trinkets and thought they must have been a recent gift, quite possibly from Cameron.

'Here's the binman,' said Cameron. 'Get yourself a glass and sit down,' he said, motioning in the direction of an empty armchair.

'Hiya, love,' said his mum, reaching up to cuddle her youngest child before placing a kiss on each cheek, then a longer one on his forehead. 'Your dad has just nipped out for a quick walk, but he'll be back soon,' she added, looking towards the front door.

'We were just talking about Annette over the road when you came in,' said his mum, placing her glass down and beckoning for Ellis to take a seat beside her. 'Did you see the van outside? Two months later and still no further forward with the veranda! Do you remember she spoke to us about it last year when she dropped off the Christmas card? I wouldn't be surprised if it's still not finished by next December!'

The living room window looked out at the houses opposite, a variety of new builds that had steadily increased in both quantity and size since Ellis and Cameron had called Elm Walk their home.

'Still,' she added, pausing while she took another sip of wine. 'She brought over a pair of lovely mallard ducks just last week to apologise for the noise. You're both lucky you're not here on a Monday morning as you'd soon know all about the racket then,' she scoffed.

'Eve,' called his father from the hall. 'That van is there again,' he added.

She rolled her eyes jokingly and called back, 'I know that Finlay, but come in here now please and stop staring because the boys are here!'

Finlay placed an umbrella in the corner of the hallway and walked with purpose to see his two sons who were now sitting on the sofa.

'Great to see you both,' he said, touching a hand on both of their shoulders and giving each of his children a light squeeze of affection. 'Lunch will be ready in an hour, so I'll open another bottle of wine,' said Finlay. 'Cameron, tell us all about this promotion then. Your mum mentioned something on the phone, but we want to get the whole picture from you. It really is great news and I'm sure Amanda will be delighted too,' he added.

Pouring himself another glass of wine, Cameron stood up and spoke. As he did so, Ellis was aware that he had to force himself to listen to what was being said. As the story progressed and the voice of his brother grew louder, arms gesticulating to emphasise and illustrate each point, he found it harder to take in and understand the words. He knew what they meant, but the order and intonation made his palms sweat and head spin. He swallowed three times to clear the dryness in his throat, then once again tried to focus. As the explanation continued, he thought how easy it was to measure success when it had followed one around so readily, and how simple and enjoyable a Sunday afternoon could be when the conversation focused on promotions and travel, or of mallard ducks and red wine. He held a faint sense of pride in his brother, yet at the same time, he wanted nothing more at that moment than to stand outside the living room door and bury his fingers deep within his ears. He thought that he could hop up the stairs two at a time, then hide in his childhood bedroom, now redecorated for the occasional guest, until the conversation had ended. Instead, he remained where he sat.

'That's great to hear, we're both so proud of you,' said Finlay.

'Of both of you,' his mum quickly added, placing a hand on Ellis' knee.

The remainder of the afternoon passed in the usual manner: with the glasses of red wine and sparkling water, slightly overcooked food, and music playing in the background. After accidentally knocking over a glass of Merlot, the wine pouring across the table in all directions, Cameron broke the growing dullness of the afternoon.

'It's always the next thing with you, Ellis,' he said, slurring his words slightly over mouthfuls of roast beef. 'Start something then stop it; start and stop. When you know what it is you're looking for, be sure to let the rest of us know,' he said, aiming a wink in the direction of Ellis.

Both parents stared at their eldest son, chastising him without words. 'Ah, he knows I'm joking, don't you

Ellis?' asked Cameron, reaching over his fellow diners before emptying the contents of the bottle into his glass. Ellis, with no interest to drag out the conversation, or worse, let it lead to an argument, nodded and smiled. 'Of course, yeah. Of course!' he lied.

There was a pause, as he mashed a piece of carrot with his fork. 'Dad, this is great food by the way. Thanks again for cooking,' said Ellis, forcing a smile.

Lying in bed that evening unable to fall asleep, Ellis tried but struggled to place his feelings from earlier that day in the living room. His heart raced as he picked his phone up, scrolled to nothing in particular, then put it down again. He took it up again, opened a new app then did the same, opening a search engine, looking at some pictures, then locking the screen. After a minute he was staring once more at the screen, its white light contrasting heavily with the black room.

He thought back to the words his mum had said to him on the doorstep as he left. 'Ellis,' she had called in the direction of his back, waiting until he turned before saying what she had wanted to. 'Ellis!' Taking his hand off the gate, Ellis had looked back to see his mum smiling at him. 'Not every cloud brings rain, son. Remember that.'

Chapter four

As he lay on his sofa that morning, Ellis thought how straightforward and unexacting it was to hide away from the world. His boss had not appeared to mind him calling in sick as badly as he had feared, but he was still certain that they were unhappy with him. He wondered if the well-placed cough was perhaps too contrived, but there was no point in dwelling on it now, he thought. Despite that, he knew he would be ruminating over it for the duration of the morning.

Pulling a blanket he had taken down from the airing cupboard during the night tightly under his chin, he stared at the ceiling and planned what he could do with the day ahead. The nervous anxiety that sat in the pit of his stomach was fading, so he went to the kitchen to make himself a cup of black tea. The cupboards and fridge, while not overflowing with food, had enough provisions to last him a week, perhaps more if required. Peering towards the back of the top shelf, he mentally took note of the assorted tins, jars, powders and packets. If all he needed at that point was food and water, then Ellis had all that was required. With books to read, the companionship and noise of the TV as numbing background noise, and the knowledge that a daily walk could be taken should escapism be sought, he reassured himself that yes, should he want to hide away, he could.

He was unsure if he wanted to, but he could. The thought both worried and reassured him in equal measure.

He considered for a moment how much easier life was when he did nothing. When he achieved nothing. When nothing filled his day, other than the routine he knew was safe, yet delivered nothing. Days where he woke up, showered, ate, worked, ate, then filled the four-hour void before sleep.

On inspection of the fridge, the sight of an unopened bottle of milk and six eggs, with two weeks until their use-by date, gave him a strange sense of contentment. With supplies he could leave the door of the flat closed, shutting himself off from the world outside. He knew that someone, no doubt Mrs McCafferty from the flat below, would come looking for money to clean the stairwell, but even her incessant banging of the door could not last forever. All things pass and that would too, so yes, he told himself, he should hide away. But not too long, of course. Days like today were paths that Ellis had walked many times before.

He understood that his was a dangerous game. He sensed that a dark wave was on the cusp of sweeping him up, but at that point, he was at least close enough to the shore. Better to stay in the shallows than get swept out to sea by the growing swell; out to a place where his toes no longer touched the sand. Yet he still sensed this wave growing inside him and his heartbeat grew faster with the recognition.

He waited, as he always waited, for his breathing to calm. He waited with a patience that was slowly fraying at the edges for something to change. For a letter to arrive or a phone call. A chance meeting or event to signal that a new experience was approaching and that this was not his lot in life.

But Ellis thought he knew a secret, indeed, a piece of wisdom understood only by him. He realised that he could live this life now because the life he was owed, and that was surely to come, was a life that happened elsewhere. Yes, life happens elsewhere, he thought, kicking the sofa cushion onto the floor before lifting it back with both feet. It happened in the past with his memories, or in the future with what were left of his dreams. But it was not happening now, that much was clear. Ellis thought that as the days turned to weeks, then the weeks into months, that the decision to pause and wait was his own. Life happened in another place, and it was his to find, as and when he wanted. Somewhere away from the buses and bin lorries, and far from the scrolling and forced conversation. But until then he waited, as he had always done.

Yet perhaps not for long. For the kernel of an idea had begun to form and grow over the last few days, but he had steadily pushed it to the back of his mind.

However, the roots had taken hold and he felt himself being pushed upwards as they stretched towards the light. The robin Christmas card had filled him with such a feeling of joy that he knew that it was by no means an accident it had been found. Truly found. No, Ellis pondered, as he stood motionless in the flat; this was a message meant only for him. He knew where his guidance was to come. Life may very well happen elsewhere, but he knew that he was one step closer to finding where elsewhere was.

   The sound of boiling water shook him from his daze. The thermostat had broken the week before, and Ellis now found himself listening keenly to the elongated boil before flicking the switch off with his left hand.

   Walking to the kitchen window, he stretched over the sink with its dripping tap, reaching upwards to release the catch that sat below the white painted frame. A small clicking sound signalled it was ready to be pushed open. Outside, some council workers were mowing the short, well-kept line of grass between the car park and the offices. Ellis watched as the two men, each wearing black ear protectors, marched in opposite directions. Working from the outside, they slowly closed in on the darker, wetter grass in the middle, walking with their lawn mowers until the patch was a uniform, clipped, light bottle green. High above them in the offices, workers of a different kind sat at their desks staring into screens. The window glare from the morning sun hid those on the second and third floor, but Ellis could see clearly into the first. In a separate room, a group of six sat around a table, a mass of blue and charcoal grey suits. His own no longer fitted him as they gathered dust on a white clothes rail that stood lopsided in one corner of his bedroom.

He thought of his own time spent in offices like the one that now cast a deep shadow over the two grass cutters, both of whom had stopped to drink from thermos flasks. He remembered the noises of that time; of the language used to signify importance that mattered only to those who used it. The talk of deadlines, actions, KPIs, outputs and traction. Mornings with emails, calls and quarterly breakdowns, and afternoons filled with meetings, none of which ever went anywhere. Meetings where men and women in similar blue and grey suits to those he now saw wrote on whiteboards about audiences and data, telling the faces that looked back at them about the importance of market share.

Ellis wondered if they had believed it all. He had not. He looked back and tried to understand or recall if the passion, opinions and zeal of the people hunched over the whiteboards and laptop keyboards was real. He questioned whether if what he had seen at that time was a genuine interest in the work by his former colleagues, and if their demeanours were sincere and honest. He suspected otherwise, but what did it matter? Of course, Ellis knew he had worn the mask as well. He understood that to go back to university would be expensive, but it was what he had wanted to do at the time. Even then, he found he could hide away from it all. The smiles and nodding. The best regards. The Monday morning tales of weekends filled with nothing much.

  Pouring the hot water into a white mug, he watched as it mingled with the teabag and darkened. Opening the fridge again, he took out two eggs from their cardboard box and a packet of smoked streaky bacon before setting the food on the countertop beside the hob. A non-stick pan was taken out from the dishwasher, its coating increasingly flaky with each passing wash. Ellis watched as the fat from the bacon rendered, casting small droplets of hot grease across what was an otherwise clean hob. Two eggs were cracked in the pan, their edges browning in the bacon grease. Flipping the eggs for a second or two then turning them over once more, he sprinkled the semi-solid yolks with salt and pepper before sliding the contents onto a plate. He hungrily ate the food in less than two minutes. Finishing his meal, Ellis made his way to the bathroom at the end of the hall. The tiles felt cold on the soles of his feet, and he moved his toes back and forward in a movement that welcomed the chilling sensation. There were still some of her toiletries left in a box under the sink, so he knew not to look there. One day he would sort them and bin them, but this would not be that day.

Taking off his t-shirt and underwear, he stared at his naked body in the mirror as his dull, tired eyes looked back at him. He looked thinner than he had at the start of the year and the faint tan on his forearms, neck and face gave a sharp contrast to the paleness of his legs and torso. In the shower, he changed the temperature between hot and cold in the hope that it would rejuvenate his mind and body. It did not, but he had been told it had been good for his heart, so he dried himself with a once fluffy towel with that knowledge at the forefront of his mind.

While in the bathroom, someone had placed a Church newsletter through his letterbox and it lay bent and solitarily in the hall, partly hidden underneath a storage heater that was never on, even in winter. He left it where it was and walked into the living room, taking a selection of books down from a shelf and placing them on the end of the coffee table. An email he had received that morning made it clear that all three had to be returned to the library by the end of the month.

Conscious he would have little time to finish one, let alone the others, he went back into the hall to retrieve a green backpack from the hooks where his coats were hung. She had drilled the holes two summers before as he was fearful that his own efforts would hit a water pipe, or worse, an electrical current. Pausing to consider what would be one of the only meaningful choices he would have to make that day, he placed two of the books, including an Italian phrasebook, back in the bag ready to be returned when he next visited the library. Walking back to the kitchen to close the window, the sound of lawnmowers signalled that the duo of workers had finished their break, and he looked again towards those who sat in the office opposite.

    Making his way back into the living room, he picked the remaining book up from the coffee table. Opening 'And Quiet Flows the Don' at page two hundred, he moved the blanket to one side and sat down to read. It was then that he once more recalled the memory of the Christmas card. Perhaps, he hoped, but his hand had thumbed the pages of the book before he could even finish his own thought. It was empty of all but the words on its pages.

Chapter five

The yard was quieter than usual when Ellis went back to work. He reasoned that many of the workers were now using some well-earned annual leave, taking time off to be with their families, or partners, or even just to spend some time alone. Time away from the bin lorries, pavements and rubbish. He had expected someone to make a comment about his absence the day before, but he was the only one in the canteen when he went to get what had now become his staple cup of stale-tasting, gritty coffee. He wondered when the machine had last been cleaned, then pushed the thought to the back of his mind through repulsion at the expected answer.

Making his way to the truck, he could just make out the faint reflection of the driver in the side mirror, his head turned towards the direction of the passenger. Ellis rarely saw him speak other than to signal a missed bin, the planned time they would stop for the next tea break or lunch, or much more commonly, a two or three-word warning. The radio went off when it was the latter.

However, on this occasion, the movement of his hands suggested that he was deep in conversation with someone. Ellis wondered if Jordan had brought in a bottle of vodka again, or worse, had stepped in dog shit and brought his soiled boots into the cab, seemingly oblivious to the smell as it spread in the warming air. He thought the topic of nationalism could have once again raised its head. A discussion that left Ellis sitting between the deathly silence that only seemed to grow with each passing day, until one day when all had seemed to move on from, if not forget, what had been said. Jordan's nose, though no longer visibly misshapen from the blow when seen from a distance, took longer to calm, the deep red mark still visible on its bridge.

As Ellis got closer to the lorry, he could make out the focus of the driver's attention much more clearly. It was Andy who sat in the middle passenger seat. 'Jordan's sick today so Andy's with us,' the driver said, giving Ellis a little nod as he slammed the heavy door behind him.

'Maybe he had what you had,' said Andy. 'I hope you're feeling better now,' he added.

'Thanks, yeah, a lot better now,' responded Ellis.

Starting the engine, the driver made his way slowly out the yard and into the working day that lay ahead of them. As he had anticipated, Ellis did not have long to wait before Andy spoke.

'We had just been talking about places we wanted to see before you came in, Ellis. Did you know that Archie used to live in Helsinki?'

This was the first time Ellis had heard the

driver's name.

'No, I didn't know that,' said Ellis. 'When was that, Archie?'

'Oh, a few years back now,' croaked the driver, both hands gripping the wheel, eyes focused on the road ahead. 'I used to do a bit of contractor work when I was younger, mainly just doing the odd bit of construction here and there. It was all sorted through a friend of a friend. He'd met a Finnish girl in a bar before that and that was it, he was off! Settled down with a wife and kids now the last I heard of him. It's not so easy to stay in touch these days, is it? You both know how it is. To be honest with you, it was Espoo where most of the work was, but it's easier to say Helsinki, isn't it? People know Helsinki,' he added.

Slowing down to meet a red light, Archie took out a mint from his shirt pocket and flicked some of the more notable pieces of fluff that clung onto it with a well-placed movement of his thumb. Ellis listened as he crunched the mint between his teeth, sucking on the remnants and swallowing loudly. It was gone before the light turned to amber and the story continued.

'It was only really a couple of months that I was there, but I loved every second. People often say that don't they? I mean of course there were some hard times, but you soon forget about all that when you've left a place. Have you ever been in a sauna, lads? A real wood-fired sauna?' asked an increasingly amiable Archie. Andy went to speak, then paused to allow Ellis to answer. Ellis was unsure if his experience with the infrared and electrical saunas that came from his incredibly rare hotel stays and long expired gym membership counted, but Archie left no space for either of them to respond.

'It's a real part of their culture,' said Archie, pushing the indicator up and slowly steering the hulking lorry to the streets where they would soon all have to work.

'All of the lads that I worked with had saunas that their families had owned for years, and I'm talking ten, twenty, thirty years here. In the summer they are all at it. After work with a few beers or Saturday afternoon with the family. I got a lift back with one of them and he had all these birch twigs lying on the back seat. The boy told me it's for making sauna whisks. A couple of good whacks with that really gets the blood pumping, you know?' said Archie, smiling to himself at the memory.

Andy nodded along to what Ellis understood to be all the right points in the story. Ellis was enjoying the casual, informal conversation, a welcome if unusual break before the work started. Where in the past he would have played along, trying to include supporting noises, this occasion saw him simply listen.

Archie, now aware he had an audience,

continued. 'I'd say that when you break it all down, I mean really focus on why they do it, then it's all about respect. A real respect for and awareness of their health, and a respect for nature, I suppose. I don't mean going into the woods and meditating, nothing like that. But there's a feeling that comes from it. I don't know, I can't really explain it,' he said. Pressing down on the accelerator, the lorry sped ahead on its way. They would soon be at the first street.

'I'll tell you this though,' he continued. 'When you first go in, feeling the heat on your skin and smelling the wood smoke coming off a roaring hot fire you feel something. I don't know how to explain it, but there's a different feeling there. Something primitive. I don't know if that's the word but it's something like that. At that moment, it's just you and the heat. They're usually quite dark, silent places, so your eyes and ears are drawn to the orange glow of the fire and the crackle of the logs. I'm making myself want one now just thinking about it! Here we are though now, lads. Let's crack on and aim to stop at ten, maybe ten-fifteen for a cup of tea and something to eat,' said Archie, his amiable tone suddenly turning serious.

A steady overnight rain had caused most of the boxes not sheltered under the awnings and garages to be filled with an inch deep slurry. Loose beans floated in the shallow pools alongside bits of newspaper and lumps of congealed jam. The occupants of five Shandwick Place had put used cigarette ends in a half-drunk bottle of Beck's beer. The smell of old beer and stale tobacco made Ellis retch, standing back as he lifted the heavy box onto the side of the truck. Pouring the contents into one of the lorry's compartments, he took the box down and kicked it across the garden in anger at the occupants. He thought of them sleeping warm in their beds unaware their actions had assaulted his senses. Ellis felt his jaw tighten and he clenched his teeth.

'Teatime, boys,' came a shout from the cab.

There was a welcome and contemplative few minutes of still silence as each man drank slowly from plastic bottles of steadily warming water, or from cups filled with tea. Archie took out a small bar of chocolate from his bag and after breaking off a piece for himself, he offered the bar to Andy and Ellis. Both took a square, thanking Archie as they did so. Andy was first to break the silence.

'Archie, you said something about Finnish culture earlier and,' he stopped mid-sentence to lick some of the melted chocolate off his finger, 'and well, it's got me thinking back to something I heard about years ago. The Kalevala.' Archie and Ellis looked up from their drinks, both showing a keen interest in what was to come next. 'It's about identity and, no, wait.' He looked at his now clean finger then up to the eyes of Ellis and

Archie. 'It's easier to say that it led to the construction of a Finnish identity before it really existed. The author travelled all over the country collecting notes, old folk songs and poetry. Real tales and stories from the people. Don't you think that's important? To collate the traditions and tales of your country and build and shape an identity from it?' he asked hopefully. There was a silence.

'Can I have a sip of your water, Ellis?' asked Andy. Ellis handed over the bottle and he drank readily, placing the top on and handing it back.

'Mastered by desire impulsive,' began Andy. 'By a mighty inward surge. No, not surge. What's the word?' He rubbed his finger along the dashboard, leaving a five-inch trail between the dust. 'Urging, that's it. By a mighty inward urging. That's right. By a mighty inward urging, I am ready now for singing. Ready to begin the chanting of our nation's ancient folk song,' recalled Andy, lost in thought. Taking two deep breaths, he exhaled loudly.

'I don't know if the translation is correct but that was the version I read,' he added. 'Do you think that matters?' he asked. 'Do you think you'll ever get the full meaning of something that's been translated? Really get to the meaning of a piece of work... a real piece of meaningful writing that wasn't written for your eyes, tongue or ears? You only truly get the feel for something, and I mean really feel it, when you understand the tone and its intonation. I don't know,' Andy sighed. 'I just don't know. I suppose it doesn't matter.'

'So, what is it?' asked Archie. 'A big story?'

'A poem,' said Ellis.

'That's right,' said Andy. 'A poem of mythology. Of lust, love and death. Powerful stuff. It's a creation story really. But within the context of a people that until then were either sandwiched between the Russian or Swedish empires. Celebrating culture and language and looking at their own history and ways of thinking.'

'That's twice in a month this cab has heard talk of poetry,' laughed Archie. 'Just last week, Jordan was speaking about poems from school. Your name got a ment...' Archie swallowed the word before it came out.

'Did Jordan mention me?' Andy asked.

Archie had taken out his tobacco and cigarette papers and took a couple of extra seconds to meaningfully lick the glue, before rolling it up, showing a level of focus unnecessary for the task. Taking an orange lighter from his pocket, he lit the tip and took a long drag.

'Ellis, do you remember what he said, I totally forget to be honest with you both,' said Archie sheepishly.

Ellis looked unblinking at Archie but responded quickly, aiming a softly spoken reply at nobody in particular. 'It was just school stuff really. Nothing more than that. He said you were mates growing up,' said Ellis.

Andy nodded. 'Let's crack on and try and finish by one today. I could do with an early finish,' he said. They all worked quickly that afternoon, walking at a brisk pace that became a jog towards the end of each street. Three streets lay before them and the journey back to base. A drive that would see the loosening of tight leather boots that had swollen in the warm rain. Strained leg muscles would be prodded and rubbed as the lorry trundled back, caught up in the slow-moving commuter traffic. The remaining tea in the flask, long turned bitter and lukewarm, would be cast out onto pavements and gardens.

Ellis hauled recycling boxes up and down and lifted heavy sacks of paper and magazines. The lorry swelled with the waste of thousands of people, once used and thrown away. As he worked, his thoughts swirled with the images of creation stories. Of beginnings and ends. Andy walked ahead of him, a steady pace keeping a good distance between the pair. Ellis wondered what he would be thinking about and thought it strange how on what an otherwise normal day, a piece of epic Finnish poetry would be discussed in the cab of EB56 87N.

After the shift had ended, the drive back to the base was filled with the usual level of non-committal discourse. The sound of the radio filled the void. The three workers focused on their own thoughts, Ellis and Andy each taking the time to inspect their dry, weathered hands. Ellis could still make out the faint scar from the cut on his finger. He rubbed a thumb across the scab. Sliding his flask into the back of his bag, he peered beneath a spare t-shirt at the two books that lay on the bottom. The spine of one had been bent slightly so he took the time to straighten it. Andy looked across at the book, scanning its title as he did so, but said nothing.

Chapter six

A cream-tabby cat lay sprawled outside the library, sunning itself and remaining firmly in place as the afternoon visitors stepped over and around it. Inside the building, a librarian sat at a solid-looking desk, her eyes fixed on the screen of a computer. Two plants sat at either side of the screen with both looking in dire need of water.

Children ran and played noisily with their parents on the building's lower section, rummaging around for books about adventuring lions, magical castles and sea creatures who swam and sang with sharks and dolphins. Beyond them sat a variety of readers who were gathered around low-lying tables on a mixture of deep red, tan and brown armchairs. Reclining for an hour or so of afternoon tranquillity and comfort, they read from a scattered pile of daily newspapers, magazines, and journals. The room carried a strange odour that was almost popcorn-like in its scent.

A set of wide stairs took those who walked up them to row upon row of books new and old. Hardbacks and pamphlets, paperbacks with glued spines that peeled at the bottom, and large collected works behind glass cases, the fingerprints of previous visitors smeared and smudged and acting as a reminder of those who had come before.

The second floor housed everything from romantic and contemporary literature to prose and autobiographical works. Quieter than the lower floor, a woman in a grey knitted sweater took one book from the second shelf, row BB. She looked at its front and back, felt the spine between her fingers, then placed it back into its rightful place. Taking a step back, she paced slowly along the carpeted floor before pausing once again. Reaching up to the highest shelf, she took a much larger book down and opened it to scan its pages, then placed it in the crook of her arm, this time clearly happier with its contents.

The last flight of stairs of the library took those who ventured up to the historical, political, sociological and nature sections. Flora and fauna met tales of revolution and of civil rights, while theses on homelessness were closed in tightly between tomes on religion and spirituality. Ellis stood with his back to a large bay window, looking down on the floors below and the readers as they sat. The old heating unit that lay at his feet was on, steadily humming and rattling as it sent out a rising wave of warm air in the direction of his shins. Ellis thought this unnecessary but was thankful regardless as it quickly dried his still damp, previously rain-soaked, work trousers. Having returned the books that were close to their due date, he now scrolled over his phone at the library's online catalogue. Skimming past 'Empire of the Past,' 'New Neighbours: an Armenian Story,' and 'Ghosts of the Mountain: the Story of Georgia,' he added 'Lenin's War: advance on Poland,' to what was an already growing list. He copied its details down into the notes of his phone and stood up: Third Floor - History of Europe - Eastern Europe - 567,084 POL. His short journey took him beyond Belgian political theory and historical Danish books on royalty and social welfare. A sojourn with the Norwegian resistance and issues of corruption in North Macedonia led him finally to his destination.

'Zero...eighty, zero eight two, zero...eight...four,' he whispered to himself. Finding the book with a small numbered yellow sticker on its red and white spine, he pulled at its top and lifted it out to form a space in the otherwise uniform row of books. The movement and the gap created led to a bookend falling, causing three books to slowly slip and awkwardly fill the space vacated. Ellis put everything back in place and held the book he had chosen to fill his evenings with after work. Opening it to read the chapter listing, he flicked his thumb over the pages in a well-practiced movement to gauge the word count and time he expected it would take him to finish it. If indeed he did finish.

As he did so, a fluttering movement caught his eye and he watched as a small scrap of paper fell from the pages, taking some seconds to land on the library's faded burnt-orange carpet. He looked around his surroundings, in the hope that nobody had seen what could have been perceived as his littering. His eyes were met with an empty room. Reaching down to pick up this piece of wastepaper, ready to be crumpled between his damp palms and pushed into a now dry trouser pocket, he noticed there was some scrawled writing on it. Flicking the pages of the book once more to see if it contained any other makeshift bookmarks, he stopped at page eighty nine when he noticed a small amount of blue ink on the top right of the page. Turning the scrap of paper over in his hands, the ink had bled slightly across what he could now make out to be a sketch of a mountain. The book's previous reader had clearly read enough before the chapters on Bolshevik volunteers, the Kiev offensive or the Treaty of Riga. Though small, the drawing was detailed and sat in the centre of a sheet of lined paper. Ripped at one end, the other corner forcibly folded over in a neat line by the weight of its neighbouring pages, Ellis could now make out the writing at its base: 'See now, see later, but see.' Ellis felt his heartbeat increase and a cold sweat grew across his back. He placed the slip of paper in the sleeve of the book and took it downstairs to check out.

  The library was close to his flat, so he took the decision to walk home. Welcoming a break in the rain, he made good pace, paying little notice to the streets which he had long walked over. He remembered meeting someone in a pub some years ago, who had lectured Ellis and his friends on the importance of always looking up. Ellis thought it strange how this memory would come into his head now, but subconsciously slowed his pace regardless.

Raising his field of vision beyond the people who busily crossed his path, jostling and bustling around him as they hurriedly made their way home, or to something more important than right now, he looked up. The buildings above cast a delicate shadow on the street opposite. From inside flat windows he saw wooden shutters and the edges of curtains, the bulk of which were hidden from view. To his left, he saw ornate, triangle-shaped roofs that sloped steeply, making him feel slightly dizzy. Light brown stonework that was aged darker in the middle merged with rusting drainpipes and faint patches of grass or other foliage that grew from between its cracks.

His own flat was on a street just like this one. Not knowing his immediate neighbours by more than their names, he wondered who they were. He contemplated how they spent their weekends and about the conversations they had when they made their way up the stairs and closed themselves in for the night. He questioned whether they took the same joy that he did in filling his cupboard and fridge with supplies, shutting off the outside world so he could hide away in safety. Would the people on his street call that a life? Did he? Ellis was unsure. He thought it strange that in being so close to other people, with flats built below, above and at each side, that he should still feel so entirely alone. Looking back at the faces of those who sped across the pavement, he asked himself if they shared his fears, or worries. How could they, he thought, for they were his alone. He knew that they all had their own lives to enjoy when enjoyment was available, and their own stress to overcome, face, or hide away from, when the need arose. But the feeling of loneliness filled him with a growing sense of dread, and he no longer looked up on the walk back to the flat.

Finding his appetite gone as the front door closed behind him, he walked into the kitchen and took an orange from the fruit bowl, telling himself that he had to eat something. A birthday gift from his brother, the bowl contained a handful of grapes, three overripe bananas and a single green apple, its wax coating giving it a look that Ellis took to be an unnatural shine. Taking a knife and plate into the living room, he sliced the orange into four pieces and sucked slowly on the first segment, looking around the room for the TV remote as he did so.

Sitting in that moment, his heart racing and breath shallow, the juice of a segment running down his arm, he looked at his faint reflection in the black of the

TV screen and cried. The tears were short lived, but they came with a ferocity he had not experienced for some time. As they steadily rolled down his face, he slowly regained his composure and soon found himself wiping away the last visible sign of a period that had been filled with little but worry and hiding. Months of insignificance, he thought.

    The previous summer held a promise that he had not felt since early childhood. Memories of pushing sticks into hot tar and running in the woods. Ice cream and family holidays. Of his father and the wood pile and his mother and jugs of iced orange squash. Early afternoons that turned to night on the football field, smelling the cut grass and cigarette smoke as the sun set on Ellis and his friends. The summer of last year led to memories that were as evocative for him now, as he sat on the sofa, the orange peel and pith all that remained of his makeshift dinner.

    He could still smell the after-sun lotion on her skin and only had to close his eyes to picture the way her hair looked when she came out of the swimming pool. He could taste the assorted food of the plentiful picnics in the park, and the refreshing bite of sparkling wine taken from buckets of ice. He questioned if that was happiness. If she was happiness. He knew now she was not. Ellis thought how everything, or at least everything he had known, touched and felt, had a beginning and an end. She was the summer but the seasons can never be halted and summer moved to autumn, then the wind, rain and snow of winter.

One evening, while in the last throes of love and before either had accepted the truth that the end was near, she wrote the words 'teach us to sit still' in the back of her black notebook. Ellis gave it little thought at the time, but the words now clung heavy in his memory.

Catching his reflection again in the black TV, he thought of the tears and the fights, and of his inability to make her happy. He looked back to the start of the growing dark wave looming on the horizon, where he had gathered his life and selfishly thrown away everything that could not keep him afloat. The job was gone, as was the post-graduate degree. But more importantly now was that she was gone, and it, whatever Ellis took to be it at that moment on the sofa, was gone too.

In bed that night, as he drifted off into a fitful sleep, his mind turned towards the last twelve months. Of the missed calls and rejected invitations. The day the notes were torn up and the files were wiped, in anger and frustration only at himself. He thought of the hours of video he watched of others as they lived their life, travelled, had sex, explored and learned, while he spent his watching them. He understood that some, perhaps most of this was an act. Ellis was aware that a natural part of being human is to do what others would see as nothing. To understand and to live life is to live in those moments. But Ellis had removed himself even from that. His was a year of unfinished books and abrupt conversation. A year of hiding away and removing himself from everything that before then had been a part of who he was. He wanted to participate in and be the author of his own story, but as he fell asleep, his thoughts filled with a weary sadness and the unsettling fear that he was powerless to do so.

Chapter seven

The low-lying hills lay to the west of the city. Beyond them, a distant mountain range loomed over the green, rounded ridges; its jagged, snow-capped summit contrasting against the ever-changing colours in the canvas of the sky. The picture steadily changed through the seasons. In spring and summer, the light illuminated the western side of the mountain with a deep orange glow. During the autumn and winter, when it was visible at all behind the fog, rain cloud and snowstorms, the light illuminated the eastern face, giving its peaks a majestic clarity and imposing stillness.

When the weather was cold, dry and clear, when the ice clung to pavements and the slow-moving rivers and lakes froze, the residents of the city could look through their windows, warm and safe inside, and see the imposing mountain range in front of them. The scene revealed the rocky crags with patches of trees on the slopes and scree, and the waterfalls that seemed to blow upwards when the strong north-easterly winds blew. The same wind rattled windows and cast sea foam, grey, white and thick, across the beaches and pier. It shook the trees, breaking off then scattering their weaker branches, sending them far over fields and across gardens. And it blew loose slate paving slabs from the residents' roofs, with the ease of a dentist removing a decayed tooth.

The slate came from quarries that sat in the foothills of the mountain range. In the 1800s, the men of surrounding villages dug, cut and trimmed the slate that was to shelter their children, grandchildren and great grandchildren. With gunpowder, hammers and picks, they spent their days at the quarry face, lifting slate of all sizes on damp wicker baskets to ponies that waited impatiently below.

  Eight wooden huts sat below the site of the quarry, each filled with six low wooden beds, a small stove for heating and cooking, and little else. The men would heat water over the stove, burning dried peat that they had carried up in huge sacks in the spring. Barely fortified by a diet of brose - the boiled oats, barley and beans that filled their stomachs during the morning and night, they took comfort in contraband bottles of whisky stored in the awnings of the roof. It did what their woollen blankets could not when the temperature dropped. In the autumn and winter, their hands cut and raw from the quarrying and hard manual labour, they lay in their bunks and listened as someone read the Bible by the light of a smoky paraffin lamp. The stove glowed and comforted the hut's inhabitants in their makeshift home as it stood strong against the wind, rain, sleet and snow.

  1914 saw the quarry abandoned, its workforce volunteering to fight in the trenches of Belgium and France. Perhaps some knew even then that they would not be back home by Christmas. Some may have wondered if they would make it home at all. Little now remained of the miners' huts. A keen eye when out walking may notice the faint scraps of weather-beaten beams that lay half swallowed and petrified between heather and bog. Those who knew where to look could see the rusted mass of old railway lines, sinking further into the soil with each passing year and leeching orange-brown rust into the groundwater.

Ellis awoke in the early hours of the morning, the sun just beginning to rise on the horizon. Getting up from bed, he stretched and heard a welcome crack in his lower back and right shoulder. His earphones, which he had fallen asleep with still in his ears, now played the closing chapters of an audiobook. He pulled them out and cast them on the bed. The narrator's voice, though faint and some distance away, still carried across the room.

Making his way across the hallway, the floorboards creaked under his weight. He saw a mouse, no bigger than the core of an apple, running quickly away in his presence, squeezing itself under a gap near the bathroom. He went down on one knee and rubbed his finger against the slight spacing in the wood and felt its roughness. Where there was one mouse there would be more, but the pressure on his bladder took his mind off the worry.

Going back into his bedroom with the intention of getting a few more hours' sleep, perhaps even having some luck and being treated to an enjoyable dream, his sleepy eyes caught sight of the early morning sun as it hit the peaks of the distant mountains. Just then, he remembered the piece of paper he had taken from the library. 'See now, see later, but see.'

As he sat down at his kitchen table, blowing the steam from the surface of a cup of coffee in haste, an idea came to him. 'I can climb that,' he said aloud. While small at first, the thought slowly grew, and an energy soared through him that cast any residual tiredness aside. There was an old rucksack under the stairs, and a camping mat and sleeping bag stuffed somewhere in a bag in the airing cupboard. His work boots, though not designed for the purpose, were solid, relatively new and proved to be waterproof enough. Though ripped, the black Gore-Tex trousers would be somewhere to hand and there were several jackets on hooks in the hall, some warmer than others.

What harm can it do? Ellis thought to himself. For a minute, perhaps even longer, he might have even believed that he would do it. That after all this time he would do something. Do anything. Anything but work and read. But as he expected, and as readily as they always did, the doubts soon began to grow. Why now? I can go again, maybe even next weekend, he told himself.

It's too early. I should sleep. 'I could fall,' he said in a whisper, reassuring himself that to stay in the flat was the only acceptable course of action. The doubts grew and poured iced water on the glowing ember of optimism he had felt only moments ago.

Yet despite that, he stood in the kitchen taking down packets of dried soup mix and placing them in the side pocket of a battered rucksack. An apple followed, then some nuts. The kettle boiled and Ellis filled his flask before wrapping a ceramic mug in a tea towel and placing some cutlery in the makeshift package for good measure. With some chocolate, a box of raisins, one of the overripe bananas and a few bouillon cubes, the bag steadily filled. A sandwich of cheese and ham completed this impromptu ration.

The trousers, which looked to still hold at least the hope of waterproofing qualities were scrunched into a sausage shape and placed into the bottom of a bag. A lightweight summer jacket followed, then a heavier waterproof that Ellis had been given for the winter when he started with the council. Two hats, a pair of gloves and a spare pair of woollen socks now made the rucksack billow and bulge.

This was not Hillary's Everest, nor was it Amundsen's South Pole. Yet for Ellis, an imperceptible wind was forming that could soon propel him forwards towards his own discovery. A storm was building and for the first time in months, he had faced up to it. He would climb the mountain, and he would climb it today.

The bus station was busier than he expected at such an early hour on Saturday morning. Elderly couples sat together waiting on public transportation to take them where only they knew. A woman sat opposite Ellis; plastic shopping bags placed between her legs. Behind him he could hear the laughter of young girls, and beyond that, the faint sound of music being played from a phone, its melody drifting out over the sound of engines and reversing buses.

'Excuse me, son,' came a voice from beside him. 'I've gone and left my glasses at home and can't see the screen there. Do you know when the next number six arrives?'

Ellis looked up, squinting at an electronic board that was placed high above the departures' hall. 'You've got another forty minutes yet before it leaves,' he answered, giving a quick 'no problem' back when thanked.

He felt conspicuous by his strange mixture of clothes and his battered rucksack, and as usual, he worried that people were looking at him. However, he did not have long to dwell on the feelings as his own bus pulled into stance nine. He would take the thirty-six, then change at the sports centre on the outskirts of town. From there, it was an express bus in the direction of the park and ride. By the look of the map, it looked like a couple of hours walk to really get into the foothills and the start of the mountains proper. No more than that, he reassured himself.

Above the bus windows that appeared to be permanently shut, a line of rectangular advertisements drew the attention of passengers bored with the housing estates, fast food restaurants and retail parks that lined the route of the thirty-six. Outside of town as the bus crossed the bridge above the garden centre and its grounds, Ellis looked towards the shore and saw light wisps of smoke from a beach fire. The smoke made him think of Andy and Jordan and he wondered how each man would be spending his weekend.

Outside the sports centre, green graffiti daubed across its walls, Ellis waited with a handful of other passengers for the express bus to arrive. Soon they found themselves hurtling along the motorway, the mountain range looming directly ahead of them. After thirty minutes of driving, the passengers got off in twos and threes, leaving Ellis as the sole occupant. Turning off the main road, he watched as the homes, cars and other signs of life reduced, then seemed to cease entirely. A solitary red bus stop with Perspex red windows signalled the end of his journey, the winding road above it leading the way to another that was about to begin.

Ellis watched as the bus drove what must have only been one hundred metres forward, reversed cumbersomely into a nearby passing place, then slowly veered out back in the direction it had come from. He chose to tie his boots tightly, not looking behind him as the bus made its long journey back through the villages below. Opening his rucksack, Ellis took stock of his supplies. He was unsure of what to do next and he questioned what now seemed like a foolhardy decision. Regardless, and with a heaviness in his legs that he could not explain, he walked along the road in the direction of a path, light brown and worn by the boots of sheep and hikers, as it wound itself up the foothills of the mountain range.

    The path quickly gained elevation and looking down on the scene below as he drank from a bottle of water, he saw the city in the distance, the sea stretching out far beyond to the horizon. Boats and ships of all sizes and purpose appeared motionless on the still water. The arable land that stretched upwards from the coast contained a patchwork of different coloured fields in all shades of green and yellow. Wind turbines hemmed in the field, standing in rows that were soon hidden by an outcrop from some of the lower lying hills.

    He walked on, the wind rising and falling as he did so, and he perceived a notable drop in temperature as he gained altitude. Recognising the feeling of emptiness in his stomach to be that of hunger, he stopped to eat.

A patchwork fence, covered with wool and surrounded by pearls of sheep shit, marked out the path he had come from. He sat on a rock, two metres from the main path that now narrowed, heather and plants creeping over its edges. The growing wind made him take out a jumper from his bag, and he removed his jacket before pulling the piece of second-hand knitwear over his head. Putting his jacket back on, he pulled the oversized waterproof over his knees and sat huddled up, watching as the wind blew stalks of grass at a forty-five-degree angle. He greedily ate the sandwich in a few bites, before filling up a cup of hot water from his flask and pouring it over the contents of one of the packets of soup. Drinking quickly before the wind had time to cool it, he finished his lunch then placed everything back into his bag. The sweat from the back of his neck dried and he sensed a chill go down his body. He could smell his skin, a slightly sickly smell of unwashed hair and fresh sweat. Taking a hat from his bag, he pulled it tightly over his ears, then sat and listened.

A bird flapped its wings on a nearby rock then chirped loudly, its feathers rustling against the wind. Ellis looked at his phone and realised with some degree of shock that he had left the bus almost three hours ago. He perceived that there was a distance from the notion of time and the thought gave him a feeling of great relaxation. His mind felt silent, the rushing thoughts he had experienced early that morning settling down. Getting up slowly, he cast the rucksack over both shoulders and continued on his way. Far beyond, he saw two hikers on their way down the path coming in his direction. Soon enough, nods were exchanged and the person in front spoke to Ellis. He found this notable, given his weekends were usually spent in silence.

'The weather's turning,' said the female hiker. 'The hills aren't going anywhere so no need to push it. I'd watch yourself if you're going further,' she added, looking down subconsciously at his makeshift equipment as she did so.

Ellis thanked them and looked on as the woman and her friend, the latter trailing a less than enthusiastic Airedale terrier behind her, made their way down to the path. Looking up, he saw the mountains rising resolutely above him. At this distance, he could not see their peaks, hidden behind a looming grey cloud that promised a heavy rainfall. Standing in the plateau, he thought of the contents of his rucksack and felt the chilling wind steadily creep inside the barrier of waterproof trousers that were nearly as old as he was.

Heinrich Harrer scaled the Eiger's North Face; Desio, Compagnoni and Lacedelli ascended K2; Whymper reached the Matterhorn in 1865. Ellis Penrice had taken public transportation, walked for what was now five hours and eaten some dry bread with cheese and ham. Yet he noticed a change within, and while he could not place what it was, he knew that it had taken place. With a feeling of calm tranquillity, he stood in this spot, looking up at the majesty that lay before him. This was his adventure. No, he told himself, in an almost unbridled, maniacal joy – this was his expedition! An expedition as important as any experienced by those who came before him. His was a story that would not make the history books or be spoken about around the world for years to come. Its technical brilliance, endeavour and grit would not inspire others to push the boundaries of human strength and resilience. But as Ellis walked back on the long path to the bus stop, his feet and hands numb from the cold, eyes stinging from the wind, and mouth dry from exertion, he stopped and tried to absorb and bathe in a feeling that he had felt rising inside him. A growing feeling that made him ignore his aching muscles and the chafed skin between his legs.

Chapter eight

<u>April 1989</u>

The newspapers lay bound with brown string in piles outside the shop door. Jordan sleepily placed his key in the lock, turning it while waiting to hear the welcoming click of the mechanism. Reaching up instinctively in search for the main light switch, his fingers fumbled clumsily before he reached his target. A deft flick saw the strip lights flicker and buzz before illuminating the room with a dull orange glow. Knowing that he still had time for a quick cup of tea before the papers had to be split, sorted and stacked, he took a seat in the shop's back room and waited for the fatigue to subside.

The cup was barely finished when he heard the front door creak open. The sound of heavy footsteps came towards him before Robert poked his head into the back room.

'Jordan, why are the newspapers still outside? I'm not paying you to drink tea. This isn't the first time we've had this conversation, but I trust it will be the last,' said Robert, who was always querulous at this hour of the day.

'You're right,' Jordan muttered, avoiding Robert's gaze as he did so. 'I was up a bit later than usual this morning and didn't have time for a cup of tea. No excuses. Sorry, I'll get to them now,' he said, quickly standing upright and giving a solemn smile by way of apology.

'See that you do, Jordan,' sneered Robert, making his way behind the till before removing a brown notebook from his shirt pocket.

The shop was a labyrinth of cosmetics, food, confectionery and anything else that Robert could get his hands on, as long as he believed it could sell for a profit. In quieter periods, when the morning rush had subsided and the usual stream of regulars came in to buy their milk, cigarettes and bread, Robert would sit Jordan down to deliver short lectures on economics.

'Supply and demand, my boy, supply and demand. We do our work and earn a little something for ourselves as nobody else will do it for us,' he warned, over mouthfuls of Bournville chocolate. That morning, he had objected at what he took to be Jordan's laziness and took it upon himself to show him what hard work looked like. He marched from the storeroom to the front of the shop, lifting and dragging, pulling and sliding boxes and packages as he went. Jordan marvelled at his perseverance and drive, but not to any degree that he was willing to offer his help. Robert emptied and inspected the contents of each box with military precision. Despite that, excluding the daily essentials that would always find a buyer, Jordan had yet to see much variation or rotation in the stock and wondered how many of each respective item was sold.

Once everything had been checked over by Robert, it was only then that the warren-like structure of the shop began to change. This happened each morning with the regularity of clockwork, and anyone watching the scene unfold would have been amazed at the engineering, desire and propensity of the owner to make use of every last piece of conceivable space.

The front window and façade, which only minutes before had been visible from the street, were both now hidden by all manner of cheap plastic wastepaper baskets, buckets, watering cans and plant pots. Rows of all varieties of potting compost, Irish peat moss and seed packets, framed the plastic commodities. In the summer, which for Jordan meant even more time off school, all manner of inflatable dinghies, beach balls and other novelty props for a day at the seaside hung from the rafters, taking the place of hard and soft bristled brushes and sturdy looking mops, their strands of cotton hanging limply.

By the time Mr Grendle and his companion walked into the shop that morning, Jordan had finished stacking the papers on the shelves and was now doing what Robert suspected was a less than scrupulous stock-take. He had to leave soon to get to school but did not mind being late. 'Consistency is key,' a teacher had said to him during a well-placed, if not wholly welcome, motivational talk. Jordan thought it best he lived up to it by never being on time for the first lesson, if he made it in at all.

The bell above the door signalled the entrance of a patron. 'Morning, Robert,' said Mr Grendle. 'A lovely morning we're having, I must say,' he added, peering up from behind a hastily stacked row of baked beans boxes and manoeuvring himself into any available space.

Robert looked up. 'Mr Grendle,' he said curtly, a respectful nod thrown in for good measure.

Looking at the chocolate bars before taking a Flake, Mr Grendle's companion looked eager to continue the topic that had so clearly been a heated item of debate, which Jordan figured had now spilled over from the streets outside. He spoke quickly and with a passion that sounded strange to Jordan's ears.

'As I was saying and be that as it may, but privatisation is still privatisation, however you want to dress it up. What will be next, I wonder, or need we even wonder? For it will all be on us soon! Profit before people with no going back. Commitments to this and that mean nothing when the facts are laid out so clearly before our own eyes,' said the man, his wavering voice belying his intended outward calmness.

Mr Grendle bristled. 'Some pipe tobacco

please, Robert. And I'll get this chocolate bar for my young friend here, too. Maybe the sugar will sharpen his brain and senses!' he scoffed.

Unperturbed, his companion continued. 'Working for patients,' he said in a mocking tone. 'It should be called working for themselves, and only themselves! Mark my words!'

Mr Grendle handed over some coins to Robert, then waiting for his change to be handed back, spoke once more, this time with a notable frustration in his voice. 'Now listen here. You may take this to be some student union debate with you and your drunken Trot friends, but this is about raising the levels of healthcare for all! You are too damn minded and pig ignorant to see,' Mr Grendle said in a raised voice. He counted his change, placed it back in the top inside pocket of a waxed Barbour jacket, then bit theatrically upon one of his fingers. Jordan could see his cheeks and forehead changing from light pink to scarlet.

Mr Grendle continued. 'I can explain it to you, but I cannot understand it for you. Is it that you want to have no choice? Is that it? Would you rather we be like Poland, Hungary and East Germany? Or do you want to see Kinnock run us into the ground? You should be thankful that he bloodied Benn's nose last year, or we'd be facing even more of the red hordes right now!'

His hands shook now, and as before, he went to

bite upon his quivering fingers. Jordan noticed the wry smile growing on his companion's face. He had now received the reaction that he clearly wanted. Mr Grendle was building to a crescendo. Raising his voice to all but a loud gravelly roar. Spittle left his mouth as he continued his tirade against the man who dared to question what he saw to be the brilliance of Thatcher's NHS reforms.

'So no, it is you who should mark my words and mark them well. Clarke will see this through, you'll see. Decisions coming from the front, not by some penpusher in Whitehall! There is nothing wrong with private sector tendering, or.'

He was cut off before he could finish his sentence.

'My thanks for the chocolate but I must say, perhaps it is you who would benefit from a boost of energy? Can you not see that we are now in danger of losing a health service that will soon put people before profit? No amount of advertising, however they spin it, will change that, father,' said the man.

Robert forced a single cough. It had the desired effect and led to a welcome pause in the morning debate.

'Excuse me gentlemen but will that be all for today?' he asked.

Mr Grendle nodded, thanking Robert for the tobacco and holding the door open for his son as they made their way out of the shop. Robert watched them through narrowed eyes as they left.

'You'd best get to school now, Jordan. The work will still be here tomorrow,' he said. Jordan smiled; his fingers pressed against a stolen chocolate bar in his pocket.

'Thanks very much and I'll see you tomorrow,' he said, slinking out the back door of the shop and into the morning.

As he came towards the corner of Brandwell Gardens, where the playing field looked out at the Chinese takeaway, Jordan had already made the decision that he would not be going to school that day. He was unsure if Andy, who lived close enough that he could roll out of bed and into the classroom, would still be at home. He had not been to school since the end of last week and Jordan had begun to worry that what he presumed was a cold or sickness bug, had taken a turn for the worst. He decided he would pay him an early visit that morning to see if everything was okay, or more hopefully, that he would agree to a game of football or a salvage expedition along the beach. A recent storm had blown all manner of scrap, wood and plastic along the shore and he had not yet found the time to investigate.

The curtains were still closed by the time he made his way to the front door. A black gate sat open and swung in the breeze, knocking rhythmically against a crumbling red brickwork wall. The grass had gone uncut, and the garden looked shabby and devoid of any life. Small plastic bottles of lemonade had been cut lengthways to lay in a row of cloches, but Jordan could see that none of them sheltered any plant. The other gardens in the street looked to be coming to life. Daffodils bloomed between primroses and bluebells and the trees hung with immature green bulbs, readily awaiting the summer. Yet Andy's garden had none of this, making the contrast even greater for Jordan. It felt unloved, uncared for, and if Jordan could pinpoint the particular feeling he encountered in that moment, it felt dead.

The letterbox rattled as he knocked three times on the door. Waiting for an answer, he knocked once more, but still he found no response. Placing his hands to the side of his eyes, he pressed his face to a loose pane of glass that sat and rattled between the top panel. It appeared to be the only source of light from a house that seemed to be shut off from the outside, the curtains hiding away whatever was inside. Jordan realised that he had not been inside since Andy's dad left the year before.

Deciding to knock once more before making other plans, he tapped the letterbox and gave the bottom of the door a solid kick for good measure. A neighbour peered out of their upstairs window at the sound, looking Jordan up and down, before sticking their head back in the direction it had come.

Jordan listened closely at the faint sound of footsteps from the stairs in front of him. Looking through the glass once more, he saw a faint shadow darting back and forth on the hall landing. Seconds later, Andy was bounding down the stairs in his direction.

Jordan could see Andy's red, tired eyes. He did not know if he had been crying or had just not slept. Either outcome proved troubling and unsettled him. He could hear what sounded like the chain of a safety lock being drawn to one side, then strangely, a second one going through the same hand-drawn motions. Andy fiddled behind the door, moving in a rhythm that Jordan did not recognise as that of his friend. Peering through a gap in the door, Andy spoke first.

'Jordan, it's not a good time,' he whispered.

'Sorry, just wanted to see how you were and why you hadn't been in school,' replied Jordan, taking one step back from the stairs and subconsciously turning towards the gate.

'Hang on,' said Andy, stepping outside and joining Jordan on the path. He glanced up at the bedroom window above him. The curtains were still closed, but he noticed they swayed and swung slightly.

'It's mum,' said Andy. 'She's having one of her turns,' he said.

Jordan, unsure of what to say in response forced out 'oh... sorry.'

Andy looked around the dead garden, anywhere to avoid Jordan's dull looking expression. He whispered. 'Look, this is hard for me to ask but do you have any money on you? Even a quid would be great. I'll pay you back,' he said, his voice breaking with embarrassment.

Robert paid Jordan for his help in the mornings and weekends. What Jordan was not paid in cash, he took in confectionary and bottles of blended Scotch whisky. He rummaged in his pocket and took out a chocolate bar, a 50-pence piece and two dull, tarnished pound coins. Turning them between his fingers, he looked at the detail of their faces; an English oak tree growing between the motif of a crown.

Placing a hand on Andy's shoulder, he realised how fragile his friend's body felt. Too rigid for boys their age, he thought. Andy still bowed his head, his face looking down at nothing. Taking Andy's right hand with his left, Jordan placed the coins in his palm and gently closed it. Andy remained still.

'Thank you,' he said, though it was barely audible.

'Andy,' said Jordan, his voice sounding weak. 'You need to talk to someone about this, Andy. It...it can't go on and you need help now. Now. You need to,' his tone forceful yet he hoped supportive.

Only then did Andy look up to meet Jordan's gaze as a car reversed loudly out of the opposite driveway, blasting grey-black exhaust fumes across a nearby group of children as they walked to school.

'We got by. We were fine. It's just a bad week... I know that. Mum is alright. She's fine... it's just a bad week,' said Andy, the words forming slowly with staccato intonation.

'We'll go to the doctor again soon, but I can't force mum and there's just so much to do now. So much... and I'm scared,' said Andy, his breathing sounding forced and laboured.

The door, which Andy had not closed properly swung open and the warmth of the house met with the fresh air outside. Jordan could smell damp clothing and a strong smell of decaying rubbish. The same smell that hit him when he retrieved his stolen whisky from outside the bins. With the door open and the house lit, Jordan now saw cat shit in all stages of desiccation and decay on the foot of the stairs. Clothes lay over the floor and hung from the banisters. In the early hours of the morning, Andy had rubbed some of them with carbolic soap in an attempt to wash them in the bath. Jordan could see water dripping at irregular intervals from women's underwear, pastel dresses and three blouses, staining still evident around the neck and arms.

'We're fourteen, Andy,' he said, involuntarily placing one finger under his nose and swallowing down hard, the sense of nausea growing in his stomach and throat. 'Fourteen,' he gasped, looking once more at the scene of devastation that lay before him in the house.

Hours before, Jordan's mum had woken him from a deep sleep by gently knocking on his bedroom door. 'Here's some tea for you, love,' she had said, closing it again after Jordan had thanked her. Eating a slice of toast for breakfast, his only worry was what mood Robert would be in today, or if he would get the Bible out again. He brushed his teeth and washed his face, the remnants of shaving foam and stubble still clinging to the sink's rim from his father's early shave. He had evidently left for work early. Jordan had taken his clean school uniform down from an ironed pile that sat at the top of the stairs, waved goodbye to his mum and set off for the shop.

As he stood on the pathway outside Andy's house now, he saw his friend's red blotchy face and deep, half-moon dark patches under his eyes that had no right to be there. The sight made him angry, and he spat on the grass. He watched as Andy failed to hide the tears that now poured readily from his eyes, falling onto the dry concrete path. Reaching up to wipe his face, the sleeve from his dressing gown fell loosely to his elbow. Jordan could see cuts and scratches on Andy's arm, fresh and bright as they crisscrossed the tracks of previous scars.

  Jordan felt anger rising in him. He wanted to run into the house and throw everything he could into the bin. He wanted to tear at the overgrown grass with his teeth and smash his fists against the muddy garden and crumbling walls. Take Andy away to a place where there was toast and clean clothes. To a place where his mother would leave a hot water bottle in bed for him at winter, and cold glasses of juice and biscuits out on the kitchen counter in summer. He wanted to tell someone what was happening, but he did not know what that was, nor did he know who to tell. But most of all he wanted to take away the tears and sadness from Andy and cast them far out to sea.

Chapter nine

When one becomes caught in a riptide, the best course of action is to swim parallel to the shore. Swimming against it will do nothing except drag the unfortunate person further to sea. Ellis had finished work early and now sat on a bench by the promenade. He watched the plentiful swimmers as they splashed and paddled in the shallows, with some even braving the deeper waters beyond the pier. His memory took him back to his school lessons where he and his classmates were told about the risks of swimming in the sea.

After his experience in the mountains, he had begun to feel his very own unseen current swelling inside him, touching each part of his body at different stages of the day. A toddler waddling along the shore with her parents close behind dropped an ice cream and was immediately swarmed by the seagulls that hovered above, each one shrieking with delight and diving down in the hope it would get to the now-sodden cone first.

Taking a towel and shorts from his bag, Ellis changed awkwardly and aligned himself closely with the wall where the beach met the pavement. He was quite sure that nobody was watching, but the towel and wall covered his modesty regardless. He noted the sensation of the sand as it turned from dry and powdery to wet and clay-like, darkening in shade as he got closer to the water's edge. His toes and feet touched the tide as it lapped the beach, and he welcomed the contrast of the cool and chilling water against the warmth from the sun that covered the rest of his body. Trudging deeper until the water reached his calves, then his thighs, he stood and took in his surroundings as the water lapped against the bottom of his swimming shorts. In doing so, he realised that he had not swum in these waters since he was a child. He and Cameron had once played on this beach each summer, making sandcastles and catching the small fish that darted in the surf with small nets.

Bracing himself for the shock that was to come, he placed his hands in the water, splashed some on his chest and neck, then dived below the waterline. Staying underwater, he kicked his legs and resurfaced some feet away from where he had stood moments before. His feet no longer touched the bottom, and he treaded the water, feeling the welcome tension from the sea as he pushed against it with his hands and feet. Ellis felt the bracing chill throughout his body and tried to calm his breathing, which he knew was becoming erratic and staccato. Some seaweed on the bottom brushed against his arm and a plastic carrier bag floated below him; neither sinking nor floating.

Keeping his head above the waterline, an unpractised breaststroke got him to a point he could once again touch his feet on the sand. Walking back to the beach, he sensed his body tingle as if being pricked by small needles and his skin glowed with a bright ruby red hue from the cold water. Taking the time to experience the sensation, he pulled his fingers through his salt-water soaked hair and felt its gritty roughness. As he stood with the towel draped around his shoulders, no thoughts filled his mind. For perhaps one full minute, he stood unthinking, a calming numbness, preceded by a feeling of contentment, overtook his entire body.

The screeching seagulls, laughing families and traffic noises from all around did little to break the trance. It was only when a passing runner accidentally tripped and stumbled before him, did his soft gaze become focused once more on the surroundings and his mind became busy.

He had not yet eaten and instead of going back to his flat, Ellis wanted to explore the market that was set up each Sunday; a once regular event which he had not visited for several years. At the very least he was sure he could get a nice cup of tea and perhaps a bacon roll. He dressed quickly, drying himself as best he could, but a dampness persisted, and he tried to ignore the sand between his toes and the soles of his feet as he walked in the direction of the town centre.

On one stand, circular wheels of Edam and Gouda lay between rows of cylindrical goat's cheese and wedges of cave-aged cheddar. A brown speckled Cantal and a rectangular block of Maroilles were arranged at the front of the display, a red-and-white check covering hanging loosely and blowing gently in the breeze. People huddled around and tasted samples from others who sold bread, olives, cured meats and various types of confectionery. Ordering a coffee from a miserly looking man who seemed to scowl at those who passed his stand, Ellis walked to look at the floral displays. Buckets of red, purple, green and blue flowers filled the stands, and a bundle of rose-pink peony made him think of his mother.

Towards the end of the market, a solitary bookseller stood at her allocated plot. Ellis had not seen her before, but his absence from the market for several years made him think little of it. The stall had limited footfall and those who did walk by appeared to ignore the books, choosing instead to hide their faces away in sandwiches, takeaway coffees and mobile telephones. The woman sat down and moved her red cash box so that when it was opened, she would have easy access to the money. Ellis wondered when it was last opened.

Her books lay with their spines up, packed tightly in square wooden boxes. The sun reflected on several of their covers and the glittering made Ellis think of sardines packed in their cans. Moving closer to inspect what was inside, he discovered that there was no order in the contents. Old pamphlets lay atop weighty literary fiction, while a hardback book on the merits of fly fishing looked to struggle for space with a much smaller paperback on the Pre-Raphaelites. Even with a steady wind, Ellis could smell the aged paper and dust drifting from the boxes.

'You can take two for five pounds,' came the earnest voice. 'Well, if anything takes your fancy that is. Please... take your time,' she said, once more moving her red cash box until she found a position that pleased her.

Thanking her, Ellis pulled one of the boxes closer to him and moved his fingers across the titles, trying to get a better look among the limited space.

'I wish I could tell you what was in there, but well, these books aren't mine you see,' came the voice again, this time in an apologetic tone. 'What am I saying, sorry. Ignore me! They are mine now, but well... they belonged to my father and now they belong to me.' She glanced at Ellis and took his smile as an invitation to continue.

'It's very hard to separate the belongings of someone you love when they're gone. We all collect so very much, don't we? My father loved his books, but he shared that love with fishing and whisky. Split the passion for reading with rugby and chess. It's good to have hobbies, wouldn't you say?'

'I think so,' Ellis said, conscious that his own were limited.

'Well, you see, I couldn't possibly take all these books with me, and I couldn't just put them in a skip somewhere at the local dump. We already had to do that with so many of his things and I still feel... well... anyway, listen to me rabbiting on! I am sorry. Please, I'll let you get back to your browsing,' said the woman. She sat down again and moved the cash box once more, tapping it gently with her finger as she did so.

'Just this one please,' said Ellis, feeling a growing awkwardness at his inability to respond. He prized the first one that came loose in his fingers, slid a one-pound coin across the table and thanked her.

The cover was torn but Ellis saw that he had taken a book of Pablo Neruda's selected poems. Not wishing to throw it away but having no use for a book like that, he placed it amongst his damp towel and swimming gear, bought himself another coffee and found a bench in which to sit and people watch.

The time passed slowly but he still had no intention or desire to go home. A curious feeling had grown, and he reached into his bag in response. The book was well-worn, but he flicked across a few pages and read some of the poems within. It must be said that he found none particularly engaging, nor did any strike any degree of emotion. Towards the back of the book, where some of the shorter poems were printed, Ellis could see faint notes in pencil and pen.

The clearest of these was clearly the previous owner's attempt at his own poetry. Ellis looked across the market to see the face of the author's daughter. She remained alone with little custom to speak of. A man looked briefly in one of the boxes but was quick to move on. Ellis thought back to her high cheekbones and slightly crooked nose and wondered what her father had looked like. He read the poem:

In the evening song,

With words on paper.

We will never see,

What had always promised to arrive; in talk and dream,

Yet failed to grow.

Within a soil we furrowed, and eyes cast forwards to the seedling.

That came with rain, which left with morning,

And sorrow.

Ellis could see other short lines, phrases and apparent diary notes written down in the margins and on pages where the poem only filled half the page. He had little interest in reading any more until he saw an inscription on the back of the book:

Emma.

May this guide you on your way.

x

Ellis looked back across the market and wondered if he was looking at Emma. In her grief or haste, he was unsure which, he pictured her mixing up her own books with those of her late father. He questioned that if she did not know that this had taken place, then did it really matter? Her life would not change on the return of this book; indeed, it may even rekindle memories that she no longer wanted to remember? Perhaps, he wondered, as he noted that his mind was spiralling to a place where he had limited control; perhaps she had placed this book in with the rest of them with the intention of doing so? An easy way to dispose of something that she could not throw away herself. No, he told himself. That would be too much of a gamble. If she had wanted to get rid of it, then he was sure it would have taken pride of place on top of the boxes. She would have offered it to him for free. It was not his decision to make, and he should simply go home. Leave Emma, if this was indeed Emma, to live her own life away from his interference and influence. Yet as the thoughts within him raced, he found himself walking closer and closer to the boxes of books, the little red cash box, and the woman who consistently and with great purpose continued to rearrange its position.

She saw him walking and before he had a chance to open his mouth, she got there first. 'I am sorry if some of the pages are missing on any of the books. I really haven't had the time to properly check them,' she said, instinctively looking down at the cash box in anticipation of a refund.

'I'm sorry if this sounds strange, but are you Emma?' Ellis asked timidly.

'How did you know that?' she whispered back, looking startled. Ellis had been correct.

Opening the book to show her the back page and its inscription, he placed it in her hand. 'I'm very sorry, but I think this might belong to you?'

She took the book and sat down, staring at the words that had been written for her. To Ellis, this seemed like an eternity, yet he stood where he was without moving.

'This was a birthday present,' she said diffidently. 'For my sixteenth birthday, now that I think of it,' she said, looking down at the pages as she slowly flicked them with her fingers. 'I must have misplaced it, and it fell in with my father's collection. Thank you so very, very much for returning it to me. It's funny how things turn out, isn't it?'

'In what way?' responded Ellis, unsure of the question.

'The paths we all take in life,' she responded. 'It's funny. Do you know, ever since I was a little girl all I had wanted to do was write. It filled my very being and it helped me feel when I struggled to speak about things that I felt. I am sorry, you don't need to hear any of this, thank you again for returning this book. I had forgotten all about it for many, many years and now it is in front of me again and well... I don't know what to say really. It's like a long-lost friend has come back into my life and is showing me a photo album,' she said.

'You don't have to say sorry,' said Ellis. 'I'm just glad I could return it to you.'

'Please, now you simply must take something else from the collection? If poetry is your thing, I'm sure there are some works by Frost and Plath in here somewhere. Does that interest you? You only need to rummage around and please, do take anything you like,' she said, smiling.

'That's very kind of you but if I'm honest, I'm finding it hard to read anything at the moment.' The words shot from Ellis like water from a burst tap and as they did, he witnessed something loosen inside of him. He had not voiced this to anyone, nor had he admitted it to himself. Novels went unfinished, library books were returned and interests faded and passed to new interests, only for those to fade with the same frequency, until the lightness dimmed from them all.

'We have only just met, but that brings me a great deal of sadness to hear,' said the woman, who Ellis now knew to be Emma.

'Books will be a constant in your life. They will be with you on your journey through all the experiences you'll have, and if you are lucky, they may even help shape it. These books were with my father the year I was born, and more would have been purchased after my brother arrived. Some will have been there from when he met and fell in love with my mother, and I am very sure others will come from a time when he said his final goodbye to her. Even a poorly written book is better than no book at all, that's what he always used to say to us as children. And do you know what, he was right. I can still recall as clear as you stand before me the book that I was reading on the morning my husband and I found out we were expecting our first child. And more to the point, the pages of books, of great works that I have pondered and thought over, and of hastily read page turners, have all been a solid constant in my memory. I do so hope you can read again. At the very least, it can unlock something within you that may not have crossed your mind for many years. That is what you and this book of poetry have done for me today. I am extremely grateful to you because of it. Now because of that, may I ask you to do something for me?'

Ellis was confused. 'You can certainly ask me,' he said, fearful of what was to come next.

Scanning the boxes, she swooped down like a hawk on its prey. Taking some brown paper from her bag below the stall, she quickly wrapped a book she had taken before Ellis could see its front cover.

'Take this,' she said. 'When the time is right for you, you can read it. Only you will know when the time is right to open it, but you will know.'

Ellis took the book from her with the intention of opening it as soon as he was out of eyeshot.

'Thank you for this,' he said, resolved in the fact that he would soon know what was wrapped within the brown paper package. Yet such internal expressions so often do not come to fruition, and as the hours passed to days and the days turned to weeks, it remained covered and hidden, its contents known, at least then, only to Emma.

Chapter ten

Mid-July signalled the start of summer proper. Throngs of youngsters and families now flocked to the beach to hunt in rockpools, read by the waves and splash in the surf. Work followed the same routine for Ellis, but he filled each day with a stoic resignation, helped in part by his work with Andy.

Jordan had taken some enforced time off from the job towards the end of June. While far from encouraged, his drinking had long been known to senior management. However, after one too many slips and trips, he was finally offered the help he so badly needed. A fall one drizzly Tuesday, just outside the base, left a deep cut above his eye. Involvement could no longer be overlooked.

Ellis had not seen him for some weeks but had heard he was doing well, whatever such platitudes meant, he reasoned. Such language was the order of the day at the depot and Ellis would often think hard about what it really meant. Was he now sober, looking forward to whatever it was he looked forward to, or did it just mean that he was safe inside a hospital, in a space where the trips and falls would, he hoped, no longer occur. The thought would often come to Ellis, particularly on the days when the work canteen was filled with its usual silence.

He walked nearly every inch of the city in those long summer nights. Down long streets and through single track lanes, in parks and along hedgerows. Without music, he listened to the sounds of life around him. Of the traffic and birdsong or of the brief snippets of conversation he heard from those he passed.

'... and that's why we're considering going private...' said the woman in grey sweatpants and a quarter zip top, small weights around her wrists and ankles. Her friend, an attractive looking woman in her early fifties, nodded in agreement.

Close to the beach, so close in fact that grains of sand were visible on the path, there was a small tunnel that took walkers under the road above. Dog walkers joined the cyclists and joggers who came through at varying speeds. Ellis stood back to let an oncoming cyclist through, a shout of thanks and a welcome ring of the bell his reward. He could feel the sweat on his clothes and welcomed the light breeze that was blowing off the sea. The sensation made him think of his visit to the mountains and the feeling that it had left on him. In that moment he knew once again that the peaks and pathways, waterfalls and streams, would fill his dreams that night.

As he closed his eyes that evening, his mind drifted to the hillside path. He could hear the bird on its rock, chirping its passionate song. But most of all, he questioned why he went. 'Lenin's War: advance on Poland' had remained unfinished. Yet barely a few chapters in, he already sensed that the book had given him something that he had not only longed for, but needed. Needed with the yearning of food and drink when hunger and thirst demands. For it was no longer the book he sought, but the bookmark.

The finding of a small slip of paper on the library floor necessitated a change in his plans. He understood that while it was easy to change plans that were yet unwritten, everyone he knew attempted to try and write their own. To sketch out a rough outline and move forward, or all too often backwards from a place one found themselves in. Not everything had to be good or exciting, nor would it always induce tears of joy. He understood that on many occasions it may even deliver tears of sadness and pain, frustration and anger.

Yet despite that, and more so because of it, there was a new desire to do something; to experience and to see. The sensation grew so much that at points he was powerless to control it and his mind spun with unbridled energy. Three words ran through his head: luck, fate and serendipity. Luck relies on chance. Good or bad, it cannot be controlled by actions. Fate is also beyond our control. It is preset, and again, Ellis understood it to be both good and bad. What will be, will be. No amount of planning can overcome fate and our ultimate destination.

The thought created a brooding nervousness and a frustration that increased in severity as he pondered it during the summer. He did not want his own story to be written when he had only now recovered the pen that had been lost for so long.

Then there was serendipity. A fortunate and unexpected discovery that could spell the beginning of good luck. As his mind raced, an internal voice told him that he had not been looking for small sheets of paper in the library. But another voice deep within, much stronger than before, reminded him that he was looking for a sign or signal to change. He questioned if it mattered. If simply being and going along with whatever came his way was better than seeking something which he was unsure would come. Between his bedsheets that evening, he made the decision to visit the library once more.

He would search for - with the intention of finding - a sign. What that sign was he was unsure of, but the idea found fertile ground within. He took some paper down from his bedside table and scrawled 'library' on it, a reminder in case a change of mood took his thoughts elsewhere the next morning. Just minutes later Ellis was asleep, his breathing calm and the muscles of his face smooth and relaxed.

Once awake, Ellis looked at the scribbled note from the previous evening. Feeling well rested, he picked at the shell of a boiled egg, the yolk too hard for his liking, and drank a cup of black tea.

The strong desire he had felt the night before had not diminished, but a fear began to grow in him. Like an old friend or a regular visitor, it crept up on him and built with each passing sip. It was a fear of having this newfound hope dashed, no matter how small that hope was. He wanted to believe that the makeshift bookmark had been a sign, placed only for him. Whatever the cause or reasoning he did not understand or know, but he wanted to believe that it was placed there to be found. A secret message that would guide him along whichever path he now chose to follow. But still the fear grew. A fear of finding nothing and of falling back into a hole that he knew only too well. The hole itself was not one he found frightening, but the vast emptiness within it filled him with a horror and dread that he could not face. The darkness went on forever. But he told himself that morning that he had found a new opportunity for a way out; that final, strong and supportive hand to clasp his own and pull him clearly up and away from the shadows.

There was no cat outside the library that morning as Ellis waited alone for the doors to open. He wanted to be first in amongst the books, anything to give him a better chance of finding something. He caught a glimpse of his reflection in the mirror and if only for a brief moment, he questioned whether he still had a grip on reality. The thoughts raced and a nervousness grew, but he forced the feeling down and remained steadfast. 'This is not normal behaviour,' he whispered to himself, the sound of his own voice giving him further credence to believe it. At nine the electric doors opened with a judder. Walking inside, a gruff-looking cleaner went out in the opposite direction. He was a wispy grey-haired man with a clipped beard that was longer in the moustache.

'Morning,' said the cleaner.

'Morning,' Ellis replied, his heart beating in his mouth.

In the interest of fairness, Ellis had made an agreement with himself that he would only be able to look for books on the third floor. Skipping up the stairs with one hand on the railing at speeds that the librarian on the second floor had clearly never witnessed before, he soon stood at the gateway to his destination. Since his last visit, a librarian had clearly been placed on each floor and she was now approaching him, a smile on her face. Pushing a trolley of books, she walked up to Ellis and nodded.

'If there's anything in particular you're looking for then just let me know. I'm just over there,' she said warmly. 'Just give me a shout if you need anything pointed out.'

'Thanks very much,' Ellis replied, 'but I think I know what I'm looking for.'

This could not be further from the truth, but he said it with a conviction that even he did not recognise.

The top floor opened before him, as it had all those weeks before. Ignoring his list, he walked up the second row on the left-hand side. Rows of religious books lined the shelf. Scanning the spines, he read some of the titles under his breath: 'The World with Judaism ...Greek Orthodoxy: A History...Prepare for...' his voice drifted off. The thought occurred to him that any sign would surely come from a book that he would take an interest in. While finding some of the historical and philosophical points of religion fascinating, at least in a small part, he would be lying if he said he could pinpoint ever reading anything in detail on any of the world's major religions. He walked on, hesitating at political theory and ideology, before crossing over to sociology. Pausing to reflect on philosophy, the morning sun casting its warm rays on some of the books at the bottom of the section, he soon walked on. Stopping at history he looked back at the librarian who was placing the books from her trolley on the shelves.

He made a deal with himself in that moment. Five books. Five books and if there was nothing in any of the five then this had all been one massive folly. How foolish he had been to get his hopes up over something so stupid; something where the odds would be so heavily stacked against him, he reasoned. What way is this to lead a life, he contemplated, cursing himself for being so naive. The wave was building once more and in that moment of his indiscretion, he hated himself. He wanted to leave, to run away from that place and never come back. Sit in the safety of the flat and do as he wished. If his was to be a life of nothing, then so be it. If that meant day after day with Archie and Andy or raising a glass to the success of others, then he would do it. If his was a life of limited joy, then so be it. He would live it while he still could, embracing and dealing with whatever it gave him.

From a nearby window he could see a bus that went directly to the corner of his street. If he left now he could put this embarrassment behind him; forget all about it and hide his foolhardiness away from the world. What right did he have to believe in some other worldly force? A force that would guide his path through books. It was a proposition so preposterous that it made his head spin and he struggled for breath. He turned quickly on his heels and ran for the stairs.

Having bounded down the third flight, he could see the bus still waiting at its stop from the second-floor window. A voice from above stopped him in his tracks.

'Excuse me!' it rang out, bouncing with a delicate echo.

Looking up, he saw the librarian holding something in her hand.

'I'm sorry, but... yes, you... sorry excuse me, but is this your wallet?'

Ellis patted down his pockets and felt the emptiness. Feeling embarrassed, he slowly made his way back up the stairs and forced a smile.

'Sorry, I was miles away there. Thanks for this,' he said, taking the wallet from her and sliding it back in his pocket. He tapped it three times without thinking to reassure himself that it was there. The leather smelt damp and it was slightly frayed at the edges. Ellis felt ashamed that it was in his possession, a feeling made worse by having it handed to him by someone else.

'It's absolutely fine. I saw you drop it when you ran out there,' she said. 'In a rush?'

'Oh, well...' Ellis said, looking beyond her gaze and making something up that he thought sounded plausible. 'I lost track of time and thought I'd be late for work.'

'I won't keep you any longer then, but I must ask,' she paused, waiting for Ellis' eyes to meet her own.

'Did you not find what you were looking for? Strange, I know, but it makes me sad to see someone leaving the library without a book!' She laughed but it did little to dispel Ellis' uneasiness.

'Can I recommend something for you? All part of the service, as they say,' she said laughing.

Ellis followed her back onto the third floor, just catching the scent of what was lightly rose scented perfume. It created a sense of melancholy that he could not place, but it made him long for the comforts of his own flat even more.

'History, right?' she asked.

'Yes... thank you,' responded Ellis, trying but failing to hide his despondency.

'No problem. Now then, where are we?' She stood back to fully inspect the amassed work. Bouncing a finger off the spines, she reached behind an old-fashioned and leather-bound looking tome to reveal a light paperback. Shaking her head, she placed it back in place.

'Here we are,' she said, handing over a book on the Pahlavi dynasty. Ellis' heart felt like it was beating with a ferocity that would surely kill him. If he were to die now, he would welcome it and be thankful for the end. At that moment he cared little whether what he took to be his impending death was fate or just bad luck.

His heart kept beating. Beating at a pace that he struggled hard to control. Reaching out to take the book, he grasped it within a damp palm. Feeling the weight in his hands, he looked at the front cover, doing his best to feign interest at the kindness he was being shown.

'Looks interesting,' he said.

He opened the first few pages to read the list of chapters. Rubbing his finger across the pages, he waited with a hope that he could feel was stronger than anything he had ever experienced. Turning the book upside down, he looked closely to watch for falling notes, letters, bookmarks... anything at all. He longed for something to fall at their feet in that moment more than he had longed for anything he could imagine. Nothing fell from its pages.

'I should go, it's...' but he was cut off mid-sentence.

'Hang on. I'm sure that it's a great book but we can do better than that, I think. Please take that book out by all means, but I really want you to take something to get your teeth into,' she said.

'Let me see... ah, I've got it... it should just be here... Yes! Can you reach up and get it please?' she asked.

Ellis looked puzzled. 'You'll need to tell me which book you mean!' he said in a tone that he knew was rude. He did not care and felt all the worse for it.

'Sorry, the blue one there. Block writing?' came a voice in a light and friendly manner that Ellis' behaviour had not merited.

Taking down 'The Apple Fell,' he once again felt the weight in his hands.

'It's about the Greek Civil War,' she said, watching as Ellis turned the book over in his hands and flicked the pages between his fingers. 'Written by someone within the Democratic Army of Greece. There's a fascinating chapter on the Macedonian Issue. Truly fascinating.' She wanted to say more but trailed off, her interest and well-placed attentiveness now overtaken by a growing curiosity and, if she would admit it, a feeling of unease. She watched as Ellis forcedly shook the book. Again, nothing fell from its pages.

'That's a good book but I'll let you make your own mind up,' she said briskly. 'I hope I've not made you too late for work.'

Ellis looked at the pages of the book, full of words, but none of them giving him the answer to his questions.

'I'm sorry,' he blurted out. 'I was looking for something,' he said.

'No need for sorry. I hope you find what it is you're after,' she said, before smiling wanly and making her way back to her desk.

Ellis placed both books back on the shelf and made his way out the door, this time taking the stairs with more urgency than before. His hopes dashed, he knew that he had failed again. He was angry at himself for getting caught up in some stupid fantasy and grew more and more frustrated with each step. He had no incontrovertible proof to justify his actions and had taken a leap of faith that now slowly made him fall deeper into the black hole he had constructed in his head. Real or otherwise, it was swallowing him up.

The bus journey back to his flat felt longer than any he had taken in his life. The streets passed by in a blur but Ellis' mind, normally so quick to think and analyse every single point, now felt dull and numb. It took him some time to realise that he had not blinked in minutes, his eyes now housing the same unwelcome guest as the dryness that occupied his mouth.

Forcing a body that now ached up the flight of stairs, the muscles in his forehead and neck grew tight and sent shooting pain through him with each step. An overwhelming relief washed over him when he was at last able to close the flat door behind him. His hopes had been crushed and the feeling of embarrassment grew at this momentary lapse of rationality and reason. Emptying his pockets, the damp smell that emanated from his wallet made him relive that moment in the library. He grimaced, not only at his erratic behaviour, but at the hope that now seeped away from him with each passing minute.

Sitting on the sofa, he placed his head in his hands, then stopped momentarily as he noticed something unexpected. Underneath the coffee table and just visible beneath the stacks of paper and takeaway menus, Ellis could make out the corner of a book, poking out against the clutter. Initially frustrated at what could only be a missed library book, most probably now long overdue, his stomach turned at the thought of having to return it. To see her face again. To see anyone's face for that matter.

But the feeling subsided as the sight of the book set in motion something more powerful. A longing that this would be his chance. Frantically scattering the paper that lay atop its cover, Ellis could now at least read its title: 'Workers to Victory - the POUM militias.' Ellis had no recollection of taking this book out, but there it was, unopened.

Opening it with a desire and growing faith that his inner voice kept trying to suppress, he scanned the first few pages. Its gutter, while filled with crumbs and dirt, was otherwise empty. The inside cover and end sheets were blank, housing the remnants of neither pen ink nor pencil lead in its pages. After several flicks of the pages, each increasing in speed and intensity, he could see that this book contained nothing but the work of its author. Casting it aside in anger, it hit the wooden floor with a dull thud.

Then he saw it. The shape of the spine looked to have changed and even from a few metres away, he could see there was something sticking out from beneath its loose off-white cover and the foot band. Standing up, he walked slowly to the book, attempting to quell the rushing thoughts that came to him in fear of disappointment. Seeing clearly now, he could make out what was a credit card sized piece of paper with a vertical black stripe on it. Ferociously grasping it, it came away easily from the rest of the book, and Ellis immediately understood what he was holding. Inside of a yellow-tinged envelope he could feel a thick card within. Taking it out slowly, he moved his palm across the embossed texture and could see the calligraphy writing of a fountain pen, its message having bled slightly at the end, yet still legible.

With Compliments,

Only those who seek will find – may this book help you to do so.

E.W. Vintage Books and Collectables

Chapter eleven

It had taken Ellis less than five minutes of frantic online searching to find the shop's location. He figured he could get there in a few hours by train. He tried to think of something else, forcing the desire to leave at that very moment to the back of his mind, a consideration for another day, yet it was all he could think about. Yet he had held off. But as he walked along the beach with his parents that afternoon, he was already mentally preparing an itinerary and optimal travel route in his head.

    It had been his parents' decision to take a change of scenery and meet away from the house that Sunday, due in no small part in the belief that this would make Ellis more amenable to speaking with them. It was well meant, but misplaced, as Ellis' thoughts were focused inwards to the lanes and streets that surrounded E.W. Vintage Books and Collectables, and to the promise that lay within its walls.

    'Ellis, did you listen to what your mum just said?' asked Finlay. On this occasion it was said with a degree of concern rather than what could often be frustration.

    'Sorry, I was miles away there. Sorry, what did you say?' asked Ellis, both hands thrust deep in his trouser pockets as he dragged his feet across the sand.

'It's okay,' said his mum in a reassuring tone, reaching one hand beside Ellis' upper arm to link herself closer to him.

'Well, you know that your dad and I just want you to be happy and we've been talking. We know it's not our place to tell you how to live your life, but well...' she paused to look at her husband, who responded with a supportive raise of his eyebrows.

'But well,' she continued, 'It's just that we hate to see you like this. We know it's been a hard few months for you and we don't know why... again, we know you're old enough to make your own decisions, and you don't need to tell us why that is, but we just want to help. Well, what I mean is we are always there to help if you need us, but we wanted to offer you something,' she added, with a softness in her voice that Ellis had always found comforting.

Ellis kept pace with his mother, looking over to her when she paused and hesitated in an attempt to find the right words.

'We hated to see you leave the post-grad course as we know you loved it, so just know, if you want to look into it again next year, we will support you financially.'

Finishing what she had to say, she gave Ellis a gentle and loving squeeze of the arm.

'All of it, if need be,' said his dad. 'That's what the money's there for.'

'Mum,' said Ellis.

Both parents looked over at their son, each longing for the acceptance of the offer and of the change they hoped it would spark.

'Why are there never any flowers in your house anymore?' Ellis asked.

His father looked behind at their collected footprints in the sand, trying yet failing to stifle the shake of his head and an audible sigh. Unfazed, his mother kept her gaze on Ellis and smiled.

'I'll tell you exactly why,' she said. 'Ever since I was a little girl, I've loved flowers. I remember sitting on your grandad's knee when I was small, and your gran came in with some daffodils and put one in my hair. Do you know what, that may be one of my earliest memories?' she said smiling. Eve looked out to sea for a moment, recalling and cherishing the thought.

'Well, it's that or being scratched by our neighbour's cat! It was a bad-tempered little brute!' She laughed and her husband moved closer, smiling with her and linking an arm in hers so that the three walked together.

'But the flowers,' she continued. 'I remember the day clearly as you and your brother had left home, and your dad had cut his finger on the tin opener and was sitting on the sofa feeling sorry for himself. Do you remember that, Finlay?'

He nodded. 'If you remember, you'll recall there was actually a lot of blood,' he said.

'Perhaps,' she smirked.

'Well, I remember looking up and seeing a small bunch of daffodils that we'd taken from the garden down by the shed where they still grow now. And I looked at them in the vase and thought to myself they'll live here for a few days then they'll wilt and die. They won't thrive on our kitchen table, and I can still look at them when they're out in the garden, can't I? So that's the reason why there's no more flowers. It's silly, I know, but we all do silly things, don't we? It doesn't mean I don't love flowers any less than I did when I was a girl. If anything, I love them more,' she said, her tone soft and peaceful.

The three continued to walk along the beach, their arms linked, sharing memories from a past that was easy to live in and speaking about the various comings and goings of their respective neighbours. As the surf rolled up the beach, nearly touching the feet of the trio, it dawned on Ellis that he had not thought about books, bookmarks or libraries for the last hour. For the first time since the mountains, his frenzied thoughts now felt composed and still.

'Thanks for the offer,' said Ellis. 'You know I appreciate it, and I'll think about it,' he added, watching as the sun began to dip below the horizon, making the sky shimmer in shades of red and orange. As a boy, his parents had held him in their strong arms as he splashed in the waves and they held him again now.

Not far from the beach, in an artificially lit pub with frosted glass windows, Andy was holding court at the bar. It was one of the few pubs near the beach that did not cater to a younger audience. Music, when there was any, took the form of an open mic session on the last Sunday of each month. Since a two-inch hole had been forcibly kicked into the amplifier, the result of a disgruntled singer, the event was now strictly an acoustic one. Nor did the pub have any TVs, fruit machines, dartboards or snooker tables. It had alcohol, soft drinks, and on the days that its patrons had luck on their side, it had crisps.

Sipping from a glass of sparkling water, he and his group were engaged in lively discourse. Each participant strained their respective voices as each point was hammered home over the loud din of early evening revellers.

'Look,' said Andy, taking another sip of his water and beckoning to the barman for another. 'The only thing I said was that it's never as black and white as that.'

'Well, I'm going on what's written,' came the reply from a jovial red-faced man, his teeth slightly stained from red wine. 'You argue about truth but what greater truth can there be than what's written down for us all to learn from?'

Andy scoffed. 'It's precisely the fact it's written down that I'm contesting it!' he roared. 'History is unfinished and should lead to discussions like the one we are having right now, even if you are wrong on this occasion! There is no one truth. Who are any of us to say that this is how it was, or that is what was done when we didn't live the experience at the time?' he said. 'There's no clean cut to any of the points we've spoken about and why should there be? There are armchair historians, politicians, sociologists and psychologists in pubs across the land having the same conversations. And they'll have these very same conversations the next week, then the week after, but nothing will ever come from it. Don't you find that tiresome?' asked Andy, expecting little by way of an answer.

A woman, a lecturer at the local university, and a resolute and steadfast friend of Andy since their school days, nonchalantly rubbed a lipstick smudge off her glass and responded.

'Andy, it's for that reason that people have these conversations. Debate like this leads to greater understanding, although I must say that's not true in this case,' she laughed. 'Of course, it will never be clear cut, but you cannot seriously argue against the idea of a universal truth? Whether we like it or not, there are some things and many ideas that well... are simply true!' she said.

The red-faced man was quick to respond. 'Here here! And what's more, Andy, identity and nations are not historical constructs, however well you may argue the point. I feel my roots in my blood and no amount of naysaying to the fact will make me feel otherwise,' said the man, standing proudly, as if he had scored a point.

Andy sunk the last of the water and thanked the bar man as he placed a new bottle down before him. The heat from the pub caused condensation to run slowly down the chilled bottle, and he watched as a trickle of water found its way to a beer mat.

'I must say that I love our little get togethers,' said Andy. 'But allow me to make one last point before I really must make my way up the road.' He took another sip of water then continued.

'Of course it's all a construct, and I group history and identity in the same bundle here. Whatever has been seen has been seen through the eyes of the viewer. I dare say that if the group by the door there... no, don't turn round to look, Alice!' Andy rolled his eyes and gave her a smile. 'Well, I dare say that after a few more drinks they would be arguing about whether or not the face on the clock of the wall was white or cream. Perhaps that's not the best example, but you know the point I'm getting at, don't you?' he asked.

Andy continued. 'If someone writes something down, or if someone tells a story, it's always done with some purpose in mind. We can all look at what's in front of us and each take our own little piece from it that another wouldn't. You never just get told things for the sake of being told. You're told to inform or to influence. So no, there is no one truth, no matter if to us something appears to be right or wrong. Because whatever someone holds true to themselves, or believes in, no matter the stacks of evidence against, or the well-argued points that disprove, discredit or even mock, then it is true to them. And, my dear friends, if something is true to them, then it is true,' said Andy in closing.

'Andy, if you weren't drinking water, I'd be telling you you've had enough!' said the man with the stained teeth, as he increasingly turned a deeper crimson red in tone. After handshakes and hugs, Andy left and made his way out into the warm summer evening.

He was not yet ready to go home and so walked absentmindedly, placing one foot after the other in the direction of nowhere in particular. Yet soon, the sound of the waves rolling onto one of the small piers towards the north end of the beach pulled his attention towards it. He walked past the chip shop with its queue of hungry customers stretching out of the door and snaking its way back along the street. Two young boys fished at the entrance to the harbour, casting their lines as far as they could and slowly reeling in artificial lures of silver, green and gold. Andy watched as they pulled them out of the water ready to be cast out once more, their oval shaped discs sparkling in the light.

To the right of the pier, the water looked much shallower, and Andy could see the brown seaweed being pushed in the direction of the shore, then pulled back into the brackish water, sand caught up alongside it in the ebb and flow. He looked along the beach and watched as people walked alone or in groups, some with dogs, most without. He could make out a group of teenagers who were sitting huddled around a disposable barbeque, the smoke wafting back and upwards towards the sand dunes.

He saw what looked like Ellis walking along the shore with two people, but at this distance he could not be sure. The tide was coming in and soon the beach would be empty.

Going back to the pier, he watched again as one of the boys reeled in a fish, his rod bent heavily at the tip. Pulling it up, Andy could make out the blueish, silver and black markings of a mackerel. On the days the shoals of whitebait came into the bay, they were easy to catch. At least that was what he remembered.

Straining slightly to untie his shoelaces, he took his shoes and socks off. Walking on the damp pier, the hard concrete covered in slippery seaweed, he gingerly stepped down a small set of stairs where the fishermen with smaller boats could walk down and tie up their boats. He judged the depth to be four, perhaps five metres deep. A starfish lay unmoving beneath an empty rusted beer can and a small crab sat on an old car tire, its claws pointed towards a threat that Andy could not see. Sitting on the third rung of the stairs, Andy rolled the legs of his trousers up and hung both of his tired, cracked feet in the cold, salty water.

Chapter twelve

<u>September 1990</u>

Even when lit, the two bedrooms at the top of the house felt dingy and cold, as if the darkness had buried itself into the walls. Andy's room was adjacent to where his mother slept; a pokey rectangular space with a window where one could look out on the back garden. It contained a single bed with a well-used spring mattress, a desk and chair, a black lamp, the filament in its bulb long burned out, and little else. Some posters hung loosely from the walls, with one well-placed so that it covered the fist-sized hole in the door. The bed had originally been placed close to the wall, but Andy had moved it closer to the window around the time the crying had first started.

  The room in which his mother lived – the only space she occupied at that point - shared the same vacant uniformity. While there was a working lightbulb in the lamp in this room, Andy knew not to enter when it was on. All that remained of the artwork and photos on the walls were thin nails and picture hooks, with what they once held now stored in boxes in the cupboard under the stairs.

  One day, not long after Andy's father had left, he returned home to find that the lower bathroom mirror had been smashed. He found his mother by the trail of blood that led from the bathroom to outside the back door. The cream dressing gown did little to stem the bleeding but Mr Melford, in the house opposite, was able to drive her to hospital in his Ford Fiesta. Andy was made to sit in the front seat and felt uncomfortable when he saw Mr Melford's unblinking stare directed at his mother through regular prolonged glances in the rear-view mirror.

There were the days in bed and the weeks indoors. The half-drunk bottles of gin that lay in the increasingly yellow bath and the endless, wailing tears. Bills unpaid and the missed days of school; the lies, excuses and banging on the door. When the sofa ceased to deliver its yield of coins behind its cushions and within its crumb-filled sides, the shopping trips for food reduced in number, until they ceased entirely.

The first punch in the hall happened two weeks after Christmas and knocked Andy off his feet. The crying got worse after that day, as did the violence. Andy saw no dentist or doctor between the age of eleven and sixteen. He chose not to attend the local youth club for several reasons, most notably the entry charge. When he did attend school, he went to classes in a brain-numbing hunger. A hunger that made his head spin and his vision blur. An aching pain and longing for food and sustenance that made him question, from the moment he woke to when he fell asleep, whether this was real or a nightmare. The pieces in Andy's broken jigsaw were there for all to see, but there was nobody to put them together for him.

On the nights Andy met Jordan at the end of his street, and after he had devoured the sandwiches wrapped in tinfoil that his friend had brought him, Andy would listen intently to the stories of his friend. The couple of hours when he heard about Jordan's plans to join the army, the World Cup, and the events of school, provided Andy with a safe harbour in which he could fall into and shelter from a storm that saw no end.

'Did you hear what happened to Catherine Spittalfield?' asked Jordan.

'No?' replied Andy, pausing only to utter short responses through the bites of his cheese sandwich.

'Right, well wait until you hear this!' said Jordan, his eyes glowing with excitement. 'She went into the test, and everyone could see she kept on pulling at her sleeve and looking down at her arm. It didn't take a genius to see that she was hiding something, as nobody wears a jumper that big in the height of summer,' he laughed.

Andy nodded, wiping the butter that was smeared across his cheek and chin with his sleeve.

'So, Mr Dawson went right up to her and shouts, "Ms Spittalfield! You may see fit to cheat in your work, but you will not cheat in my class! Stand up now!"' shouted Jordan, waving his arms wildly to mimic the mannerisms of their teacher as he repeated verbatim the events of the summer.

'He goes and marches her right to the front of the class, and she's only gone and written the answers on her arm in ink!' laughed Jordan. 'She must have been sweating as the ink was running!' Jordan guffawed at the memory and looked to Andy for some acknowledgement. Andy smiled back at him and went back to his sandwich.

'That's a shame for her,' said Andy.

Looking into his backpack for something, Jordan took out some biscuits for Andy and handed them over. Then remembering that he had something else in his bag, he reached down once more to remove it.

'Here, look at this' he said, handing over a small bound diary to Andy. Its black leather cover was fraying at the edges, and it had white and grey patches over it from age.

'Dad took us into the attic over the weekend to take down the spare bed frame, so I had a little rummage in some of the boxes. Here, go ahead, take a look,' said Jordan, nodding his approval for Andy to open it.

Andy opened the book to see a neat script across the pages with doodles in the margin.

'What is it?' he asked.

'It was my grandad's notebook, I think. It looks like an old diary or something,' replied Jordan, beckoning for it to be handed back. 'But wait, just look at this one page first,' he added. Jordan took the book, licking a finger for traction, then soon found a page towards the end. 'Read that,' he said, passing the book back to Andy.

Andy popped two biscuits into his mouth and looked at the page. The pencil text read:

Dearest, Elizabeth.

Now you are gone and I am alone, there are many things that I wish I could say to you. Say to you now and wish I had said to you then. Until the day that we meet again with God in his bountiful heaven, I shall write. I wonder if you hear my prayers? I dearly hope that you do.

Our grandson was born some three weeks ago, and I have since been to visit him at home. I see Iain in him clearly and I feel your presence in him, too. He is called Jordan and is as beautiful as I sense he will be kind. There is love in him. It fills me with sadness to such a degree that I weep, knowing that you will not see him grow up into a man. My only hope is that I do, and I will give him love from us both.

Until we meet again, my dearest Elizabeth.

Andy handed the diary back. 'Have you shown it to your parents?' he asked.

'No, not yet, but I will,' said Jordan. 'I've just been reading it in bed at nights. That's probably wrong to do but it's nice to feel a closeness to family, isn't it? He died when I was three, so like gran, I never really got to know him. Sad really. By the way, have you had enough to eat? I can bring more tomorrow, if need be,' he said.

'Thanks,' said Andy.

'I meant to ask, but do you want a drink? It's not whisky this time. I don't know what it is... cream of something. Old Robert has crates of the stuff just lying around the back of the shop, so I helped myself to a couple,' said Jordan.

'Not tonight, Jordan, but please go ahead,' said Andy, his demeanour starting to show one of nervousness. A feeling of growing sadness that came when the nights with Jordan drew to a close and he thought about going home.

'All the more for me then,' said Jordan, gulping at the contents of the bottle then grimacing at the taste. 'Fuck me!' he laughed. 'It tastes like battery acid! Old Robert will do well to shift these. But like I said, it means there's all the more for us I suppose!' he laughed.

Andy looked forward to his nights with Jordan all day. He always felt they ended too quickly. The nights when he got home to hear his mother asleep, even if he knew it would only be for a few hours, were the best. When the bedside lamp glowed faintly through the curtains, those were nights that he dreaded most. On that evening after leaving Jordan, he walked back to the family home and stood in the garden, staring up at the bedroom window and the chink of light that shone from it. He did not stay long.

Making his way back down the path and along the street, he found himself standing outside Jordan's house. His parents were still awake and he could see Jordan chatting amiably with them in the window. They looked happy. Andy thought about knocking on the door but could not come up with a reason to do so that felt plausible.

Instead, he walked to the harbour. Looking down from the pier, Andy could see the sandy bottom, lit by the harbour lights. He heard the water lapping against the concrete and stared at the seafloor. The pier went further out from shore to form the harbour breakwater. Heavy concrete bollards were placed three-quarters of the way out to stop the public from going to the end. Andy knew that on Sundays the local fisherman would go up anyway, so he also wanted to see what was there for himself. The sight of the bottom faded until all he could see was the dark chopping water. There were no lights this far out and Andy felt a fear building in him, but not one strong enough to make him go home. Here he was alone, and at that moment, alone was where he wanted to be.

He sat on the edge of the pier and reassured himself that this would be his escape. In winter, he could make his way to the breakwater's edge and jump into the water. The currents might drag him down or he might get lucky and hit his head. The posters in school told all who read them about the dangers of cold water and swimming in quarries. That would surely ring true in the sea, he told himself. Yes, this was to be his escape, he thought. He could dive in on a winter's night and the unforgiving sea would take him away from all of this. He would be free. For once, he realised that he felt stronger in the knowledge that he had a way out. When he got home that night and his bedroom door creaked open to reveal a swaying figure holding a belt, he clenched his teeth, closed his eyes, and thought of the water.

Chapter thirteen

How difficult it was to wait, thought Ellis. The train would not be leaving for another two hours, yet despite that, he had replaced the warmth of his bed for the echoing confines of an empty train station. He woke around three a.m., his heart already racing and mouth dry from the nervous trepidation of a well-planned journey that lay ahead. He sat on a row of blue metal seats outside the barriers at platform six. It was too late for the drinkers, and too early for the commuters, so he sat alone as a cleaner walked from bin to bin, emptying the waste of passengers from the day before.

Sitting there, he thought it peculiar how he regularly wished parts of his life away. How he would rush and hurry to get to somewhere he thought would be better, only for it not to be any different than the place he had been. He wished away his school years knowing that a life of academia would follow; an outcome where he thought he would find true happiness. He did not. Nor did the days, weeks and months after his first graduation lead to the emotional and financial riches that he had expected. Yet for the four years of his study, the thoughts preoccupied him daily. For Ellis, experience and real life happened elsewhere, in a place far away from here. And he constantly moved with pace towards it. Yet despite the haste he showed, and often because of it, the thing he strived for remained elusive and slipped further from his grasp. And so, he chased it again, never staying in one place long enough to see what lay in store for him at that moment. What mattered to Ellis was far away from the present.

A lone swallow flew from the rafters above. The station's artificial lighting set it off in a shrill song that only Ellis and the mass of pigeons could hear. As the minutes passed, the row of seats filled and soon the platform was awash with people waiting for their train to pull in and take them to jobs, appointments and experiences. Ellis had booked a seat in advance, a fact that now caused him great anxiety in case someone was sitting in it before he could find it. He decided then and there that he would rather stand in the carriage than go through the embarrassment of asking someone to move.

When the train arrived, the throng of passengers swarmed at the barrier gates. Men with briefcases battled with women clutching handbags to their chests, while others with bicycles, roller suitcases and young children in tow, were pushed aside by those who at that moment, had no greater priority in life than to get to work. Ellis found that strange but hurried no less, a strong desire to make it first to his seat spurring him on.

Finding his place at a table, two rows of two seats facing each other, he placed his bag on the rack above and sat down. Within a minute, an elderly couple walked up and down the aisle, straining their eyes between the tickets they held and the numbering system that sat in line with the top of the windows. They walked past Ellis twice, then finally finding their place, sat down beside him.

'Hello,' said the woman, as her husband took both their jackets and placed them in the rack above.

'Hello,' replied Ellis, placing one hand in his pocket to feel for the small envelope and its printed message. A sense of relief washed over him as he felt the embossed paper between his fingertips. The doors beeped then juddered shut and soon the train was crawling slowly over the bridge near the harbour, small boats bobbing up and down with the ebb and flow of the waves. It passed the factories and the school, then gained speed as it left the town. Flat countryside filled the view of both windows and in the distance, Ellis could just make out the shape of the mountains, gloomy grey cloud cover hiding the peaks.

'Are you going all the way?' the elderly husband asked, passing a Tupperware box filled with sandwiches to his wife. She had already emptied the contents of a plastic carrier bag on the table: a pen, crossword book, some scones in a bag, a flask and two ceramic mugs.

'Right to the end,' said Ellis. 'And you?'

'We'll be with you all the way then,' replied his wife, brushing some of the sandwich crumbs that had fallen from her blouse. Ellis caught the scent of strong, vanilla-scented perfume when she did so. 'We're off to see a specialist, aren't we, Harald?' she said, her convivial tone not matching the words she had said. 'Harald has been quite poorly, so we're off to see someone about it to see if we can find some answers,' she added.

'I'm sorry to hear that,' said Ellis, feeling genuine empathy for the couple.

'A young strapping lad like this doesn't need to hear about our worries, Lorriane,' bellowed Harald, giving Ellis a wink when he did so. 'What are you, son? Twenty-six? Twenty-seven?'

'I'm thirty-four,' replied Ellis, 'but I'll take the compliment.'

'Ah, thirty-four, Lorraine. Do you remember thirty-four? We had three children by thirty-four. Do you have any kids yourself, son? Are you married?' asked Harald, reaching into the Tupperware box to remove one of the sandwiches for himself.

'No, none yet, and no, I'm not married,' said Ellis, with less enthusiasm than before.

'Well, I'm sure it will happen soon,' replied Lorraine quickly. 'A nice handsome man like yourself won't be on the shelf for much longer,' she said, giving Ellis a warm smile as she did so.

'Thirty-four...' said Harald again, looking along the distance of the corridor and catching eyes with a young mother who had a baby held close to her chest in a sling. 'At thirty-four I don't suppose you even think about your health. When everything still works that is,' said Harald. He laughed then smiled at Lorraine, before looking down solemnly at a newspaper that lay on the table. 'Still, I'm sure I'll find some answers soon and we'll get to the bottom of this, won't we Lorraine?' he asked.

Ellis watched as she gripped his hand in hers, squeezing it tightly and placing her head on Harald's shoulder.

'We certainly will,' she said, her voice breaking slightly. She looked out the window as she composed herself. Ellis could see her lips tremble, yet there was a welcome sense of relief when the tears he expected failed to arrive.

'Can I give you some advice, son?' said Harald.

'You can,' replied Ellis, looking briefly at Lorraine to check if she was okay. There were still no tears.

'I remember being your age and being told something by someone who was much older than I. And what's the first thing you do when you hear such advice, neither asked for nor wanted? You disregard it.' Harald coughed into the crook of his arm, then continued. 'Well, what I'm asking you now is to at least consider what I say to you. That's a big ask, you're sitting there now, having only met Lorraine and I this very day. In fact, we don't even know your name?'

'Sorry, it's Ellis,' he said.

'Well, Ellis. As you may have heard, my name's Harald and this is my wife Lorraine.'

A man pushing a trolley of biscuits and hot and cold drinks walked up and down the aisle of the train, its squeaking wheels mirroring the rattle of the train on its tracks.

'The thing with advice is you only really take heed when it concerns or means something to you. So, I hope that one day, when you need it most, what I tell you will rise up within you and help you. Life goes in a flash, son. A flash. One minute you're on a train, going to wherever you may be going, and the next, you're our age. Life is happening now. It's not what happened yesterday, nor is it what's to come in the future. It's what's taking place right now, at this very moment. When you understand that, you'll truly appreciate the value of it,' he said, his voice straining towards the end. When he had finished, he looked across at Lorraine. Ellis could see in her eyes that they were glassy with tears, yet they still shone brightly.

'Pay no attention to us, Ellis. We're just a little bit emotional today,' said Lorraine, giving him a compassionate look.

'No, no, thank you for sharing that,' responded Ellis solicitously. 'If I can help with anything, please let me know.' The words had not even left his mouth before he regretted what he had said. He knew that he had nothing to give by way of meaningful help to these two strangers.

'Thank you,' said Lorraine.

'We appreciate that, son,' added Harald.

'If you will excuse me once more there was another thing I wanted to say to you,' said Harald, now sitting upright in the chair, his back straight and his chin protruding slightly from an otherwise rounded, welcoming face. The cover of the headrest had fallen off the seat and now hung loosely from his shoulder. Lorraine brushed it off and sat with the same dignified straightness. Her chest puffed out as she looked at her husband with pride.

'I say this now not only to share the knowledge, but to remind myself at this moment of how I should approach my situation,' said Harald. 'You see in life, it's important to think with your whole body. Let me be clearer,' he added, speaking with a thoughtfulness that immediately gained Ellis' attention and respect.

'Take this,' he said pointing to his head, 'and this,' slapping the top of his wrist. 'They are both connected, and so is everything in these fantastic vessels that we inhabit. Think with the mind but listen to your body. Often it will tell you what your mind is thinking before you have had the chance to think about it. If you are ill or sick, it is only one part of you. Never tell yourself that you are sick or ill, only that one part of you is, understand? Your feelings, sensations and thoughts are never solely one thing. A part of you can be happy or sad, excited or fearful, but it is never the whole of you. Remember that, as I am trying to remember it now,' said Harald.

The train slowed before stopping at the next platform. Ellis, Lorraine and Harald watched the passengers come and go then steadily went back into their own lives. Harald's eyes grew heavy and soon he was asleep, his head falling gently to the right. Ellis thought he looked peaceful. Lorraine took up the crossword puzzle and spent her time looking between the pages and the face of her sleeping husband. Ellis too began to feel tired, lulled by the movement of the train and the nondescript fields and pastures that had met his vision for the last two hours. His eyes grew heavy and soon he had drifted off into a deep sleep, the deepest for several weeks. He dreamt of a flowing river and of his parents who had gifted him a silver coin, only for it to be cast into the fast-flowing waters. Try as he might, his attempts to hold the coin in his hands proved fruitless.

An announcement from the train's conductor awoke him from his slumber. Looking at his phone, he saw that he had been asleep for an hour. The table in front of him was now empty. Briefly coming to his post-sleep senses, he wondered if their presence had been a dream, but then he saw them. They both stood in the carriage vestibule by the train doors. A row of passengers stood behind them, each one impatient to reach their destination, breathe the fresh air and stretch their legs. They looked over at Ellis and both gave him a pleasant smile that he found reassuring. Soon they were gone, lost behind the sea of bodies that swelled on the platform.

Ellis took his bag and made his way to the exit. The carriage was littered with crisps and nuts that had spilled from mouths and from packets on the three-hour journey. Plastic bottles, the odd beer can and newspapers and magazines of every size, colour and genre littered the tables. Ellis suppressed an urge to pick up everything and cast it all into the nearest bin. He stood on the platform and breathed in deeply, feeling the warm air fill his lungs. Soon he had caught up with the throng of bodies as he made his way to the exit, and whatever it was that lay ahead of him.

After his meticulous research, Ellis had calculated that he could walk to the shop in an hour or so and still make it back in time for the last train. By taking the earliest train he could, he had given himself a slot where he did not have to feel rushed. Having never been to this specific town before, he thought he could take his time and make it as much of a day out as he could.

After he left the train station, he found a small river path that snaked down into the village. To his right in the distance lay former red brick factories and mills that had been turned into apartments and commercial offices. A smattering of houses on the left bank of the river had thatched roofs, two half-moons cut into their front, so the two windows caught the morning sunlight. Ellis wondered how much they would cost and thought his answer of little use, seeing as he would never be able to afford such a property.

Cameron had bought his own flat after university, a simple two-bedroom on an investment banker's salary, even at entry level. The flat had since been sold for almost double the price he had paid for it, making him a sizeable profit and leading to a short spell as a semi-successful property developer. He had asked Ellis to help out, but the offer was strongly rejected, leading to the two not talking for the best part of a month. Cameron's appointment in a senior position for a large multinational went some way to defrost the iced tensions and it was never spoken about again. It was thought of though, both by Ellis, and as he suspected, his parents.

There was a café further down the winding path and Ellis thought he would stop in for a glass of sparkling water and something to eat. He could see some people in the window eating soup and sandwiches, or in hearty conversation with those who sat opposite.

At that moment, and it was just a fleeting moment, he longed for human interaction with a trusted friend or a lover. He wanted to hear the laughter of someone who knew who he was and what he stood for; to listen to others and to be heard when he spoke. Someone with which he could share his experiences; the highs and lows and the general daily nothingness that comprised all that made up life. Yet as with most things concerning Ellis, the feeling soon abated. It was replaced by an urge to eat and drink, two sensations that he could at least address himself with some degree of control.

Control had been important for him ever since the breakup but despite his best efforts, he found himself unable to command or master even the smallest of his wishes. He was unsure if others could, or even if they tried to as he did. Touching his stubbled chin, he again thought of this strange quest he had imposed on himself. A dream of something better guided by the hope that it was being controlled for him by someone, or something else. Of looking for signs and following their guidance, no matter how small the clue and regardless of the outcome. Until now this had been a positive experience, but he was unsure what would come next, or indeed if anything would come at all. The mountain had made him feel like he had clarity again; like the dulling numbness in his body had dissipated with each step he took. The feeling stayed with him for several weeks, but he could feel it fading once more.

His experience with Emma at the market was the closest he had felt to a real human connection in as long as he could remember. Again, the catalyst for this had come from a book. If books were the answer, he was determined to find whatever it was he was looking for in an old bookshop.

A small bell above the café door rang as he opened the door. The noise led some of the diners to look up from their early lunches.

'Just sit wherever you'd like, and I'll be with you in a second. Go ahead, there's plenty of space,' called an unseen voice from below a counter. Soon a man popped up holding three thin looking baguettes. Patches of white flour clung loosely to his apron and were soon whipped into dust by the brush of a strong hand. Once he had sliced the bread into thick chunks, he lifted the lids of several steaming pots on the range behind. He wafted the steam across his nose with a practiced, almost theatrical movement, then plunged a spoon in each pot. The tasting and seasoning undertaken to his liking, he took a menu from the top of the counter and placed it in front of Ellis.

'Don't worry, I make everything fresh each day and it's all delicious,' he said assertively. 'Take your time and I'll be back to take your order as soon as you can say

Michelin star! To drink, Sir?'

'Can I have a sparkling water please?' asked Ellis.

'You certainly can,' came the response, before he trotted off in the direction of the other customers, stopping to speak to each one, pointing and gesticulating with his hands. Ellis thought the behaviour more than a little odd, even disconcerting, and made more so by the fact that to his eyes, most people appeared to only be eating soup and sandwiches.

Soon he was back behind the counter once again tending to the steaming pots and pans. A girl in her mid-twenties came towards Ellis with a bottle and glass on a tray.

'He trained in Lyon, you know,' she said, as she placed down his order. 'In France,' she added.

'Did he? He must be very experienced then,' replied Ellis, sounding slightly wooden as he did so.

'Well, at least that's what he likes to tell everyone,' she laughed. 'In saying that though, his soup is second to none. If you're looking for something to eat beyond the water, as filling as I'm sure that is, I'd certainly recommend the soup with some crusty bread. He makes both himself,' she added. 'By the way, where's that accent from? You're not from around here and even if you were I'd have seen you before; it's certainly a small enough place to know most people.' Ellis replied. On hearing the answer, she raised her eyebrows and said: 'Ah, the big city. Well, I won't hold that against you. We welcome everyone here.'

Ellis ordered the soup with bread and in the time it took to arrive, he watched as three other couples in the café paid their bills and left.

'Here you go,' said the waitress, placing a plate and bowl down in front of Ellis. 'We're actually closing early today due to a family gathering so it's good you've come when you did. Just excuse me a moment while I put the closed sign on the door.'

Flipping it to read closed to those who read it from the street, she pulled the blind down and asked the man who continued to tend to his soups to do the same at the counter side.

'Do you mind if I join you?' she said. 'We don't get a lot of new faces in this town and it's always nice to have something new to talk about, don't you think?'

'If you have the time and won't get in trouble from your boss,' said Ellis, meekly.

'Ha!' she scoffed. 'My boss? There's only one boss around here and I'll have you know that this is my café,' she said.

'I'm sorry... I just assumed that... never mind. I'm sorry,' he added, bashfully.

'It happens more than you would think,' she said, rolling her eyes as she said it. 'How's the soup?'

'You were right about the soup. It's really nice,' said Ellis.

'I did say it would be,' came her response, an impish grin on her face. 'So, tell me, what do you do?'

'Do?' answered Ellis.

'Yes, do! What is it you do?' she asked again, speaking to him now in a friendly, if slightly condescending tone.

'Well, if you mean for work, then I'm a binman,' he said, feeling pressured into a response.

'Why does everyone you ever ask that question to automatically think it's about work?' she said mockingly. 'Why are people so quick to give themselves a label all the time?'

Ellis, who was usually quite level headed and quick to avoid any conflict, felt irritated.

'Excuse me, but I was actually just in here to have some lunch and to relax for a bit. I'm not used to, nor do I intend to progress with a sociological conversation with someone I don't know, or in the minutes I've spent with you, would want to get to know,' he snapped back. It was uncalled for, and he knew it as soon as the words had left his mouth. Yet his growing anger remained.

'Jesus, lighten up, will you!' came the reply. 'I was only trying to chat for a bit. No need to take yourself so seriously,' she said, her frustration now also growing.

'Well, I'm sorry but who randomly approaches

someone and attempts to strike up a conversation then goads someone over their response? Do you not think I know that people are not one single thing? You may spend your evenings polishing rocks or drinking in bars and singing karaoke each weekend. You may be a mother, a gardener, a singer... hell, you might even be a pilot!' Ellis felt the anger subsiding with each word and felt better for it.

'There's nothing wrong with being a binman,' she said.

Ellis, who had paused to eat some more of the soup, which to his displeasure, he did find absolutely delicious, looked up at her with scorn in his eyes. 'What are you talking about?!' he barked.

'A binman. I said there's nothing wrong with being a binman. You seemed a bit hesitant to tell me,' she added.

'Well, if I was hesitant, it's because I'm not used to strangers approaching me and asking me what I do for a living!' he shouted back at her. Those who remained in the café were now focused on the argument that was taking place at the small table, a plastic carnation in a turquoise vase the only thing separating each of the bickering parties.

'I'm sorry, but that's not what I asked, I just asked...' Ellis cut her off before she could finish what she wanted to say.

'I don't know if you behave like this with all your customers, but I find it strange, rude and now this has all escalated into something that it didn't have to become. And if you must know, then yeah, what do you think? Do you think I want to be a binman? Do you think that that's always been my dream in life and that I fall asleep each night looking forward to the days of excitement that lie ahead of me? Because I don't! I haven't for years and I don't now. And what do you have to say to that? Is this what you wanted to know?' Ellis took a gulp of his water. The owner stayed quiet, her silence urging him to tell more of his story.

'You asked what I do. Well, I do nothing. I wake up, drink weak gritty coffee, go to work, come home and wish my evening away until sleep takes me away from it all, if I'm lucky to sleep, that is. Then I wake up and do it all again each morning. There was a time where I lived for the weekends, but I don't even do that anymore. Look at me, a man of my age travelling all this way in the hope there's something else in store for me. Something that isn't this monotonous void of non-existence.' Ellis pushed his chair back hurriedly, spilling the half-drunk bottle of water in doing so. The man behind the counter, who had been listening all along, used the pause to go back to slicing excessive amounts of bread.

'I am many things,' said Ellis, a tightness growing in his throat that made it hard to swallow. His lips felt dry and his hands trembled. He looked the owner in her eyes, taking some solace in the fact that she was not looking back. 'I am...' he said. 'Many... many things. Only now, I feel that the good things have deserted me, and the bad grow daily,' he said, in all but a whisper.

'I'm sorry,' she said, with a tenderness that Ellis felt was unmerited and undeserved.

'No, I'm sorry,' he replied. 'I'm not feeling myself at the moment.'

'Please, sit down. I can get you some more soup if you want. I'll leave you alone this time, I promise,' she said with a hopeful smile that disguised her concern and worry for this strange visitor to her café.

'No, no, please. This is your business and I've been quite rude to you. I really should be leaving now anyway. I have an appointment,' he lied, making his way to the door.

'We look forward to welcoming you back soon,' said the now imperious man behind the counter. The owner did not look at him again, and opening the blinds, turned the handle of the door before beckoning for Ellis to leave.

Chapter fourteen

The mark of a bad listener can be judged in how long it takes one to hear what is said, before bringing the conversation back to themselves. The café, its owner, and the needless argument Ellis had had with her had filled him with a great deal of disconcertment.

Walking idly once more along the banks of the river, he felt a sense of relief, much as one would when a splinter is pulled from a deep wound in the skin. He thought it both troublesome and timely that the argument from moments before had been the first time he had spoken to someone about his feelings. He had felt something shift and in doing so, he felt energised and giddy. Ever since he had left that morning there had been a growing nausea and aching in his body, but for now, it had temporarily lifted.

What was it to feel normal, he wondered. To wake up with purpose and a vision for the day that lay ahead. To find something that gave cause to celebrate, rather than just being, doing and seeing for the sake of it all. To feel an energy that would ebb and flow through the course of twenty-four hours, but still remain, even when at its weakest.

The banks of the river thinned as he got closer to the centre of the town and he was soon met with the bustle of daily life. Shoppers filled the cobbled streets, throbbing in and out in waves and into the artisan bakers, knitwear shops, cheese and fishmongers and various upmarket fashion boutiques. A pet shop on the corner had a selection of rodents in the window. Ellis watched closely as one hamster ran on its wheel. It walked off, stretched a little, drank purposefully from its upturned bottle, then got back to its run that led nowhere.

Ellis thought that a hamster gets two years of life; perhaps three with luck on its side. In a fleeting moment that left almost as soon as it had arisen, the thought struck him that in the last two years he had given as much to the world as this hamster had. At least a hamster was capable of inspiring love in others, he thought. Of providing outcomes that created memories for someone.

With a capability that shocked even himself, he was quick to pull himself out of his inner chastisement. He walked, turning over a question in his mind: if someone were given the chance to begin life again - stripped of every memory and every hard-earned lesson - would they still arrive at the same place? Would the spouse beside them still be their spouse, the children remain their children, the job still wait for them tomorrow? Would they find themselves in the same chair, the same room, reading the same words? Or would it all be different? The thought troubled him and with a well-practiced ease, he pushed it deep into the confines of his mind to be deliberated over another day.

For reasons unknown to him, the movement of the hamster in its wheel had led Ellis to think of Archie and his time in Finland. He thought of how little he knew of the people he worked with and how what he did know very rarely came from the person it concerned. In his time working in the refuse department, he had heard tales of what was and what could have been, and of affairs and of divorce. Stories were passed back and forth, or whispered in corners, telling those who listened of debt, or of real or – he believed - quite often imaginary sexual conquests.

    The one narrative that was a mainstay was anything to do with travel. At the time Ellis had put this down to simple escapism; even a sun lounger on a rainy day in a seaside coastal town was better than a day traipsing up and down pavements, lifting the waste of others. But the more he thought of it, and the more the feeling took hold, he thought that those who spoke of travel did it for one reason that was greater than all others: to say they had. These men travelled on package holidays or took hiking trips in the mountains of Scandinavia; they saw desert and dune, ocean bottoms and foreign sunsets. And they did it so that when they looked back on their life, they had proof in their fading memories and in clearer photographs that they had seen and they had done. That their life did not consist only of a job that many, if not all of them, hated, and that they had discovered and experienced more than what had been offered to them.

To his right at the end of a small street leading off the main shopping area, Ellis could now see the sign for E.W. Vintage Books and Collectables. Reaching the entrance, he walked in with purpose and audibly gasped at the cavern that lay in front of him. The space, of what little remaining space there was, was filled with all manner of items: red vases, glasses and paperweights were presented in a lower shelf beside the door, with creamy blue glassware in the middle and translucent blue at the top. Ellis could smell the decades' worth of accumulated dust with each footstep, giving off a slight staleness as he crept forward being careful not to knock into any of the trinkets and ornaments. A writing desk lay in the middle of the floor, boxes of pamphlets and magazines scattered and thrown upon it without any visible order. On its top, two large tribal looking vases teetered close to the edge, while ashtrays, rolls of old posters and sketchbooks, sat in the middle. Another desk, this one with a shelf hastily screwed onto it, held precariously positioned crockery and kitchenware.

At the back of the shop towards the counter where an older man sat smoking, row upon row of books were gathered upon hazardous looking shelving.

'Can I help you or are you just browsing like most of the others?' called a grumpy voice, harsh and gravel-like from apparent years of smoking.

'I'm actually looking for something in particular,' said Ellis, moving closer to the desk and the occupant who sat hunched over it. A small lamp illuminated the smoke that rose with each exhalation.

On hearing this, the owner drew heavily from his pipe and closed a book that he had been reading absent mindedly.

'Is that so?' he said. 'Well please, I do love to hear such requests, so do let me know how I can help.'

'Well, I found something,' he said, reaching into his bag, 'in a book I was reading about the Spanish civil war. About the POUM?' questioned Ellis.

'Ah, how interesting. A fascinating topic. Well, if it's the POUM you want I may have something on Joaquín Maurín hidden away somewhere. In fact, someone brought in something just last month on The Independent Labour Party. If it's simply anti-Stalinist writing you want, I can probably find you a few things too; the same goes for Trotsky, but that will cost you,' said the owner. 'Well, everything will cost you these days,' he added for good measure.

'No,' said Ellis impatiently. 'It's not that, I was actually wondering if you remember writing this?' He handed the small paper slip over the man who studied it carefully. Taking the pipe to his mouth, he took a series of small puffs, then blew a stream of smoke over Ellis so that it rose into the air, accumulating in a grey mass towards the ceiling.

The man took the card in his hand and looked it over cautiously. 'Only those who seek will find,' said the owner quietly. 'And just what is it you want to know? I'm not quite sure that I understand?' he said, bringing the pipe to his mouth once more.

'Well,' said Ellis, his heart racing. 'What does it mean?' asked Ellis.

'It means just what it says. It's no deeper than that, to be honest with you. It's something I write for all those who buy a book from me. I've not had to write it for some time, so if you don't intend to buy anything, I have things I have to be getting on with,' said the shopkeeper abruptly.

Seeing Ellis look defeated, and wondering why that was the case, his mood softened. 'Look, it's just a little message I write into all the books here. If you're a reader, and you look to me to be every inch of one, then you yourself will know what it means. Not everything has to be specifically aimed at you, you understand? We can all take our own different meanings from things and that's what makes life that little bit more exciting, wouldn't you say? If you want to buy a book, how about I write a little message for you? Something that I've never written before?' he added.

Ellis thought he was being mocked and remained quiet. The shopkeeper spoke once more.

'As I say, the fact you're looking for something in the first place is the important thing. I'll be honest with you; I still don't understand why you're here or what deeper meaning you're trying to find in my compliment slips, but you're clearly looking for something. I'm sure you'll find whatever it is soon, and the important thing is not to give up.'

'Thanks,' said Ellis. 'I appreciate you taking the time to speak to me, but I won't take up any more of it today. Thank you again,' he added, wandering aimlessly to the light that crept under the heavy wood door. Out on the street, his heart raced with an intensity that scared him.

His thoughts blurred but steadily settled to a place where he could focus. A throbbing on his skull made him hold the flat of his palms against his head, a move that was powerless to stop the increasing pain that now shot through his forehead, neck and shoulders. Placing both hands on the wall for balance, he made his way unsteadily up the street in the direction of a nearby bench. Feeling helpless and lost, he sat down and tried to calm his rapid breathing. Exhaling slowly through thinly pursed lips, he watched the clouds above blowing across the sun and covering the street in a gloomy shade.

Seconds later, the sun shone again, and he watched the clouds pass in front of it three or four times more before he regained the strength in his legs to make it back to the train station.

The last train was a couple of hours away, but he wanted to get there in good time. He also felt it easier to wait at a train station where waiting would be done by the majority of people, rather than out on the street where those he saw were going about their lives.

Ellis was unsure what he found that day, but he was sure of one thing: his resoluteness that this quest, whatever it was and however short lived it had become, was at its end. There would be no more looking for answers in places where there were no answers to be found. Yes, he repeated, as a pigeon picked crumbs from between his feet on the floor. If he kept on repeating it to himself, he may even come to believe it.

On his arrival at the station, he was pleased to see it emptier and without the bustle that he had anticipated. His was the last train of the evening and as he took his seat, he looked with tired eyes at the glowing lights from the town he knew he would never return to. His hand brushed against some discarded chewing gum that had found its way onto his seat. He rubbed his hand against the adjacent headrest, avoiding the judging glare of the train inspector as he passed the empty carriages. Watching as the lights dimmed and the darkness of the countryside showed his reflection in the window, he listened at the growing rumbling in his stomach. He had not eaten since earlier that day and even then, the soup was only half finished. Making his way to the buffet cart, his head once again beginning to throb and spin, he reviewed the sparse menu.

'Can I have a sandwich please?' he asked. 'Just whatever you have left is fine, and can I have a can of cider as well please?'

'You certainly can. How does ham and cheese sound?' said the affable man behind the counter. 'This train isn't usually a busy one so I'm afraid we don't have a lot in stock for the last trip of the day.'

'That would be perfect,' said Ellis.

Handing over the sandwich, the man took a note from Ellis and gave him his change.

'So, what brings you all the way out here then?' he asked, pointing outside to the darkness. 'Just what is it that you do?'

Ellis winced at the question and the events of earlier that day. 'I do a lot of things,' he replied. 'Well, at least I try to. I'm trying to do a lot of things at the moment.'

'Well, that's an answer I haven't heard before, but good luck to you!' came the reply. 'Enjoy your journey and safe travels home.'

The journey back was a lonely one. Yet despite that and perhaps because of it, the hours of silence and of staring out the window delivered a feeling of clarity and clear-headedness that Ellis absorbed with every cell in his body. He had always known that something had to change, but in that solitary, fleeting moment, it was the first time that he believed that it actually could. He just did not know how and when.

Chapter fifteen

<u>April 1992</u>

The coroner ruled the death to be accidental.

When the silence in the house had reached a point where to ignore it became unbearable, Andy crept upstairs, gently pulled against the bedroom door, and saw the lifeless body of his mother. He stared at it; the half that was visible under the sheet looked contorted and the skin was ashen. Despite the frailness of her limbs and a body that looked paper-thin and brittle, Andy told himself that the unmoving corpse was now at peace.

That afternoon, Andy did not yet know that the scene before him and the lifeless body of his mother would creep into his daily thoughts, accompanying him as each year passed. But for now, he looked vacantly and confusedly at the body. A cocktail of sedatives, sleeping pills and painkillers had finally done what the alcohol alone could not.

He had never seen a dead body before and had no cause or desire to ever see one again. He made a pact with himself that nobody would ever find him one day in his bed, bottles cast around the floor, in a room that smelled of damp clothing, vomit and stale air. He decided that he would not be dragged bloated and blue from the bottom of the harbour.

When the minister came to school and Katy Young asked about her grandmother, he said she was in heaven with the angels. Looking at the fragile body of his mother, as light and delicate as a leaf when it's cast from the tree in autumn, he questioned whether she would be joining her. In that moment he did not think she would. He wished he could have asked the minister that if a person is troubled in life, do they bring those troubles to whatever comes next when they die? The minister may not have known the answer, but Andy wished that he had asked it all the same.

    Unhappiness can arise from any number of things: from a missed bus to a barbed comment, aimed with vitriol designed to wound. Andy's confusion arose from an inability to summon tears over the woman who had shared her body with his own as he grew in her womb. What pictures there were, and those that he had seen, pointed to some brief moment of peace and calm. But Andy had no memory of that; his thoughts filled instead with fear and seeking shelter; constantly searching for a place, or a person, he could find safety and solitude within. Reassurance, kindness, warmth and opportunity were all strangers to him.

    During the term of school where Andy regularly attended his lessons, Liam Conroy had told him during one English class that when the Soviets entered Berlin, they gang raped women and young girls. They did it hunting in packs, he said. His grandad had told him, so he knew it was true. He had said that age did not matter. They burned and mutilated and hung corpses from bridges. Thomas Norwood did not know what rape was, but Andy told him.

Andy could still recite the lines that his mother had shared with him when he was younger. To tell the friendly doctor that he had fallen holding the glass. That the bath was too hot, and he had hurriedly rushed in, ignoring the pleas of a loving, caring and compassionate mother.

On the day of the discovery and his first experience of death, the phone had been disconnected. Andy remembered knocking on the door of number eight, explaining what had happened, and sitting in their living room watching from the window as the ambulance removed the lifeless body. He had never had sugar in his tea before. To this day he still could not drink it without wanting to vomit.

Barely twenty people filled the church on the day of the funeral. Andy had only seen a couple of those in attendance before, including one uncle. Jordan and his parents had come, and Jordan sat beside Andy for the entire short ceremony. Because nobody else spoke, Andy read a poem he had written in school. It was not written for his mother, but that point mattered little either to him, or to those who had heard it.

Two eggshell yellow stalls in the back of the church housed the toilets, only one of which worked. A small metre-long urinal had been placed underneath an unclosed window, and the stale smell of urine and old urinal cakes filled the room. Andy sat on the closed seat of the broken toilet, picking dirt from his fingernails and taking a moment in which to try and process his thoughts, something which proved to be impossible.

The door creaked open, and Andy could hear the conversation of two men as they came into the room. Through a gap in the door, he recognised one of the faces as that of a distant uncle; the brother of his father who had left the family home when Andy was younger, though he could not remember when. The other voice sounded less mature, and its cadence carried a joy that sounded out of place at the funeral.

'We can get out here soon, can't we?' came the voice of the younger man, a steady stream of piss vibrating off the urinal and creating a dull metallic hum.

'Shhh, will you?' came the voice of his uncle. 'We are here to show face; the least we can do is stay for a bit longer. I want to speak to Andy before we go,' he hissed.

'That's fine,' came the younger voice, 'but just you remember why we're here today. You hated her as much as your brother did, so spare me with the pleasantries, will you?'

Through a crack in the door, Andy could see his uncle zip up his fly and walk over to the sink. The tap did not release its promise of water when pushed, so he wiped his hands on the black suit trousers and wandered slowly back to the door.

'Whether you like it or not, family is family. That may not mean anything to you now, and that's very sad for me to have to say to you, but it will mean something to you one day. Regardless of what has been and gone in the past, he's still your cousin,' said Andy's uncle.

The voice sounded familiar to Andy and sparked a memory in him that he could not place. Waiting until they had left, Andy tried the broken tap and was met with a trickle of strong-smelling water. He washed his hands as best he could then dried them with the rough blue paper towels that were scattered around the room.

Jordan stood with his parents and met Andy as he came out.

'We can take you home now if you want?' said Jordan's Mum. 'Home to our house, I mean. We're going to have you as a guest of ours for a few days, maybe even longer, if that sounds alright with you?' she asked kindly.

'Thanks, that sounds good,' said Andy, as the consoling hand of Jordan's father rested on his shoulder.

'You don't have to worry about anything anymore,' said Jordan's father. 'I'm just very sorry about today and I hope, well we all hope actually, that you are feeling okay. As well as you can be feeling, I mean. I know it can't be easy,' he added.

'That's okay,' said Andy. 'Thank you.'

'Andy... excuse me, Andy. Can we speak?' came the voice of his uncle.

'Hello,' said Andy bluntly. He noticed a boy of his own age standing towards the entrance to the church. He guessed that this was his cousin but felt a great deal of relief when his presence failed to be referenced, let alone introduced.

'Andy, I'm so very sorry about your mum. This can't be easy. I just wanted to pay my respects. I don't know what else to say, but I'm sorry,' his uncle said meekly. 'If I can do anything, you only need to ask.'

Andy looked at his uncle and saw the face of his father; a face that he now only recognised from the photos that he had kept hidden between his spring mattress and the bed slats. Once they had fallen and a breeze from the window had blown them into the hall. He had had little luck in his life up until that point, but he knew he was lucky that day having been able to find them before his mother did.

The minister at school had said that angels were the messengers of God. On that day, Andy went home and prayed to the angels, and to God, and to anyone who would listen. But his prayers always went unanswered.

'I have done everything alone until this point and I will continue to now,' Andy said candidly. 'I know who you are, but I do not know you,' he said.

The two held eye contact before his uncle held out his hand. Andy looked at it dismissively and shook his head.

'You can leave now,' he said.

Andy had often heard in school about what it was to be a man. None of the playground chatter on sex, drinking, fighting and driving had ever contained even the smallest reference to what he had experienced. Yet at that moment, he no longer felt that he was a boy.

Late that night, as Andy lay in Jordan's bed, his friend lying on a blow-up mattress, he watched car lights cast their dull beams of light through the curtains before they dropped away then vanished.

'Are you asleep?' asked Andy.

'Nah, I can't sleep,' said Jordan. 'Are you okay? Do you need a glass of water?'

'No,' said Andy through an elongated sigh. 'No thanks. Jordan... what do you think happens when you die?' he asked.

'Well,' said Jordan hesitantly. 'You go to heaven, don't you?'

'Everyone?' asked Andy.

'Well... I think so? I think if you speak to God when you are about to die, you can say sorry for the bad things you've done, and you'll be taken into heaven. Is that not right?'

'I don't know, I'm asking you,' said Andy. 'What if you don't know you're about to die?'

'Then you say it when you're outside heaven. Good or bad, whatever you've done, you get to go into heaven. You just need to say sorry to God for all the stupid, nasty and evil things you've done and then you get let in. We are all sinners; you just need to say sorry for your sins,' Jordan said.

'And you believe this?' asked Andy.

'I don't know. I don't think so. I just thought it was what you wanted to hear. Do you believe it?'

'No,' said Andy resolutely. 'I've been thinking about it. I think some people are good. They do good things, you know? Care for others, are kind, generous and give things back. I think those people go wherever it is they think they go when they die,' said Andy.

'What do you mean?' asked Jordan, sitting up on the blow-up mattress and peeling a sweaty leg off the plastic.

'I mean that if you've been good and you believe in heaven then you go to heaven. If you think that you get buried or burned and that's the end of it; eaten by worms or turned to ash, then that can happen too. I don't think there is one thing set in stone for everyone. If it's something you believe, then that's what happens,' said Andy.

'And what happens if you're bad then?' asked Jordan warily.

'I've been thinking about that too. I don't know. I think that some people know they are bad and some people... well they don't know they are. If someone hurts someone and knows they are doing it... well...that's evil isn't it? I mean really hurt someone with the intention to hurt them; revelling in the hurt and doing it with purpose. Well, I don't think they get what they believe. I don't know what happens, but it's not a choice they get to make,' said Andy.

'What does revelling mean?' Jordan asked.

'Well... like, to take happiness from something, you know?'

'Okay, well then yeah, I suppose that's true then,' said Jordan, stifling a yawn.

'But there are others who don't know the things they do are bad. They could hurt someone; really hurt them. Physically. Mentally. But they may not understand that they are doing it, you know? I don't know how to say it, but their brain might not work like yours or mine does. If you don't know what's wrong from right, then I'm unsure what happens next. They should be punished but how can you punish someone who doesn't know why they are being punished?' asked Andy. 'Anyway, I don't know what happens with them when they die. Do you?'

'No,' said Jordan. 'Are you sure you're okay talking about all of this today?' he asked, in a sincere and sympathetic tone.

'Of course,' said Andy.

'Andy,' said Jordan, before hesitating. 'My grandparents are in heaven.'

Andy watched another set of headlights cast a dim light that swept across the curtains then disappeared.

'I believe you,' whispered Andy.

Chapter sixteen

It was late autumn and the leaves had turned from shades of orange, yellow and red, to decaying mulch that coated the parks and pavements. Jordan had returned to work and his process of recovery - a duration he dared not put a time on - continued to progress as he had hoped. He would tell anyone that would listen, and there were several people at work that were more than willing to do so, that his hardest days were behind him. While that was true, he knew he was only at the very start of a journey that he understood would be never ending.

The plastic bags had been replaced with a longing for talk and connection, but the transient nature and mundane conversation of the base did little to fill the void he searched for. In a quieter moment, when he knew Ellis would be in the canteen, he informed him that he was trying to take long walks each evening. Beyond that, he told Ellis that he was considering joining a reading group. He asked if Ellis would also be interested in joining, and while he had no interest in doing so, Ellis agreed, safe in the knowledge that he would always have some excuse ready at hand so as not to attend. After the debacle with the book hunt and a desire to find whatever it was he was searching for, he had become even more languid. However, he woke each morning and stoically approached his situation as that of his own making and one he could live by. He no longer felt empty or pessimistic. Instead, he harboured a feeling that his present state of affairs were his to own and his alone.

In September, when the students went back to university and some of the casual workers had been let go, there was a restructuring of the teams. Andy and Ellis now worked together alongside Archie the driver. The three got on well with Andy and Ellis in particular forming a close friendship, despite what must have been more than a twenty-year age gap. While initially put off by Andy's impulsive tendencies, erratic conversation style and a level of deep discussion that had no place in the early hours of wet autumnal mornings, he had grown close to him.

On one particular Friday afternoon, Archie, who had taken up the welcoming habit of having the truck's radio on each day, took something out from his coat pocket and gathered Andy and Ellis around him. They both hoped that he was about to share some long-lost secret, or a treasure that had been hidden away for centuries, now found and safe in his possession. Instead, he opened his spade-like, rough hands to reveal a cassette tape.

'What is it?' asked Ellis.

'It's an apple tree, of course,' Archie replied mockingly. 'What do you think it is? It's a cassette tape. Surely you know what a cassette tape is at your age?' he asked. 'Yes, Archie, of course I know what a cassette tape is. I just mean what's on it?' Ellis asked earnestly.

'It's my own music,' came the reply from Archie, his chest puffed out at the reply.

During that afternoon, Andy and Ellis gained a bond that neither had expected when they drunk their first cup of coffee earlier that day. For thirty minutes - Andy still argued it was closer to forty-five - the two listened to the demo tape of Archie's folk rock band. Prosaic lyrics met an out of tune bass guitar, while the background din of a tinny sounding hi-hat drove the musicians on and on with no end in sight. After that afternoon and the stifled laughter that followed, the tape failed to make another appearance.

Other than the day at the pet shop, when the owner had let them in early for a cup of tea after clearing the bins, only for Andy to run out when he saw the caged birds, it was an otherwise fairly uneventful few months. As they drove on their last shift of the week, an early morning news bulletin caused the three to hush from what was already muted conversation. The silence was so complete that Ellis had questioned as to whether any of the men were breathing. War had begun. Not a war on their doorstep, but a war nonetheless and one that would soon fill their TVs, newspapers, radios and their collective consciousness.

As a wet October turned to a cold and blustery

November, they worked on the same routes and streets as before, their lives unchanged by the events that were taking place far away. They worked, ate and slept, in varying degrees of contentment and fulfilment, but they were safe. They stood unflinching at windows and turned on electrical appliances. They sat in bars, drank milky tea with sugar in cafes and watched those around them, the people whose rubbish they cleared, in an otherwise unguarded fearlessness.

Each day and before the news reports were read, the pictures were looked at in newspapers and on mobile telephones. The maimed and displaced, the dead and dying. Each morning, Ellis would share an update in the cab. Andy no longer looked at the pictures.

'A crying shame,' said Archie. 'Those poor, poor people, but what can you do?' he asked nonchalantly.

'There isn't a lot we can do,' said Ellis. 'There rarely is,' he added.

'Why is that?' asked Andy.

'Why's what, Andy? What do you mean?' Archie asked warily, already sensing the relative calm of the morning was about to be broken.

'Why is it we can't do anything?' Andy spat back. 'I know why we can't in the literal sense, after all, what can three binmen do to stop a war? But how many dead babies being pulled from the rubble of buildings will it take for someone to do something? Why when these acts of war, no, I don't mean that... I mean these atrocities! Why when these atrocities are taking place do we all seem to place our heads in the sand? Ignore it in the hope it goes away? Is that it? Is that what you want to know, Archie?' Andy's face flushed in anger and frustration.

'No, that's not it,' said Archie, with a degree of calm control that Ellis had not anticipated.

'That's what our governments are for. It's not for us to get involved and, more than that, this is a war between two countries. It's not a football match where you can cheer on from the sidelines; one where there is a good or bad side and we should all pick who we support. Killing is a sin and it's evil, no matter the context or the killer,' he said, staring intently at Andy as he did so.

'We have a long and shameful history of turning a blind eye to these things,' said Ellis. 'It's easier to know something is happening and not to think about it. Everyone would give the regular platitudes when they see such things. It's sad, horrible, awful, we'll all say, but we all have our own worries after all, don't we, so we go back to them. We all have bills to pay, health issues, or a family member to worry about. There's always something else. The economy is going down the pan as well and it's always easier for people to look the other way. Thirty minutes on the news after they've eaten a warm dinner is enough for them. Make it as concise as possible then throw some numbers in. It's watched knowing full well that nothing remains impartial and balanced, but we all eat it up regardless,' said Ellis.

'Not everyone,' said Andy sternly.

'No, you're right, it's not everyone,' said Archie, jumping back into the conversation. 'But it's most of everyone and that's why nothing changes and that's why nothing will change. Because we don't will, wish or want it for ourselves. What other reason are you looking for here?' asked Archie.

'We should all be protected,' said Andy, his anger changing to what Ellis could now sense was sadness and distress. 'These people have done nothing wrong and when they lay down at night, if they are lucky enough to still have a roof over their heads, they close their eyes knowing that they might not wake up again. That's not a life,' he added.

'Sadly, it's a life for thousands if not millions around the world,' said Ellis. 'This is no different to what's gone on in the past and will be no different than what's to come in the future. The important thing is not to dwell on it, or you would drive yourself mad,' he added meekly, knowing his response would anger Andy. Ellis was unsure if he even meant the resigned words that were spilling from his mouth.

'The important thing,' said Andy, blowing his nose in a dirty handkerchief, 'should be to change that way of thinking. What sort of life is it when action doesn't align with our compassion? Our sympathies and prayers will do nothing for these people. And yes, you're right. This has been what's gone on in the past and what will follow, and I'm all the more ashamed to be a man because of it,' he said.

'Ashamed to be a man?!' Spat Archie. 'You're ashamed? What preaching nonsense. I think it's high time that you got off your soap box and got back in touch with reality. What are you doing to change things? Do you think a self-important lecture to me and Ellis here will make any difference, because I'm telling you now, Andy, that it won't.'

He paused to forcibly swallow in an attempt to overcome a dryness in his throat from a voice strained with anger.

'And it's not just this war,' continued Archie. 'How many times have you seen something and turned away from it? Pretended it wasn't happening as we all know that it's easier that way? That's just how we are; all of us. Only some of us choose to actually do something and there is little anyone can do to change that, apart from taking their own action. That's the situation and nothing you can do or say will make any impact whatsoever to it,' he said, taking stock to sit back in the driver's seat when he realised he was now looming over Andy in an aggressive manner.

The three men looked their own separate ways, each taking a moment to reflect on what had been said. Archie's exasperated nasal breathing accompanied the contemplation. Ellis was first to speak again.

'When I was younger,' he said, 'I had terrible pain in my arms and legs. Each morning when I woke, there would be shooting pains that went across my body before it settled heavily in my limbs in what felt like a dull ache. Even now I can't describe it, but it felt like my joints were being rubbed with sandpaper and pushed from an unknown force.' Ellis paused then continued, sensing that his words were quelling the angry mood that had arisen from within the cab.

'My parents took me to any number of doctors and specialists, and each time I would try to describe the symptoms as best I could. I find it hard to do it now but you'll appreciate that when you are only fourteen, it's a much harder task. Everyone I spoke to said something different to the last: it will get better, or that it's growing pains from puberty. Test after test to be told not to worry and that my worrying about it will only make it worse. Do you know how hard it is when all you want is for someone to tell you that you have this or that, just so you can label it and reassure yourself and others that it's real and you're not making it up?' he asked, the question aimed at nobody in particular.

'To be told that it will get better is something, but how can you believe something like that when you wake up and try to fall asleep with a pain that until that point never ceased? We all have our own worries and things to focus on. Do you know something? I've never actually told anyone this, well at least not anyone but my parents, and I don't know why I'm saying it now. I guess it's just to say to you that you know what, people have their own worries and problems that perhaps only they know? I'm sure that most of us would want to change how things are in life, like war and famine, or persecution and injustice. But it's hard. When you are fighting your own battle each day it's hard to do something for others, even if you know that what's happening is wrong. We need to remember that. All of us should,' said Ellis, his voice strained.

'I wish I knew how to talk when I was younger,' said Archie, pausing to reflect on what he had said. 'I bottled things up, didn't I? Bit of a cliché really, but that's how it went. I don't even know if you'd call twenty-three young these days, but looking back, it feels young to me. When my son was born and my wife and I took him home, I went into the bathroom and cried. I still don't know why but I did it and it certainly wasn't tears of joy. I felt like something in me had changed forever and I didn't know if that was a good thing or something that well, wasn't so good. You couldn't voice these things or say that type of thing at the time as much as you can say things like that today, but you can still feel them, can't you?' he asked, looking over at Ellis and Andy for reassurance. Ellis nodded.

'Don't get me wrong, I love my son with everything I have in me, both of them, but at that time on that day it didn't feel like love. It felt like I'd lost a part of myself rather than gained something. I've never told anyone that either and I have no idea why I'm telling you both now, but well, that's how it is.' A hush fell over the cab. The silence drove Archie on to say more.

'This was so, so many years ago now and I didn't know how to speak about it at the time. I don't know why I cried but I did and once it was over with, it was done. I just felt it building and the tears came.'

Archie's gaze caught the gloomy dark grey clouds that were growing on the horizon. 'I've never told anyone that before, like I say, not even my wife, but now you know. It doesn't make anything any different. Everyone feels in their own way and only that person will ever know what that is,' he said.

The cab fell silent again. The radio was soon turned on and the music mixed with the sound of heavy rain as it beat down on the cab's roof in continuous waves. The growing storm was gathering speed and strength and soon the winds took the rain eastwards, over to the next village, town or city, then off into the sea.

Chapter seventeen

The artificial glow of the floodlights against the men below cast long shadows across the football pitch. Andy stood with Ellis on the touchline, their breath condensing and lifting skywards on the cold winter's night. Neither had gloves and their red swollen hands were cast into the depths of jacket pockets. Not far from them, a man with a shaggy-looking red-haired dog blew hard on whatever it was that filled his polystyrene cup. The earlier sleet was now accompanied by persistent wind that unfalteringly blew at the corner flags and against the spectators, blasting against any exposed skin it met. What shelter there was came from a small terrace at the other end of the pitch; ramshackle seating bolted onto its crumbling concrete base.

    Ellis had spent the previous weeks buried in half-finished books, drinking cheap red wine and watching life pass him by from the vantage point of his window. He now lived his life through the actions of others, either making up stories for those he came into contact with, or reading about them in novels, historical fiction and poetry. He had ceased visiting the library after the embarrassing incident with the librarian and aside from the workplace hours each day spent with Andy and Archie, he knew he was becoming increasingly reclusive. While that concerned him, it worried him more that he did not appear to mind this outcome. It was to be his next chapter on the downwards spiral, he told himself. He was resolute in his belief that there would be nothing notable to come, and that for now, this was his lot. Trying to change it would not do him any good, he reasoned.

And it was with those thoughts coursing through his mind that he stood with Andy on a late winter's evening watching two teams of amateur sportsmen play football. One of the players in a light blue and amber shirt kicked the ball in the direction of the goal. He missed his desired target, and the ball bounced off the sodden turf, careering under one of a smattering of advertising boards and finally settling in a nearby field. One of the opposition players, a burly looking defender with cropped black hair and tape across his shin guards, placed one hand on the farmer's stonewall dyke, hopped over in a move that resembled a gymnast on a pommel horse, then stood looking between the long grass for the ball against the backdrop of semi-darkness. It was soon found, and the solid thud of his kick saw it launched back into the field of play, its arc disrupted by the growing wind.

'I can't say I had you down as a football fan, Andy,' said Ellis, shivering and pushing his chin further down into the collar of his jacket.

'I'm not,' replied Andy, 'only this pitch is quite close to where I live and whenever the floodlights are on like tonight, I've always wondered what it would be like to watch a game under the lights. I must say, it's not the experience I had expected it to be. Do you want to leave? We can go and get a drink?' he asked.

'I was surprised when you asked me to come,' said Ellis frankly. 'I know there was a bit of an argument in the cab, and well, I didn't expect you to want to do anything after that,' said Ellis. 'I'm quite tired so not too sure about grabbing a quick drink to be honest with you, Andy,' he added.

'I asked you to see if you fancied doing something different,' said Andy warmly. 'What happened in the cab was good for us all, I'm sure. It's not beneficial to keep things bottled up and emotive subjects like that will lead to some disagreement. I don't want to get into it all again now,' he said hastily.

Ellis did not yet know Andy fully, if it was possible to ever know somebody fully, yet he was quite sure he had never met anyone more mercurial than the man he stood beside that night. He found it more than strange how someone could become so impassioned about something, only for the subject to get brushed over at a later date.

'Look, tell me to mind my own business here but is everything okay?' Andy asked.

Ellis winced. Everything was not okay, but he had no cause to discuss that with anyone, least of all Andy. Yet for reasons he did not understand, he had still become accustomed to him over the last few months.

'Everything is fine, Andy,' he said, 'honestly it is. I'm just a bit tired with work and everything.'

'Of course, I understand that,' said Andy. 'Just know that if you ever need to speak about anything, whatever it may be, then know that I'm here if needed,' he added.

'Thanks, Andy. I appreciate that. And yeah, likewise. That goes without saying,' said Ellis, who by now felt increasingly awkward. 'One quick drink won't hurt I suppose,' he said, ducking instinctively as a stray ball flew close to his head.

'That suits me,' said Andy. 'I know a good place by the harbour.'

Despite being relatively close to the football pitch, the walk to the harbour felt longer than either of the two had anticipated. It was not the wind that made it so, nor was it the irregular rainfall that came in waves and soaked their already frozen bodies: it was an uncomfortable feeling of unease. While the warm confines of Archie's cab and the comfort and security of both his and Jordan's role as the interchangeable third person in their initial friendship provided a welcome buffer, both now realised they had never spent significant time together away from work. It was beginning to play heavily on both men.

When the small talk about Archie, Christmas plans and politics had dried up, Ellis anticipated that Andy would spring some deep and meaningful question on him at any moment. He did not feel capable of becoming embroiled in a serious debate, nor did he have the mental wherewithal to engage at a level he thought would please Andy. In keeping with his expectations, he did not have long to wait.

'Ellis,' said Andy, wiping his rain-soaked fringe and tucking it in the direction of one ear. 'What do you think it means when someone perceives something? What does perception mean to you?' he asked.

Ellis, who was in no mood for the question and the change of direction in the conversation, answered back curtly. 'You know what it means, Andy. Is that the pub you mean there down by the corner?' asked Ellis.

'Yes, yes, that's the pub,' Andy said impatiently. 'I know what it means, but I just wanted to see if you thought it meant the same. Sorry, I didn't mean to fill the void with noise,' he added. 'It's a trait I have, but no harm meant by it,' he added.

Ellis kicked an empty can that lay on the pavement and watched as it bounced three times before landing in a puddle. He could see Andy looked hurt.

'Andy,' he said, trying to force a positive tone in the hope it would raise the mood. 'Where do you want me to start? I'll answer the question,' said Ellis.

'The beginning is usually best, my friend,' replied Andy. Two smokers stood outside the bar, stubbing the ends of their spent cigarettes against the wall. A shower of orange sparks filled the air and were blown down the street. Ellis watched as the colour quickly left them and the remnants became lost in the darkness.

Andy wandered over slowly to the small table, placed his drink beside Ellis, then sat down beside him. The cold beer took little time to warm Ellis. Drinking his usual bottle of sparkling water, Andy instead chose to warm himself on an old bar fire. Ellis watched as his companion rubbed both hands over the glowing bars, his gaze unflinching from the vivid red that emanated from the electrical glow. Its bars produced a smell of burning dust and of piping hot metal. In the dimness of the bar, Ellis could see in his stance and posture that Andy looked like a much older man, not in keeping with his relatively young age. The shadows cast against his face produced a dull greyness and it brought out deep-set wrinkles around his eyes. Ellis felt there was a fragility there and he found that it paired uncomfortably with Andy's erratic comments and sensitivities.

'So, Ellis,' he said. 'What was that you were saying about perception?' asked Andy.

Ellis sighed unintentionally, then watching as Andy's smile faded, quickly spoke in the hope a response would change the mood.

'Well, it's, I think, eh,' he stumbled over his words. 'It's more than feeling, isn't it? I mean it goes beyond sensation,' he added.

Andy nodded but did not answer, hoping instead for Ellis to continue.

He did. 'I suppose a lot of it will be based on your life experience, won't it? You and I won't have had the same experiences growing up so we will view certain things differently. Don't get me wrong; blue will still be blue, and rain is wet, but it's about emotion, I suppose, isn't it?' Ellis asked.

'I'm asking you,' said Andy, taking a sip from his glass.

'Well then yes, it's about how we as people view things based on our own experiences. On our own values, moods, how we feel at that particular day. It's a fairly nuanced question and to be honest, Andy, I could do without these faux intellectual questions, okay? Can we not just have a drink? You asked me how I was feeling earlier so I'll ask you: are you okay?' Ellis found himself growing frustrated at the mercurial Andy who was now smiling again, unsettling Ellis as he did so.

'What do you think of if I said the word treasure to you?' asked Andy.

'I'd say that what I took for a quiet drink would have turned into some cliched philosophical debate about how one man's treasure being another's rubbish,' said Ellis, eyeing up the remnants of his pint glass and considering if now was the best time to leave. He wanted to like Andy and if he was honest with himself, he had welcomed the company and an excuse to finally leave the imposed confines of his flat. Yet at each turn, Andy had the ability to change his mood for the worse, or to send his thoughts into a downward spiral that he could well do without. While he continued to feel a growing unease around their discussions, he realised that he harboured a stronger emotion towards him. It was the feeling of pity.

Andy smiled. 'No, but that would be quite apt for our line of work, wouldn't you say?' he laughed.

'Andy, you clearly have something to say so just come out with it please. I'm going to make a move soon and try to get an early night,' said Ellis, stifling a yawn that was building. The warmth of the pub when mixed with a slowly drunk beer had caused a genuine fatigue to set in. His limbs throbbed and he felt a growing pressure building in his forehead, as his thoughts drifted to the image of his bed and the escapism that four, perhaps even five hours of sleep would bring.

'Okay, Ellis,' Andy said quietly, beckoning him to move closer while looking around the bar to gauge if any of the patrons were in earshot. 'When I asked you about perception it was to see if you understood the world as I do. The fact you realise we'll see things differently is the main thing I wanted to hear, and I welcome the words as you said them. Rest assured; I agree with you. But with the treasure question then that's something quite different altogether,' Andy added, a wide grin filling his aged face, the deep wrinkled grooves growing between his temples and eyes.

'But for now, Ellis,' he continued, 'you and I must discuss the treasure I mentioned.'

Ellis knew now that Andy was, to use a term widely used on the base, slightly unhinged. He did not like to hear him being spoken about in that way, but the term was one that had picked up in frequency during the last few weeks. Andy's erratic behaviour had increased and as the two sat hunched around the small table, he found himself attempting to get as far back as he could. Andy's eyes shone with an intensity that Ellis had not yet seen over the last few months. He was filled with regret. Regret at accepting the invitation to watch the football game and a deeper regret and fear that his presence had released something in Andy that was uncontrollable.

Andy, who wore a tattered herringbone jacket, stained darker at the bottom with the earlier onslaught of rain, reached into his pocket and removed a handkerchief. Placing it onto the table, it unravelled slightly, and Ellis could make out the faint pastel colours that still clung to the frayed fabric; a miracle given its threadbare state.

'And what's this then, Andy?' asked Ellis, with a conciliatory tone rather than genuine interest.

'Inside that handkerchief is something that's going to change my future, and yours if you'll let it. One of several little pieces I have that when put together, will cast new light on the ways of the world,' he said, unblinking. The dim lighting of the pub made his grin look maniacal.

'Andy, are you feeling okay? I mean that with sincerity when I ask it, but is everything okay?' asked Ellis, moving closer in the hope his presence would calm Andy.

'I like you, Ellis,' said Andy, moving back in his seat and sliding the handkerchief and its contents over the table. 'Please rest assured that while I am tired, and while I would be the type of person some may refer to as complex, that yes, I am perfectly fine. Go ahead. Open it. What's stopping you?'

Ellis stared at the small package on the table with an emotionless gaze. He felt nothing other than concern for Andy and a growing sense of wariness that increased in intensity with each passing word. Taking the handkerchief in his hand, he opened it with a nonchalant movement.

'It's open, Andy. Happy now?' he asked. Ellis looked down to whatever was in the handkerchief as it shone and glimmered in the pub's lighting.

'Oh no,' said Andy, with a sardonic grin. 'I won't be happy until you know what it is.'

'In that case, what is it?' asked Ellis curtly.

'It's a map. Or at least it's part of a map,' replied Andy. 'Go ahead, look at it.'

Ellis delved into the fabric and could clearly see four small metal shards. Each looked to be cut unevenly, and their serrated edges clung tightly to the handkerchief's fabric, as if almost fearful from the light. Andy continued as Ellis held one of the flakes of what looked like silver in his hands, tracing his finger across embossed writing that he could not make out.

'Many years ago, long before you and I were born, there was a ship that ran aground just off the coast there,' said Andy, his eyes growing wider and his voice hushed to a whisper. 'A Royal Navy man-of-war, laden with a cargo of gold and silver coins. It took on water and went down in a winter storm, all of its crew lost to the high waves and freezing waters,' he said.

'I don't have time for these fairy stories,' said Ellis, interrupting Andy.

'Well, you will when you hear what I have to say,' replied Andy. 'Men of the town knew about the wreck and what it contained for years but none of them had the means to recover what went down with the ship. Over the years it was forgotten about. Well, not completely, of course. There was always some wreckage that was cast up on the beach with each winter storm, but that was all that remained of its memory. But those who knew about the treasure and the location of where it went down never forgot. And what's more, they made a map to remind them. A long time ago there used to be a large slate mine in the hills far from here,' he said, nodding in the direction of the mountains. 'One of the tinsmiths of the mine knew the stories from his father and his father before him and embossed the location on a sheet of metal. That's what you're holding in your hand. A piece of a puzzle,' said Andy, sitting back in his seat.

Ellis looked at one of the thin pieces that lay in his hand and wondered how old they could be.

'Why are you telling me this, Andy?' he asked.

'Because I want you to help me find the other pieces,' he said. 'I need your help. What do you say to that?'

Ellis had spent the last four evenings toiling over the question as to why Andy had asked him to a local football game. He told himself that he had no intention of coming to meet him on each of the subsequent mornings when he woke from fitful sleep, yet here he was, sitting with him in the pub. Even if he did not care to admit it, something was pulling him in and closer to Andy, whether he wanted the unseen force to do so or not.

Ellis watched as a group of three noisy drinkers left the bar, the strong winds rocking the door against its frame and sending a chill through the room. He had read or been told that in life everybody gets one opportunity to do or achieve greatness. Others may get more than one opportunity and yet more pass up the chance when it arises, either through fear, its demands, or simply, not understanding that this was their moment. Ellis was adamant he would not fall within those categories. After searching for so long, he wondered if this could finally be the point where his life would change for the better.

'Okay,' Ellis said, looking once more at the shining pieces on the table. 'You look after these,' sliding the package over to Andy who gently wrapped it meaningfully then placed it in his pocket.

'I'll do it,' he said, rubbing some of the dried beer foam from the top of his pint glass. He saw it reflected in the polished brass ornament that lay behind Andy's head. Before he had time to think about it, he observed that his grin now mirrored the maniacal look of his companion which he had so harshly judged before.

Chapter eighteen

Jordan sat at the bus stop and twirled a blue strand of wool around his right forefinger. The wool had been buried under a pile of coins, rubber bands, old birthday cards, pens and electrical fuses, all of which were crammed tightly within a drawer in his kitchen. He had hoped to find some safety pins, or at the very least some paperclips that he could fashion into a pin, but neither were to be found on this occasion.

A young couple dressed in their school uniforms kissed passionately against one side of the bus stop. The boy stopped, spat out some chewing gum onto the pavement, then continued. Jordan could see that the girl's eyes were open, and he became uncomfortable and felt more out of place because of it.

Jordan wore thin suit trousers that were slightly too big for him, held solidly in place around the waist by a shiny belt that he had punched an extra hole into that morning with a corkscrew. The safety pins were required for some much-needed support, but as yet, their absence had not caused him any embarrassment or discomfort. Neither the belt nor the corkscrew had been touched in several months.

A gentle breeze blew across the road and made his trouser bottoms billow. A white shirt, only marginally creased where the elbow met the forearm, lay under a tweed style blazer. In its upper inlaid pocket, he carried an old pocket watch left to him by his grandfather. He had kept the diary he had found as a youth and now read from it most days. This routine had only been a recent one but had now become a practice that gave him great solace. He himself was trying to write each day, sometimes more successfully than others. It was important to get your thoughts and feelings out on paper, he was told. On the nights when the words flowed freely from his black biro he would write until his hand ached, and sleep filled his tired eyes. At other points, he would stare blankly at the empty pages, trying but failing to express how he felt in that moment. He accepted both scenarios to be acceptable and embraced both with compassion. He had also been told that this was important.

  The street opposite the bus stop had a betting shop on its corner and a steady flow of customers streamed in and out. A man with a cane stood beside the door, smoking a cigarette purposefully and with a vigour that failed to match his otherwise sour, run down appearance. His back rested against the wall and Jordan could see black rings that lay heavily under his eyes, even from several metres away.

  Two pigeons fluttered above a lamppost, swooping down low to the pavement then gliding upwards to sit on the top of the shop's sign. Feathers and bird shit covered it, but the customers were not there for the building's interior or exterior aesthetics. The betting shop was once the place where Robert Prestwick had traded, but long gone was the assorted bric-a-brac, newspapers and pints of milk. Jordan felt the sting of nostalgia that hung low in his throat, and he found it hard to swallow. The new occupant and its steady stream of customers made him feel a sadness deep within and one that he told himself would soon fill the pages of his notebook.

A new mobile phone that he purchased with cash only two weeks before rang loudly in his pocket. The shrill tone appeared to wake him from his depressive daydream. A woman's voice was on the other end.

'We're just about to leave now,' said the muted voice, in what he could already tell was a slightly forced tone of friendliness. 'You're still feeling …' she hesitated, and Jordan heard her dry mouth swallow. 'You're still feeling okay, aren't you?'

'I promise I am,' said Jordan, with a conviction that belied the nervousness he felt. His arms and legs trembled, and his full bladder felt like it was screaming to escape from his body.

'I mean it, Kirsty,' he said. 'I feel good but if you are having second thoughts about today, I'll completely understand if you want to postpone. We both know that it's important that we get this right and you are the one in control here,' Jordan said. He meant every word of it.

There was a long silence before he again heard the voice on the other end inhale deeply, then forcibly blow out a sigh.

'No, it's not that, I just...I just wanted to check that you would be okay with everything. That everything was still on track. As I say, we're just going to leave soon so I guess we'll see you in thirty minutes or so?' said Kirsty, Jordan's estranged partner.

Along one side of the street, down beyond the butcher and greengrocers, and past the doctor's surgery, there stood a short red brick wall. The wall enclosed the base of a large oak tree; its structure crumbling in parts and misshapen thanks to the strength of the roots that pressed against it. Jordan could not see it, but he knew he was close. It was there that he had split his forehead open and cut his hand. His head hit the wall and his hand, the shattered glass. Long before that point it had contained vodka. At least that was what he had been told. He could not remember being picked up, or the looks of the worried shoppers as they moved in to offer help. Many others simply looked then walked on, busy with their own lives.

He remembered when it started but had little memory of the last time he had drunk. He thought of all the mornings where he would wake, his mouth dry and a sickly-sweet staleness seeping out from within the layer of sweat that covered his body and bedsheets. On most days he would be careful and organised enough to have something in the house that would take the edge off. Pull him back from the precipice and settle frayed nerves, a racing heart and the black desolation that filled him. Anything to silence the growing anxiety and anguish and make the day ahead more bearable. With a can or two drunk from the safety and confines of a warm, if dirty bed, the day would instantly become more manageable. In those twenty minutes, he could silence the side of himself who hated what it saw in the mirror: the absent father; the addict; the destroyer of his own body and all he had been gifted. But when the alcohol wore off the feelings grew, and so he drank more.

There had been a tipping point: when the stolen whisky was no longer glugged down for bravado, but for necessity. This did not happen overnight, nor was there any particular reason that Jordan could pinpoint as to why it did. An otherwise poor academic performance at school was met with a hubris for life. The lessons were not places in which he could learn, but a space for laughter and for friendship.

His home life was settled and happy and as a boy he had been given all the opportunities that his loving parents could provide for him. There was one moment, when Andy had stayed at the family home following the death of his mother that burned deep in his memory. Andy was snoring softly one evening, a sleeping bag pulled tightly over his chin and shoulders. The streetlights outside the bedroom window shone through a gap in the curtains and he watched the sleeping figure rising and falling with each breath, guttural gasps and groans rising from the back of his throat, nose and mouth. There was no malice for his sleeping friend and instead he listened sleeplessly with a steady degree of curiosity. He wondered what if anything Andy may have been dreaming about at that point, then watching as he writhed and whimpered, an action that halted the snoring, he no longer wanted to know. Jordan pushed the question to a hidden place that he had found could not be accessed when he closed his eyes and gently hummed to himself. The thoughts would often come back, but he knew how to suppress them. At least in the early days. Unable to sleep he crept downstairs and stood in the kitchen, the cool tiles numbing his feet. There was a bottle of white wine in the fridge, three quarters full. Staring into the light from the fridge, he sensed the cold air drop and waft against his naked stomach. He took the bottle, drank it down in barely a few gulps, then wiped his hand across his mouth. He smelled the sweet bitterness of the grapes and the alcohol. He stood in the kitchen, his friend and parents sleeping upstairs, and he became at ease with himself. A ticking wall clock in the hall filled the silence and he stood for some moments, thinking about nothing in particular and scratching his head, some dry skin from his scalp falling gently before him and his thin, wiry body illuminated by the waning moon.

Making his way back into bed, he pulled the cool sheets over his body and closed his eyes. A warmth grew from within and soon filled him entirely with a sense of dull, numbing contentment. The snoring grew louder then ceased, stopped by another involuntary movement of Andy's body. Jordan felt the pleasant sensation grow and soon he fell into a deep, anesthetised sleep.

When school was over and friends found apprenticeships or went to college, he met Kirsty, fell in love, worked a steady, if unfulfilling job and made a life for himself. The alcohol had always been present in his life but soon it became the only constant. A shared bottle of wine after work was no longer enough, and every possible opportunity for a drink was sought after with a desire that was soon to overwhelm any of his other endeavours.

The morning drinks to pick himself up and iron over the lows were only a temporary measure, he had promised himself, but its grip was already too deep that he could not escape. When the holiday money was stolen, Kirsty had known all along that he was the thief. Yet she had played along in the hope that by fooling herself the money would make its way back to her along with any remaining empathy she had for Jordan. Neither did, at least not then. While it had taken her some time to move out of their communal bedroom, three weeks spent on the downstairs sofa was all the thinking time she needed to make up her mind that she was leaving.

Neither knew at that stage that she was pregnant. In quieter moments, a rarity in Jordan's restless mind, he often wondered if his decisions would have been different if he had known then she was. He asked himself if the drinking would have stopped if at that point, he had the opportunity to hold his baby daughter in his arms only months later. He told himself that he would have stopped, but he knew otherwise. He realised that he wanted to but he understood that he was powerless to do so, and the thought made him hate himself. On those days, three bottles of wine would turn to four. His dishevelled husk of a frame would make the trip to the shop. The same story would be told to the shopkeeper in so far as that the party was ongoing, he had guests over, or that he was stocking up for the weekend. He knew he was not believed even then, but the shame and embarrassment soon left him. It was the first of several lies he would tell on a daily basis.

Jordan had spent five years living that way, and each year saw him see his daughter less and less. He and Kirsty had agreed that that was the best approach to take.

It had been half a decade that was marked initially by unreliability and letdowns, and steadily spiralled into dysfunctionality. He knew that he would always be an alcoholic but even with the small degree of clarity he now held after five months of sobriety, he had come to realise that its grip was diminishing. He couldn't yet look forward without glancing back, making sure the distance was still too great for it to catch him. Yet with each month the grip loosened, its once-unyielding hold steadily weakening. He could see his future now and it was one that he no longer had to hide from.

A red hatchback came around the corner, indicated and slowed to a stop. Jordan jogged briskly to the passenger door, opened it swiftly, and quickly sat down in the passenger seat.

'Daddy's here, mummy!' called a child's voice from the back.

Jordan looked at Kirsty, seeking permission. She nodded and gave a faint smile.

'Hi, sweetheart,' he said, turning round to look at his daughter. 'It's lovely to see you,' reaching into the back seat with his right hand and giving one of her ankles a gentle, loving squeeze.

'That's tickly, daddy!' came a giggle.

'Everybody ready?' Kirsty asked. They drove off; the cheering and laughter from the back seat merging with the sound of the engine. Jordan placed his hand on the pocket watch to check it was still there, then put his hand once again on his daughter's ankle, rubbing a gap of skin between her sock and trousers with his thumb.

Had Jordan looked out the passenger side window at that moment, he would have seen the backs of Ellis and Andy as they stood at the foot of the beach, kicking patches of seafoam and waiting for something that only they knew. As it was, his gaze was fixed on the rearview mirror and the bright azure eyes that went from a stuffed teddy bear to the window, then met his own, glowing with the happiness of a child.

Chapter nineteen

Two pairs of shoes, long sodden with sea water, hung precariously from laces that were tied tightly to a piece of gnarled driftwood. The dying embers of the fire glowed and shifted from bright orange, red and yellow, while smoke hung on the air in the calm of the night. Andy took another piece of wood from a pre-prepared pile and cast it onto the low flames. It was damp and the smoke billowed as its wetness choked the fire. It was soon overcome by the heat and energy of the flames and caught light, just as those pieces that now lay in scattered embers had done before.

Ellis looked in a daze at the now roaring fire as it contrasted with the blue-black sky, the faint glimmer of lights from the fishing boats far out to sea doing much to create a calming scene. Taking a small flask of whisky from his pocket, he removed the cap with semi-numb fingers and took a sip. He basked in the warmth as it coursed through him, a dry heat from the fire radiating on his face, stomach and legs. Each man stood on dry pebbles and loose rock, halfway in the cavern of a sea cave. Its entrance was filled with every conceivable type of plastic waste, dried seaweed, fishing nets and all manner of rubbish that had been cast out into the sea, then pushed back to land by wave, current and wind, by an unwelcoming host.

Hours before, they had walked along the shore waiting for the opportune moment: a manageable swell and as little an audience as possible. On and on they had walked on that late afternoon, beyond the harbour and its curved breakwater, then on further past the marina and out towards the end of the town. The beach narrowed after that point and the two had scurried over sand dunes and small hillocks, scrambling as loose soil and foliage fell around them in clumps with each laborious footstep. They walked with intention and hung on tightly when required to do so with purposeful grips. At points they had found themselves clinging on with all the strength they could muster, hanging at the precipice twenty feet above a small cove, the murky blue-grey of its cold waters the unwelcome reward for a loose foot or misplaced hand.

  Step by step, they had edged closer to the end of the body of water and climbed down with a jump and onto the safety of damp sand. The tide was out and all that stood between them now and their destination was three hundred metres of peaceful solitude. Far from the crowds of preying eyes and now hidden by steep and looming sea cliffs on a half-moon-shaped beach of stone and sand. They had walked in the direction of the cave with desire and anticipation coursing through them. And it was there they stood now, warming themselves by the fire and drying off their shoes.

'Do you know that Jordan and I used to do something like this most evenings in the summer?' asked Andy.

Ellis turned and smiled. 'Jordan told me the exact same thing, just when I started working on the bins,' he said.

Ellis had practiced what he was about to say next for some time. He was unsure if it was a question he truly wanted to receive an answer to. Whether it was curiosity or for an understanding of why things were the way they were, he was unsure, but it did not matter, he told himself. There would be no better time than now.

'Look, Andy. I've never asked you this before and don't feel you need to answer or anything. I just think that we're both standing here with our shoes off in the middle of a cave, so as situations go, it's not what you would call normal is it? But seeing as we are here now then I might as well. What happened between you both? You and Jordan, I mean? I don't even know if anything did happen, so please do tell me to mind my own business if I'm way off course here,' he added quickly, sensing a change in Andy's facial expression as the shadows danced across his face.

Andy wiped his nose with his finger, inspected it, then wiped the remnants across the sleeve of his jacket.

'Nothing happened, nothing at all,' he said, with a calmness in his voice that put Ellis at ease. 'Jordan went his way in life, and I went mine. We were very good friends at one point in time. I think people would have called us best friends, but I've never really gone in for that term myself. Every friend who crosses your path in life holds the same degree of merit as any other, or at least that's how I've always seen it,' he added. 'Now you may say that that's because I've had so few cross my path in life. Real friends that is, not just the casual acquaintances we all make in life,' he said.

'But as people we often just grow apart, especially when you're younger and your focus is changing every day. I mean at that age it's so easy to move onto different things, vary your surroundings a bit and meet new people,' Andy continued.

Ellis was unsure if Andy had done any of what he had mentioned but he had not long to wait before he found out.

Andy rubbed his nose again but this time his finger remained dry.

'I went to university,' he continued. 'I went and Jordan didn't. Then with each passing summer, the time you spend together becomes less and less. It's not that it ever becomes forced, but I don't know...I don't know how to put it into words. There comes a point where you're looking across at someone and something is different. You can still have experienced so much together and seen and done so many different things, but the feeling creeps up on you all the same, or at least it does with me,' he said.

Andy moved down to the fire and tossed a couple of the dry branches on the flames. Both men watched as sparks flew and swirled in the night sky.

'Look, Ellis. Jordan and I experienced a lot of...' There was a momentary pause as Andy bent down again, rubbing his hands purposefully close to the flame to warm his chilled fingers.

'We experienced a lot of things together when we were young that nobody should have to experience. Neither of us chose to have those things happen to us but I made a choice to bring Jordan into my experience,' said Andy.

The lights of a passenger ferry moved slowly in the distance and neither man spoke for some time, each choosing instead to focus on the ship as its bow dipped and rose in the swell.

'You know, Ellis, and I'm sure you'll have heard this before, but when people say their life has been a living hell, I often wonder if they really mean it. My life was a living hell but even calling it that won't do the things that happened to me any justice. I don't know how else to put it or if there's any need to after all these years? Why do we always have to compartmentalise and label every feeling and experience?' he asked. 'But for want of a better turn of phrase then yes, my life was a living hell, and I chose to bring Jordan into that hell. Do you think that's selfish? To share an experience that you know will expose a friend to something that they should never think about in life, let alone hear firsthand?' Andy looked expectantly at Ellis, the light from the fire dancing over his face.

'No,' said Ellis. 'I don't think that's selfish. Not now and certainly not when you are younger. When you are growing up you don't have any responsibility. No accountability to anyone. That means that friendship is in its purest form, I suppose. A friendship of genuine support and concern, before the dirge of modern life takes hold. Before the worries about bills and the state of the economy, or lack of career progression keep you awake at night. It's a friendship at its purest when you're young, and you're lucky to have had that with Jordan,' he said.

Ellis took out the whisky again, but it was empty. He blew over its opening with dry lips and listened as a gloomy, owl-like drone reverberated from the empty container and filled the cave. Andy looked at Ellis and smiled.

'Thank you,' he mouthed, though Ellis could not hear the words.

'Do you ever think it's all an act?' asked Ellis.

'What?' asked Andy.

'I mean friendship. I suppose I mean, love, too. I don't think those things are real. How can they be?' said Ellis.

'Go on,' replied Andy. 'Say what you want to say.'

'It's just...' said Ellis, looking down at his shoeless feet and scrunching his toes up and down on the cold rocks. 'It's just, I understand that it feels good to be with other people sometimes, of course I do, but it all seems too forced to me, as if we're all just going through the motions with it all. You could be close friends with someone then if one of you decides not to put the same level of effort in, or you simply don't want to do anything, then the friendship falls apart. Friendships shouldn't need a set number of meetups, calls or messages each year, should they?' he asked.

'They shouldn't and I don't think they do,' replied Andy. 'Even excluding that, what's wrong with a transient friendship? Of a little while friend? You should enjoy the people that bring joy into your life for what it is, as those moments are fleeting. You don't have to label everything, Ellis, as I was saying earlier.'

'How many people have you ever known in your life that have been in love only for it to come to an end?' asked Ellis.

'Several, and I know where you're going with this,' replied Andy, giving Ellis a smile as he did so. 'Just because something ends, it doesn't mean that the thing, in this case love, wasn't there at some stage. If love is there even for a fleeting moment, then you can rest assured that it's been true and real for the person that experienced it,' he said.

'Anyway,' continued Andy, 'we can speak about this any time you'd like but are you not wondering why I've taken you into this sea cave? I would have expected that that would have been the predominant thought in your mind right now!' Andy laughed heartily and his head and stocky shoulders shook, casting a dull shadow from the fire that filled all the way to the back of the cave.

'I know why we're here,' said Ellis, 'or at least I think I do. It's to find the part of the map, isn't it? I have no idea why else we would have come all this way if it didn't have anything to do with what you told me in the pub,' he said.

'Ah yes, I see now that you've been paying attention,' Andy said mockingly. 'I know you know why we're here, but I don't think you know specifically why I've taken you all this way and why we stand here now, our shoes drying over the fire in an old smugglers' cave. Did you know this was an old smugglers' cave?' he asked.

'I did not, but I expect that means you're going to tell me more about it,' said Ellis, who still had his doubts whether all of this would actually lead to something. He imagined their names splashed across the front page of the local paper, with 'treasure hunters' placed somewhere in the headline, before his inner voice chastised himself for the act of fanciful whimsy.

'HMS Illustrious,' said Andy, 'that's what she was called.' He pointed out to sea and watched as Ellis' eyes followed. 'A fourth-rate man-of-war with cannons bursting out from her broadside and stern. Laden with Spanish gold, silver and sixty men when she went down in rough seas just off the coast there,' he added, pointing to a different spot out in the deep black. 'She was sailing away far from her fleet when she took on water, sinking fast and offering safe haven to none. Many said that it was a mutiny, and the crew were heading north, trying to escape whatever it was that followed. I don't know what they planned to do when they got to whichever port they had in mind, but I can't imagine it would have been a positive outcome. Well, more of a positive outcome than having your boat swamped by a roaring, raging sea in the depth of winter. Some say there were even French and Spanish sailors on board. Can you imagine the treachery? But they hushed it up, you see? Even then they wanted to keep it silent. All done to keep the good name of the Royal Navy in its customary high esteem, of course. But the stories passed down from generation to generation led to the creation of a map of the wreck site and that's why we're here today to find the missing pieces.' Andy looked into the fire at the end of his speech, waiting eagerly for Ellis' response. It sounded polished and Ellis thought the words that were spoken jarred with Andy's usual style.

'So how do you know it's here then?' Ellis asked.

Andy smiled. 'Ellis,' he said. 'You're here because I need your help, and I thank you for coming. I've told you the parts of the story that you need to know but for now, that's all you need to know, at least until we can find some more of the pieces. If we find anything, as I'm sure we will, then whatever we recover will be as much yours as it is mine, I promise you that,' said Andy.

Andy meandered slowly towards the glowing fire and placed his fingers inside each of the footless shoes. He took them from their wooden props and was clearly happy that they were now acceptably dry. Small semi-circles of granular sand clung in patches on the fabric. Stepping into his own shoes, he marvelled at the warmth as it spread across his toes and feet, then up across his ankles and shins. He tossed Ellis' pair across the cave towards him, and they dropped with a thud on a large stone, smooth and oval.

'Well,' said Ellis, sounding only marginally exasperated, 'where do we look?'

'That's the point,' said Andy, 'I don't know that, but I do know they are here. I can feel it with every inch of my body; I can almost sense that they are, hidden away in some nook or cranny just waiting to be discovered. Can you sense it?' he asked.

The flames of the fire had once again reduced down to ember and Ellis now stood shivering in the sea cave, his nose running from the cold and lessening the smell of damp wood smoke that clung to his clothes and hair.

Raised some feet above the shoreline, any would be smuggler, malcontent, village romantic or those who wanted to keep things hidden, would have to lift themselves up across the sharp rocks. When the tide was low this was possible, but at high tide the entrance was partially hidden and only the bravest, desperate or most foolhardy of souls would venture into the ebbing water and its cavern, that was either beaten or caressed by the waves, depending on the mood of the season.

'I don't know how far the cave goes back but we have time before the tide comes in. You don't need me to tell you that we don't want to be at the back of this tunnel when that happens. It can't be more than fifty feet until we hit the rock at the base so we should spread out and each take a side. Look for any crags in the rock or obvious places that someone would hide something,' said Andy, his voice trailing off as he turned his back on Ellis.

Ellis carried a look of discontent but nodded his response. He stood silent for some minutes before placing batteries taken from a damp rucksack into an old cycling headlight. He had found it in a shoe box on the back shelf of his airing cupboard earlier that morning.

He watched as the beam from Andy's torch lit up the cave, showing its true majestic form. Ellis saw then that it was much larger than he had realised, and the thought disheartened him. A gust of wind from somewhere, he could not tell where, suddenly blew upwards, and the temperature dropped. Andy's light shone brightly, and Ellis listened to the sound of his footprints and laboured breathing as he stumbled over rocks, flotsam and jetsam.

The cycling head torch illuminated each crag, cut and curve of the cave with a muted, deep orange tone, the rectangular beam spreading across the fissures that dripped with icy water from above. Ellis edged himself alongside the face of the rock, feeling with his arms and knees as he did so; feeling for something that felt out of place, within the unsettling environment where every inch of his body was screaming that he himself was not supposed to be there. Yet he pressed onwards. Somewhere ahead of him he heard the nasally whistle of Andy, the high notes dulled by the echo.

'Any luck, Ellis?' he shouted, the question booming throughout the cavernous tunnel and out into the night sky.

'Not yet!' Ellis responded, accidentally stepping into a small rock pool as he did so. He looked down to see the dried shells of long-dead limpets scattered around his feet, the glow from his torch highlighting their creamy white iridescent nacre.

The two trudged on in their respective tasks, pulling out loose rocks and reaching worn fingers inside gaps in the face of the cave. Ellis wondered what had brought him here and how strange of a situation it was to find himself in. How in an otherwise uneventful year, and one in which he had felt a great degree of sadness, that he was now skirting the walls of a sea cave looking for parts of a long lost treasure map. It dawned on him that for the best part of that day, he had thought of nothing in his past, only of the present - a rare occurrence. The fear and overthinking had reduced, and his thoughts of failure and of a life wasted had not plagued him as he strode over the beach. Nor had they reverberated unwelcomely as he stood gazing into the fire, listening to Andy tell stories of shipwrecks and sailors. For the first time in a long time, a noticeable contentment took hold of him, made stronger by the semi-darkness of the cave and the whistling of Andy. Andy had had no cause other than his own desire to ask Ellis on this adventure and to share his tales with him, and it gave him a level of gratitude that he sensed building with each step.

Ellis' fingers caught something sharp in the rock and he pulled his hand back quickly, wincing with the pain that shot across his hand and made it swell and throb. He waited for the blood but when it did not come, he smiled at the strangeness of his actions and how they took place within the dark confines of a sea cave. On closer inspection, he saw that the crack in the wall housed a long-abandoned bird's nest, sharp pieces of plastic woven intricately into its desiccated wood.

His ears pricked up suddenly at the quick moving footsteps that rattled in a wave of sound from the foot of the cave.

'Ellis!' came a roar, 'Ellis!' the voice of Andy rang out, making Ellis turn quickly as the clear white beam of light from Andy's torch cast broken light from wall to roof, then the floor, then to himself. Soon Andy was standing before him panting in the artificial brightness, steam rising from his mouth with each forced breath. His trouser legs were soaked to the knees and Ellis could see his body was trembling slightly.

'What's wrong? Did you fall? Is everything okay?' Ellis asked at quickfire speed.

Andy moved closer to Ellis but remained silent. Some liquid dripped from his nose into greying stubble and his breath continued to rise above him as he sought to cease the burning sensation and strain that was building in his lungs. He held his closed hand out to Ellis and dropped a fibrous material that appeared to be loosely coated in patches of strong-smelling wax. Ellis closed his palm around it and felt the sharpness of shards of metal that pushed out from what he could now tell was rotting fabric.

Both their torch beams merged into one, focused on the package and Andy's fingers as he pulled and tore at the parcel. It ripped with a wet tearing sound, like sodden paper, and a glimmering light shone back at them from within their putrescent bundle. Ellis smelled the strong odour of paraffin and tar. While some pieces were tarnished and sullied with age, others still shone in the torch light. In his hand, Ellis could see seven pieces of metal, each roughly the size of those he had seen in the pub. Now he held what he hoped would be the final pieces of that puzzle.

'Let's go,' said Andy, a grin beaming across his face. He placed a hand on Ellis' shoulder.

'We've done it, Ellis. The tide will be in soon, we have to go, but we've done it. Everything we need is in your hands, my friend.'

Chapter twenty

At precisely three forty-two a.m., Andy and Ellis sat hunched over a well-worn wooden kitchen table, every sinew of their body aching. The sweat from the long walk home had soaked what the sea water could not, and both men now sat in damp clothes. Neither could discern whether the strong musky odour that rose from their armpits and groins, or the smoke that clung to their clothing, were the prevailing scents on that quiet and still morning. A clock ticked on the wall to accompany their thoughts, and the dull hum of an otherwise empty fridge filled the remainder of the silence.

Andy lived in a small bungalow at the end of a sleepy lane. On its approach, visitors were met with weeds and wildflower spread wilfully across its path that wound itself up towards the deep brown wood-stained front door and brass knocker. The window frames of the house were painted white and the mantle of each provided a home for two flower pots that sat at each end. A small bedroom lay behind a living room, while a toilet and shower room greeted the guests who turned right. At the end of the hallway, which hosted a variety of sketches, drawings, prints, photographs and framed mementos, lay the kitchen. On an old stove, a pot of soup sat, long cooled from its hours of simmering earlier that day. Ellis had already rejected a bowl and while Andy had poured himself a large portion, it remained untouched on the kitchen countertop.

'We're missing a piece,' said Andy, staring unblinkingly at the centre of the table. 'Who was to know?' he whispered.

The shards of metal had been pieced together like a jigsaw puzzle and now resembled a circle; only a circle with a sizeable chunk taken from within its centre. 'More than just one piece, by the look of it,' he added. 'It looks like we need at least four more pieces, maybe more,' he said, his gaze still focused on the unformed circle.

Even before the contents of the package had been emptied readily on the table, and as each shard was inspected before being meticulously placed together to form the shape before them, Ellis feared it would not provide the answers he had waited for. He now saw with his own eyes that it did not. The metal shards, some dulled with age, others shining in the kitchen lamplight, painted an incomplete picture. Across it were the rudimentary scrawls and scrapes of waves, a compass, some apparent headland and line upon line, their dark crosses nearly forming their own circular shapes in the centre. None of this meant anything to either man.

'We'll just have to keep on looking,' said Ellis. 'I don't know, but perhaps you need all the pieces to really understand it? Really get to the bottom of what it's trying to tell us and where we should look next?' he asked hopefully.

Andy wandered aimlessly to the stove and lit the gas ring. He emptied the soup he had poured earlier into the bubbling mass to reheat and waited. Once again scooping some into his bowl, he took his place at the table, this time slurping noisily with hunger at the contents.

'Are you sure you don't want any?' he asked.

'No, and Andy I'm sorry, but we have bigger things to be preoccupying ourselves right now than eating,' replied Ellis.

'There's nothing we can do tonight, or should I say this morning, Ellis,' said Andy, his eye catching sight of the clock as its hands moved ever forward.

'I can't make head nor tail of this map, and I know you can't either. If I'm being honest with you, and I have been up until now, I think I also expected there to be more pieces that we must find. As is, I've been proved correct in that regard. The good news is that I think I know where we can find the missing pieces,' said Andy.

Some soup had fallen on the front of a loose-fitting t-shirt, the sight of which made Ellis feel unease and anger in equal measure. His body ached and his eyes felt heavy from the exertion of the day and the lateness of the hour.

'Where?!' spat Ellis. 'Why did you not tell me this before?! If you knew that we would have to search more than one location, then you should have said at the very beginning!' he roared.

'Well,' said Andy. He rubbed his chin and loosened the soup stain before licking it off his fingers. Ellis suppressed the urge to retch.

'I think we have to go to where the river meets the ocean. We have to go to the place by the estuary and to the old huts that are scattered around there. I'm quite sure that our missing pieces will be there, buried or hidden in the mud and clay. Look at the map,' he said.

Ellis was unsure if what he saw could be called a map, but his eyes followed Andy's fingers regardless.

'The missing pieces look to be where the sea meets the land,' he said, pointing to the gaps. 'I think that whoever it was who hid these pieces knew that there would always have to be a second part of all of this. And what better way to tell the finder than to leave the section blank? he added. 'If this is the sea, then this is the coast, which means that yes, yes, but how...' he muttered to himself and trailed off before he regained his train of thought. 'Look,' said Andy once more. 'We look at the estuary. We look there soon, and we'll find what we need, I'm sure of it.'

'And how do you suppose we find them in the mud and clay, Andy? Do you know how long the estuary stretches? Its banks alone stretch out for as far as the eye can see. How do you suppose we can find such small pieces of metal, if indeed they are there in the first place? This could take months, years even!' He slammed a fist on the table, scattering the pieces so that they fell and broke the already imperfect circle. 'How will we find them, Andy? Please do tell me,' said Ellis pleadingly.

Andy, who had expected, yet was saddened by the outburst, sought to calm his tableside companion.

'How long have you waited for something to change?' he asked.

Ellis looked down at the scattered pieces but said nothing.

'Have you ever longed for something so much that you wanted it to happen there and then, knowing full well that it can't?' Andy continued. 'That's what this is, Ellis. Neither of us can fully comprehend or understand the potential riches that lie ahead of us, but we must wait that little bit longer and search just the smallest distance further until it is ours. Because rest assured, it will be ours, but getting frustrated and angry won't get what both of us want in our hands any faster. It is patience that's required now, patience and a sense of calm. You have waited long enough, and you will have to wait some more,' he said.

'Well how long have you waited for something to change?' Ellis asked angrily. 'I have nothing, Andy, nothing at all. I need this more than I have ever needed anything and you're right, I do want it right now. There's nothing wrong with feeling that way, is there?!' he shouted.

'No,' said Andy, 'no there's not, but you have plenty, let me tell you that. I can tell you that, but I cannot understand it for you. If you have waited so long for something to happen in your life, then be grateful now that it has. Enjoy the search and the path to the final outcome as moments of joy are all too fleeting. Enjoy what's taking place now. This should be something that excites and enthrals not an idea to get angry and frustrated about, or rush towards its end. Do you understand?' asked Andy.

'Of course I understand,' replied Ellis, 'but I'm allowed to feel the way I do.'

He sat gloomily at the table and glanced up at the clock on the wall. He was unsure if it was now at the stage of being much too late or far too early. The pot of soup and the dried remnants that clung to its side made him feel a sickness that only grew as the morning progressed.

'You can stay the night here and after a short sleep, we can go out again when the sun rises,' said Andy. 'We don't need to go to work today. What do you say?' he asked. 'I can't offer you a four-poster bed and continental breakfast for your stay this evening, or should

I now say for the morning, but there's an old camping bed, some toast and hot tea and a shower, if you want it. You're more than welcome to stay and we can continue what it is that we both so badly long for in the next few hours.'

Ellis wanted nothing less than to spend the next few hours on Andy's living room floor, breathing in what he expected would be dust from an old sleeping bag, and having a rickety old camp bed knock his joints out of place and bruise his skin with its harshness. He wanted to go home, run himself a bath, then crawl into his own bed. He longed to wash away the salt water and smoke that coated his skin and hair, and watch as the perceived failings of the last twenty-four hours ran down the plug hole with the rest of the dirty water. From outside, he heard the gentle falling of rain and a light breeze that even if not of great strength, seemed to blow and warp Andy's single pane windows. Despite the longing for his own bed and flat, he soon felt his anger reduce until it was replaced with a sense of guilt and ungratefulness. What right had he, he wondered, to be so rude to Andy in his own home and to think of him so poorly when all he had tried to do was to help him; to bring him into an adventure, that to Ellis, had given him some purpose again where any motivation, cause or ambition had been null and void?

And it was for that reason that at five in the

morning he found himself awake on Andy's floor, a threadbare sleeping bag pulled tightly against his throat and chin. He stared into the darkness but for a small glimmer of light that remained at the foot of the doorframe. He heard what he thought could be mice scuttle and run along the floor, but his body screamed with such a degree of fatigue that he gave them no further thought.

When he had first entered the living room, he was taken aback by how little of anything there was within it. There was a sofa and two armchairs, each with a light that hung over them from the wall, but there was little else. There was no TV and no sign of a radio or hi-fi. The photography that filled the hallway was not present in that room, and it appeared that not even the tiniest speck of dust was present on the floor, skirting boards and window frames. If Ellis had been asked about it, he would have said that it appeared that it was a room that was not lived in. It had no sense of purpose, no reason for being there, in an otherwise cluttered – but homely – bungalow. It made him think of himself and the thought stayed with him as his eyes grew heavy and sleep took hold.

He awoke two hours later, shocked for a second at the strange surroundings before remembering where he had spent the early hours of the morning. The wind caused a loose branch to tap against the window and he saw the silhouette in the curtain of a tree blowing in what was now a storm. He heard Andy in the kitchen and driven by hunger as much as the growing pressure in his bladder, he got up to investigate.

Andy had his back to him when he walked in the kitchen, preoccupied with a tea towel and the drying of a variety of cups, mugs and crockery. He pushed the mugs towards the back of the cupboard, reaching up on the tips of his toes to do so, then stopped when he heard the welcoming clink of mug against mug.

Turning, he smiled at Ellis. 'How did you sleep?' he asked.

'Well thanks, although I wouldn't usually call two hours of having my eyes closed sleep,' said Ellis, rubbing the sleep from his eyes and yawning. His breath smelt stale and putrid, and he thought how his teeth had gone unbrushed since yesterday morning.

'There's some unopened toiletries under the bathroom sink, so please take what you need,' said Andy.

Ellis thanked him and left, then returned to the kitchen, feeling slightly cleaner if not yet fully awake.

Andy took a mug from the drying rack and set it down on the table. The pieces of metal still sat in the centre of the table, but nothing more was said about them, at least while breakfast was eaten. Hot coffee that smelled strongly of nuts was poured and refilled before Andy brought four slices of wholemeal toast to the table, two of the slices offering greater heat than the others. They munched on the food hungrily and with vigour, neither finding cause to speak.

That morning's newspaper lay on one end of the table. Ellis picked it up and skimmed its pages.

'Why did you do that?' asked Andy, breaking the silence.

'Oh sorry,' said Ellis, 'did you want to read it first?' he asked.

'No, not at all,' replied Andy. 'I've already read it before you woke up. What I meant was why did you turn so quickly from the front page?' he asked.

Ellis, who had the newspaper with its back facing upwards so that he could read the sporting headlines flipped it over on itself, so the paper's front was visible to himself and Andy. On it was a picture of a little girl, barely a toddler and with her face blurred. She lay motionless. She was dead. Her body was misplaced in broken masonry and rubble. Men and women were huddled around her, their faces contorted in grief.

'Why do people turn away when they see something like that? Something that they know is so immoral and wrong? The death of a child, famine, abuse, hatred, persecution,' said Andy, his face reddening. 'Why?' he asked, pleadingly.

'I don't know, Andy,' said Ellis, 'I'm sorry.'

'The worse things become, and the more people

are shown it, the more they hide away. Yes, of course, they know that what they see isn't right, but what do they do about it? Mutter in pubs or workplaces about how awful it all is, but what do they really do about it? They do nothing. They do nothing because they have their own lives to lead,' spat Andy.

'What can they do about it?' asked Ellis.

'They could question it for a start,' said Andy. 'Question why we live in such a world that allows small children to be blown to bits as they sleep in their beds, dreaming of their parents and of their toys. Question why we stand by and let it all happen around us, tutting or feeling a bit sad for a couple of minutes, then going about our business as if what they had seen was just a story from a book or the plot of a film. You ask me what we can do Ellis, and I will tell you; I do not know, but it has to be more than that.'

'I'm sorry, but I don't know what to say, or even what you want me to say,' said Ellis. 'It's early, Andy. I'm sorry, but we've spoken about this before and I'm sure we will again,' said Ellis.

The entire situation had begun to feel incredibly strange, and he knew that soon he would have to make some excuse to leave. He longed for the safety of his own home. Yet a separate feeling of hope and adventure was growing within, and this was not found in his own flat.

'I don't need you to say anything,' replied Andy. He placed an uneaten slice of toast back onto his plate. 'Only when everyone wants change will it happen,' he added.

There was an uneasy silence as the two sat across from each other, all attention now placed on the newspaper's front page. Ellis was first to move, taking it up in his hands in a gentle motion that was not required, then placing it on the kitchen counter. Walking back to the table, he rubbed his palm across the shards of metal and felt their sharpness.

'Are we still going to go today?' he asked, looking at Andy whose eyes now stared unfocused on the floor.

Inhaling slowly, Andy rubbed the back of his head with his hand and cleared his throat, taking the last sip of now cold coffee for good measure.

'We are,' he said. 'We'll go to the water and see what we can find there.'

Ellis looked down at the crumbs on the table. 'Let's go now then,' he said.

Chapter twenty-one

Long before Ellis or Andy had been born, the remains of a body had been found on the banks of the wide stretch of river. Several more were to follow, in all stages of decomposition, partially hidden by the deep mud that met the rough patches of grass and stone. Wet meadow lay far beyond this in all shades of green that changed with the passing seasons.

The first discovery was found to be that of a man who had fallen overboard from his fishing boat in rough seas. The second was a similar story: that of a young man who was accidentally dragged down by a loose rope, his body resurfacing on the shoreline several months later. The others mattered only to those who knew them, but everyone who knew the tales would speak about the dangers of the water. People spoke of the strange and unpredictable currents, or of things unseen, that could drag even the strongest of swimmers down into the darkness, a fable long told by mothers and fathers to their children. It worked, as the area was one that saw little visitors, and certainly no swimming from the people of the surrounding towns and villages.

It was on this damp, sodden marshland that Andy and Ellis now trod, slowly and with great care. Their path to the shoreline was regularly held up by the need to retrieve already mud-soaked footwear from the soft ground underfoot.

'Let's be honest with ourselves,' said Ellis, a grimace across his lips. 'We both know that this is pointless. I don't know why I even agreed to do this in the first place,' he said, pulling the heel of a boot out from the ground with a squelch.

The coffee that had been drunk earlier had done little to alleviate his fatigue and he was in a foul mood.

'Have some faith, man,' said Andy in a jovial tone. 'We've come this far, and we can already see the mouth of the water not far from here, so it won't be much further. Think about the prize at the end of it all!' he said, laughing heartily as he did so.

Andy unzipped his bag and took out two tangerines, one of which he threw over in the direction of Ellis. It sank down into the mud so that only its top half was visible. Ellis scooped it up with his right hand then rubbed the brown vegetation off and onto his soaked trouser leg.

It was only when the last piece of the dry and pithy segment had been placed in his mouth that they both heard a faint whistle coming from somewhere downwind. Both men looked up but neither spoke. Andy squinted and looked into the wind, the growing breeze running across his face and blowing already ruffled hair in all directions. He blinked quickly, straining to hear what neither he nor Ellis were sure they had heard.

Tiredness does strange things to the body, they thought, both mentally and physically. Ellis was just about to start walking when they heard it again, though this time clearer; a shrill, tremolo whistle that met their ears and caused a rising feeling of concern.

'There!' shouted Andy. 'Did you hear that?'

'I did,' said Ellis, 'but who in their right mind would be out here?' he asked.

At the third whistle they caught its direction and saw a man standing some three or four hundred metres away waving his arms, his shape made clearer by the backdrop of what looked like a tent behind him.

'Did you bring the binoculars?' Andy asked, in a hushed tone.

Ellis felt his frustration at the situation growing and looked at Andy with disgust. 'What are you talking about? Of course I didn't bring any binoculars and what the hell are you whispering for?' he said spitefully.

'Okay, okay,' said Andy. 'Let's go over and see what he wants. Whatever it is, he clearly wants to talk to us about something,' he said.

The figure in the distance grew clearer with each step. Soon they could make out his red tussled hair, khaki and tan clothing and a tent that sagged under the weight of whatever it was that was being hung from inside.

'You don't usually see many people out here walking,' said the man. 'Are you lost or something?' he asked.

'No, no, not lost, just out for a stroll to stretch the legs, you know?' said Andy sheepishly.

'The name's Patrick, but my friends call me Paddy,' came the warm voice, an outstretched hand placed in the direction of Andy and Ellis.

'Andy,' came the reply, as he took the dry palm of the man in his own. 'And this is Ellis,' he added. Ellis nodded but did not shake the hand.

'What takes you all the way out here then?' asked Andy. As the words left his lips his eyes reached the various detritus of a life lived away from a home. Cans of food, some empty, most not, and a tent weighed down at the corners by plastic bags of clothing and blankets. Some patches of scorched earth signalled that the camping spot had long been occupied, as did the look in Patrick's eyes.

'You know how it is, lads,' said Patrick, tucking a long strand of hair behind his ear.

Andy looked around his makeshift campsite and clocked eyes with Ellis, his face pulled into a barely concealed grimace at what he saw before him.

'It's not what you think,' said Patrick. 'I'm not homeless or anything, nothing like that. I find myself out here through my own choices and free will. I'm sure you boys are both married with lovely houses. Am I right? A nice, big, warm house, a woman to care for you and to care for, and some kids. I'm not wrong, am I?' he asked, a glint in his eye.

Ellis was sure that if he were closer he would have tried to tap him on the shoulder in a playful manner. He was glad of the distance between them. His eyes remained on the rusted tent pegs, the rows of plastic bottles and a broken fishing rod, its reel lying in bits beneath the gorse.

'Something like that,' said Andy, 'Just as long as you're okay. It was good to speak to you, but we best be getting on our way,' he said.

'Do you not want a cup of something before you go?' asked Patrick, placing a hand on Andy's shoulder. Ellis moved back but Andy did not shrug it off and met the tired eyes of the man full on. They were a deep, crystalline blue. They jarred against the deep creases of his wrinkled, aged face. Andy could smell the staleness in his breath and clothing.

'Stay for a tea. Or a rum. Or anything you want really. I'm sure I can knock something up or cobble something together,' said Patrick, forcing a smile now and hoping to have it reciprocated by Ellis. It was not.

'I'd offer you a glass, but you know,' he said, trailing off before he finished the sentence and passed a murky bottle of rum in the direction of Ellis.

'Not for me,' said Ellis. Andy looked unblinking at Ellis for some seconds, then grasped the bottle.

'Cheers,' he said, sipping the smallest amount he could from the bottle and quickly wiping his mouth with the back of his sleeve.

'That's good stuff,' said Patrick, unsure of what else he could say.

He bent down to one of the plastic bags that lay around the back of the tent. Ellis heard the hollow sound of wood being knocked against wood. The sound made him think of his childhood and his father's shed. In that moment he could smell the drying resin and feel the warmth of the sun against his face as he watched his father methodically stacking the woodpile. A strong gust of wind soon brought him to his senses.

'I was going to start a fire, but you don't mind if I save the wood, do you?' asked Patrick. 'There's little to burn here and my stock is already depleted. It gets quite cold at night, you see.'

'Not at all,' said Andy, 'but we really must be getting on our way. It was good to meet you. Please, I want you to take this.' Andy reached into a deep trouser pocket in his jacket and took out two pencils, a Mars Bar, some loose coins, an unopened packet of tissues and a small tub of Vaseline.

'I don't know if any of this will come in handy, but it's yours if you want it,' he said, dropping the contents into Patrick's outstretched hand.

The offer of the makeshift gift was waved away.

'No thanks, I don't need charity. Like I said, I'm here through my own free will. I just needed some space, that's all. Just some space away from the noise. If you two have it easy you won't understand what I'm talking about, but I needed to get away. Thanks for the contents of your pocket, but you need it more than me,' said Patrick.

'That's okay,' said Andy, 'I meant no offense by it.'

'And none is taken, none at all,' replied Patrick. 'Like I say, I'm here because I want to be. Do you ever think you're not like the others? Not made for the world as it is. You probably think I'm crazy asking a question like that, don't you? You probably think I'm a bit mad? Is that it?' asked Patrick, his demeanour becoming erratic.

'Not at all,' said Andy. Ellis was already standing further back than when the rum was first offered to them.

'Well, I'm not mad, not in the slightest,' he spat, coughing as he did so and inspecting a patch of phlegm that had landed on his forearm. He looked at the plastic bottle then drank deeply from it.

'There are too many rules in a place like that, too many things you need to do or not do. If you don't do it this way, you're a failure, or if it do that too much, then you're a waste of space,' he continued. 'Well out here it's just me and my own rules, and that's just the way I like it. Well just me and the occasional walker, that is,' he added. 'Where was it you said you were walking to? Take it from me, there's no fish here if you're a couple of poachers. I'm happy to turn a blind eye if that's the case though, I'll not say a word. Not one word to anyone. I'll just sit here and drink my rum,' said Patrick, smiling now to show a selection of rotten teeth, the gums receding from most of those still in place on the top and bottom.

'We're not here to fish,' said Ellis curtly. 'We're here to walk. Just to get some space. I dare say you know how it is?' he added, a sense of frustration at the growing stalemate and their lack of movement away from the situation. 'Like my friend said, we really must be getting on our way,' he added.

With that he turned and started walking. He looked back to see Andy still in reciprocal conversation with the figure by the tent, but he continued striding towards the water line that sat in the far distance, almost towards the horizon as his bleary, tired and red eyes saw it. Soon he heard the jangle and clanging sounds that came from a jogging Andy, struggling to make pace due to a general lack of fitness and the heavy contents of a backpack. Ellis had only heard the contents of it so far and had no further interest to know what was inside.

'What a poor man,' said Andy. 'It's sad to see someone like that, isn't it?' he asked. 'I mean sadness isn't the word, I suppose. But some people just need help in this world, and it must be so disheartening to look for it and never find it,' he added.

'We're all just a bad decision or unfortunate event away from that,' said Ellis. 'It's a shame, but there's nothing we can do. Anyway, he said himself that he's there through his own choice so it's not our place to get involved,' he added.

Andy stopped to catch his breath. Seeing this, Ellis slowed his pace and offered his walking companion some water.

'Free will isn't free when external circumstances require a change to be made, Ellis. We can all choose to do something, but when someone fails to see any alternative but one, there's no freedom in that choice,' said Andy. 'Thanks for the water,' he added. 'I don't know what that was I drank earlier, but it was like no rum I've ever had,' he said.

Both men walked on in silence, each moving purposefully towards a goal that both hoped was close. A series of fences, some electric, others covered with rusted barbed wire, had been overcome during the last hour, and the smell of the estuary's mouth met their noses on the gentle breeze. Ellis had now lost one of his boots three times to the mud and the thick mixture now clung to his trouser legs in a semi-dried state.

Some sandpipers flew low overhead, darting in the skies above before settling some distance from where Andy and Ellis stood. Ellis looked up and felt a shooting pain go down his shoulder and upper back. He stifled it with a rub of his neck with warm, swollen fingers. Looking down, his hand was a crimson pink, and his fingers throbbed. He was unsure of the distance they had covered, but he guessed it was now more than ten or fifteen kilometres. The distance felt much longer and the route more arduous given the sodden ground below him.

'What's the plan when we get there, Andy?' asked Ellis, the frustration in his voice unhidden. 'Where even is there?' he added.

'Well,' said Andy hesitantly, 'let's keep walking and we'll know it when we feel it, won't we? I'm sure people have a sense for this type of thing.'

'No, I don't,' said Ellis, 'and I think we've already wasted enough time to go any further. There is nothing here, Andy. Look around you man, for fuck's sake. Can you not see that? Can you not see that we've wasted all this time for nothing? To get wet and tired and hungry, with nothing else to show for our efforts? And wipe that smile off your face!' he shouted.

Andy was unfazed by the outburst and broke into a laugh. 'Calm down, man,' he laughed, his shoulders shuddering upwards with each guffaw. 'Can't you see we're here now? Do you not feel it, or do you need me to figure out and understand every single thing for you? Is that it?' he asked jokingly. Stop moaning and get yourself ready to dig. If you opened your eyes, you could see some uneven ground over there, and look to the shore and there's some old corrugated iron sheeting. Someone will have been here for something and I'm sure as the mud on our boots that this is the spot where we find what we've come all this way for,' he said.

Both walked towards the mounds, each covered with discoloured grass and brown reeds. As a boy, Ellis remembered rubbing the nail of his thumb over reeds just like those and feeling their soft, ivory-white, foamy centres. His father had taught him how to place long blades of grass within his thumbs and blow so that it resonated into a steady, high-pitched drone. He could never master the practice.

'Do we dig, or what?' asked Ellis.

'That's what the spade is for,' said Andy, 'or would you rather use your hands?' he asked mockingly.

The question was left unanswered. Andy was first to cast the shovel into the ground. The soft earth eased apart effortlessly under the weight of his right foot as he drove the spade into the ground, and he lifted each damp clod with a satisfaction that showed across his face. Each shovelful of mud and vegetation poured with dark water in steady droplets that gave off a stench of decay.

The contents were inspected, sometimes by hand, most times with an unpractised eye, then cast over his shoulder in an arc. Ellis watched as the object of each cast broke apart in mid-air, landing with a splattering thud on its way back to the soft ground. Andy stood amongst patches of various depths and widths, with water steadily pooling and filling each hole faster than he could excavate them. Sweat ran across his forehead and clung to his thick, unkempt eyebrows. A knitted khaki hat with some holes around the brim was placed on one of the mounds. His jumper soon followed.

'Your turn,' said Andy, passing him the spade and inspecting his warm, swollen, calloused hands. Ellis gritted his teeth as he took the spade, thrusting it into the ground with ferocity and speed. With each entrance into the soft mud his anger subsided, and soon each sinew and muscle in his arms, shoulders and back ached with a rewarding pleasure. For a brief moment his mind wandered to a place where he had forgotten why he and Andy had traipsed all the way out to that spot in the first place. He had to remind himself that he was here to find something that may very well change his life, and soon his mind was back onto the idea of buried treasure, newspaper coverage and a life of financial stability. But unlike before, it was now burning into his mind with a desire and pressure that he sensed could very soon overwhelm him.

The feeling he carried was now one of unmeasured excitement, which only grew as the shovel sunk into the soft ground. In that moment, his limbs glowed and throbbed in a sensation that spread at pace across his body; one that had been otherwise unknown since his impromptu day on the mountains and the ruins of the miners' encampment. He looked at Andy who now stood facing the slow-moving water of the estuary, one foot propped up on a nearby rock, as he gazed out at a nondescript, watery nothingness like some failed sea Captain or washed-up Admiral. He wondered what he could have been thinking and felt that it may not have been anything at all. The idea that it was Andy who at that exact moment could have been feeling the exact same contentment as he did filled Ellis with a joy that he had not experienced in some months, perhaps even years. This strange but engaging character had opened up something for Ellis that had lain dormant for some time and only now, out here on the banks of the estuary, did he realise that the last few days of planning and of doing had been some of the most exciting of his life.

Then all at once the very same thought saddened him. He was now in his thirties; what right had he to waste things as he did, he asked himself. Why did it take a man who had it not been for a chance encounter at work would have never crossed his path, to be the catalyst for him to do so? He had limited wealth but had money to spend, yet he chose not to. He had a love for music and a vague interest in art, yet with a variety of gigs and a range of art galleries to choose from near to where he lived, he shied away from ever visiting. He had friends he rarely spoke to, food he never enjoyed and love that he turned away from. But more than that, he had spent the last five years chasing an elusive calmness that got further and further away the more he looked for it. There is no worse feeling in life to never feel at your best; to never wake up and look forward to the day that lies ahead. Of a feeling of constant tiredness or a sense that your body was letting you down. Of never feeling one hundred percent, he thought to himself. And this is what had saddened him. Over the years he had wasted in enforced solitude, when all it had taken was this chance encounter with a man. With Andy. The squashed mandarins in an old hikers' bag, and the threadbare woollen jumpers. The conversation and companionship. And the understanding that an adventure taken with someone, no matter how consequential or important in magnitude, was all the better for being shared.

'Do you want any more water,' asked Andy, who had taken his foot off the rock and now stood watching Ellis.

'Are you okay? You looked like you were a million miles away there,' he added. Ellis realised that he had not dug for some minutes and had been staring at a nearby clump of custard yellow flowers.

'Sorry, I must have been in a daydream. It's all this fresh air,' said Ellis. He reached into his bag and took out the remnants of the water, still cool in the chilled air. Andy paid no notice to the temperature or to the small amount that sat in the bottle, and he drank the water down in two gulps. Sweat dried on each of the men from their earlier exertion and they stood around a patchwork of dug earth, clods of dirt, and slow flowing water that was soon to regain the space left by the ardent shovelling.

'There's nothing here, is there?' asked Ellis, without the anger and cynicism of before.

Andy inhaled deeply and embraced the cooling sensation of the air against his nostrils. In doing so he swallowed one of several small flies that had been buzzing around the duo since they had begun their task. He spat into the air and wiped his lower lip, coughing and making a succession of low grunts to clear his throat and to ensure that the unwanted visitor was no longer present.

'There may well be something here and I am quite sure there is, but it's not something that we will find today,' said Andy. 'Perhaps we need a bit more luck, or perhaps taking a more practical stance, some better equipment? Who knows, maybe we would have some better luck with a metal detector? I don't suppose you know how much they cost, or even if you knew someone who had one?' he asked.

Ellis laughed. 'You're some man, Andy,' he said. 'Nobody I know has a metal detector but perhaps we could buy one? Who knows what we could find with one and it's certainly a wiser approach to the current strategy of walking for miles and digging randomly in the ground. This is a very big space after all and finding a needle in a haystack may even provide us with less of a challenge than this,' he said.

Andy nodded his agreement.

'Maybe we can come back tomorrow?' he asked, in a tone that was hopeful.

'Not tomorrow, but soon,' said Ellis. 'Do you know something, Andy? Even after all this coming to nothing, I've had fun today. Well perhaps not fun, but it's been good. I never thought I'd be looking for a treasure map in a sea cave or on the estuary, yet here I am. Tired, sore and hungry, but I'm here,' he said.

'Then it's not been for nothing then, has it?' replied Andy, a smile breaking across his face and the wrinkles that lined his forehead creasing up over his dried, dirty skin. 'Let's see what equipment we can get together and take it from there then, how does that sound?' asked Andy.

'That sounds like a good plan to me,' replied Ellis. 'Let's take a break, think things through and figure out how we can get our hands on this treasure. I suppose most of the excitement comes from not knowing something fully, doesn't it?' he asked. 'To throw yourself into something driven onwards by a hope that can only grow until there's a solid outcome. It doesn't matter if the outcome is good or bad, does it? Of course you want it to be good. Who goes looking for something in life that they hope will end badly? But whether bad or good, both outcomes are one that will end the hope. When you have your answer, I mean. When you know something is certain then you don't need the hope to remain. You know where you stand when you've found something, or in our case, not found it yet,' said Ellis. 'By the way,' he added. 'It's too cold for this at the moment. Perhaps it's best to wait until the spring? Let's plan to do something then, when the nights are longer and the weather improves,' he said. 'We can get back on track then and see what we can discover. Let's see if we can end this hope once and for all!' he laughed.

Andy smiled and agreed to the plan. The two spoke of metal detectors and freshly baked bread, of life as a binman and of the ideal depth of a bath, as they made their long way back home. The sun dropped in the sky and the conversation continued long beyond the moment when the lights of the far distant town had first come into view.

Chapter twenty-two

It is only when one looks back and reflects that they see the movement and growth that has taken place. One cannot hasten the seasons, no matter their desire to do so. Winter's coldness changed to the hopeful warmth of spring. The space that followed the day at the estuary saw Ellis walk across the pavements of the town in a daydream, at times blissful, at others, deeply anxious, giving little attention or focus to anything other than the quest.

Ellis picked up a bin and emptied its contents into the side of the truck. He had heard that Jordan was now retraining though nobody was sure what he was studying to become. There had been talk of an electrical course at the local college, but others had said they had seen him working behind the counter of the local supermarket. No matter the story told, all who claimed to have seen him had said that he looked like a different man. Neither Ellis or Andy saw fit to discuss his circumstances in earshot of the others, but the consensus was that he had fallen on his feet and was slowly getting his life on track. A life with the absence of alcohol.

Ellis bounded from street to street ahead of the lorry that slowly followed his movement. Sweat from his brow ran into his eyes and he wiped what he could with the bottom of his t-shirt, lifting it with one hand to expose his thin, pale stomach. He left it exposed for longer than was necessary, enjoying the crisp refreshing air as it met his uncovered skin. The last few months had seen Ellis working with some new employees. His new driver, Peter, was an affable, red-haired man in his late fifties with a nondescript English accent. The other loader who sat alongside Ellis was a woman called Jaqueline. She had gone back to work when her last child had left the family home and enjoyed the daily exercise and sunshine, if not the company of her colleagues. Those negative feelings increased whenever the rain fell. Ellis liked her, as did most of those she met, despite the feeling not always being reciprocated.

At lunchtime, the three sat quietly and munched on sandwiches that had taken on the taste of the plastic bags they had sat in since the early hours of the morning.

Ellis' mind wandered as Jaqueline held court, a position that she often took during the tea and lunch breaks. He had not seen Andy in the yard that morning, nor on reflection had he seen him for several days. Yet he gave the lack of a sighting no further thought, instead looking forward to what they would find when they made their latest expedition into the wilderness. He had yet to tell Andy, but he had taken some of what little savings he had accrued over the years and bought a metal detector. Now there would be no stopping them, he thought. His mind raced with buried gold and silver and of long-lost treasures. He thought once again of the newspaper headlines and surrounding euphoria around the duo's massive haul of long lost treasure. He pictured cameras as they flashed on street corners, and the discussions that would soon be had with museums and private collectors, playing each party off against the other to secure the best price for their find.

The wind brought the smell of Jaqueline's deodorant under his nostrils, and it stirred him from his daydream. In soft tones, she spoke with Peter who looked to be as engaged and contemplative as he often was when Jaqueline spoke.

'You see,' she said, 'when some people say it's all in the mind, it really, truly is all in the mind.' She looked down at her half-eaten sandwich and plumped instead for a bite of crisp green apple. She welcomed the crunch of the fruit between her teeth and its tart refreshment.

Refocused on her point she continued. 'I can only speak for myself here and not everyone does, but isn't that an important place to start? With your own experiences in life?' She asked the question without expecting an answer to come.

Peter nodded his agreement.

'The back pain had been there since my late thirties, a dull, constant ache from morning until evening. At first with these things, you try to numb it with painkillers, perhaps some light stretching. Then before you know it, you're on your fifth appointment with the doctor saying the same symptoms over and over and getting nowhere in the process. You see specialists, exhaust the internet for answers, change your diet, your posture, and I suppose in essence, you change your life. We're always changing after all, but there's a certain degree of stress and worry that comes from trying to find a cure for something, isn't there?' she asked.

Again, Peter nodded, and she looked over at Ellis to see that he was listening to what was being said. He was.

'At first, it's not like you can just laugh it off, but it's certainly something that you can get used to. I mean it certainly isn't pleasant, but pain, fatigue and discomfort almost become something that your body just gets used to. That in itself is quite bad, isn't it? Being in pain but knowing that there's no way out of it, so you just plod on in a haze of ineffective pain relief, naps and whatever it is you can do that gets you away from your reality,' said Jaqueline.

'You're completely right there, Jaqueline,' said Peter heartily. 'There's nothing worse than hiding away from the realities of life,' he added. 'We all have our problems and our crosses to bear, but the best thing is always to just pick yourself up by the bootstraps and get on with it. A good walk in the morning will set most people straight, let me tell you that,' said Peter. Ellis was unsure if Peter had understood the sentiment or point of what Jacqueline had said but said nothing.

'Yes, I suppose that's true,' said Jaqueline, giving Peter a faint smile before getting back to her story. 'But it was only when I started understanding things more, things about my own mind and body, that everything started to get better. Don't get me wrong it's not like you wake one morning and all the pain is gone, it's nothing like that, not in the slightest bit actually. But when you understand that a lot of what we feel comes from the mind, you can start making changes, to well, change things! So that's what I did,' she said, before taking a second bite from the apple.

'You never know what someone else is thinking, or how they feel, do you?' asked Jaqueline, rhetorically. 'I mean at its most basic level I suppose we must all have some inkling that that's the case, but it's very easy to forget it,' she said.

A bird flapped its wings in a tree above, its leaves not yet green and verdant from the summer sun that was still months away. The movement sent some loose leaves scattering to the ground. Ellis watched as they dropped onto the pavement and a nearby storm drain.

'I'll tell you something else,' said Jaqueline, fuelled by what was now her second cup of tea and the now more obvious attention being sent her way by Peter.

She had her audience. 'I'll never take advice from someone. Never at all, not one bit of it. Shall I tell you why?' She did not wait for the reply and quickly launched into the point she wanted to make.

Ellis found himself drawn to the pattern on a brown and silver hair band, a piece of fabric that was struggling to hold back the stream of jet-black curls that framed her head. Ellis assumed it was dyed, not that it mattered.

'What works for someone won't work for somebody else, so why is everyone so keen and bloody earnest about giving advice all the time? I'll say this, sometimes I don't even know if it's for the sake of giving advice in the first place, but more a way of one upmanship. Your baby still isn't sleeping? Well, it worked for me. The back pain is still there. You can't be doing the exercises correctly. Why can't you be more like her?' Her voice drifted off slightly at the last point and both Ellis and Peter felt the mood change slightly. In under a minute the smile was back, and she was once again filling the lunchtime gap with her treatise of the world.

'You know none of it's real anyway?' said Peter.

'None of this, I mean,' he added.

'I'm not sure I do,' said Jaqueline.

'Well, put it this way then. Everything that we all think, or feel, or believe, it's all come from somewhere before us, hasn't it? Everything is built on little stories told here and there over the years, little fables and myths, small stories and the like. Nothing we think today is an original thought,' said Peter. 'My dear old mother used to go to Church every Sunday, come rain or shine. If there was a storm, she would still get the bus each Sunday to take her place on the pew. She's gone now mind, but the point still stands. What do you think religion is?' he asked, but like Jaqueline, he neither expected nor sought an answer. 'It's all a selection of stories told over the years, which grow and change, but somehow still remain the same. My mother could hold the same belief in God or of something that the Bible said as someone she had never met from Chile to Canada. Don't you find that a strange thought? How stories like that tie us all together?' he asked.

The afternoon passed quickly without note. All three moved with a renewed pace after lunch, each one spurred on by the reward of an impending weekend. Whatever topics Jaqueline had, be it holistic therapy or ice baths, hatha yoga or journalling, could wait until Monday.

      Ellis walked home in the sunshine after work, a route that was some distance, but he wanted to feel the spring sunshine on his face. Nor was there anyone or anything in his flat for him to hurry home to on a Friday evening. Nobody to eat dinner with or to speak about their working weeks. No one to hold or to share a touch with. That would change when he found the treasure, he thought to himself. When he was rich, he would never long for company again.

  The route to his house skirted through two parks, both of which were full of people enjoying the sunshine. The smoke rose from disposable barbeques and sent the smell of cheap hamburgers and sausages into the air. The assorted men and women tended the meat, their own skin a rich tapestry of deep-red sunburnt skin and bronzed tan. Ellis walked to a nearby shop that stood at the entrance of the park. A queue of patrons snaked out the door and across the pavement, with each person rewarded some shade from the shop's awning as they waited. Those leaving the shop left with handfuls of ice cream or large bottles of water and Coke, while glass beer bottles clinked in the white plastic bags of those held by others.

  Ellis decided to join the line and within ten minutes he had paid for his purchase: three large bottles of lager, cold to the touch from a large fridge that stood behind the counter. Condensation rolled off the neck and across the bottle. Making his way back to the park, he found a quiet spot under a tree and taking a reflective jacket from his bag, laid it down on the freshly cut grass by way of a makeshift seat.

He rooted around in his bag for something to open the bottles with and settled on a small plastic bottle of water. Having sat in his bag since Monday morning, the remainder of the water gave off a damp, stale, sour smell. He placed the bottle under the rim of the bottle top, put pressure on it with his left-hand thumb, then prized the cap off. The bottle gave a rewarding plopping sound, and a small amount of white foaming beer crept over the side and trickled down its length. Ellis took three large gulps and revelled in the taste. With the heat, an empty stomach and his earlier exertion, he soon felt the warming blur of the alcohol. He closed his eyes to soak in the feeling. The grass under his feet, the beer, the warmth of the sun on his skin. How simple it all was, but how enjoyable, too. This was life, he thought. The third bottle was gone within forty-five minutes, and he walked back in a light stupor, feeling the effects of the beer and holding in the urge to piss. The need proved too great and soon he ducked behind a garage wall of a mechanic, his urine bouncing off the walls and splattering in droplets on his trousers, before mixing with the wood, dry mud and broken glass that littered his feet. Some weeks ago, he had agreed with Andy that the following day would see them stride out to find the final puzzle pieces. How sad that this would all change when he struck it rich, he told himself.

Chapter twenty-three

The bakery at the end of the street opened at five a.m. In between the weighing of sugar and flour, the decorating of cakes and stuffing of pastries, the owner found time to have an affair. His long-suffering wife, as is often the case, was unaware of the fact, or so her husband thought. While she paid little attention as her husband's waking hours reduced with each passing month at the beginning, she soon grew suspicious. They remained together but the distance between the two continued to grow, until one day, it was she who left the marital bed early, never to return.

In the autumn and winter the glow from the bakery's window cast an orange warmth on the otherwise wet, leaf strewn, frosted or snow-covered streets. The display housed a selection of processed white flour, fat and sugar in all its various forms: pancakes and waffles at the bottom, nestled between freshly baked bread and morning rolls, some fresher than others. The cabinet at the front fenced off the workers from the customers, a well-worn wooden countertop having felt the caress of thousands of hungry and impatient hands over the years. Coins were tapped against its surface from those waiting to place their order, as it took the strain from tired arms who could no longer hold their plastic shopping bags of onions, milk, and meat in its wax paper packages. The counter housed the cakes in one side, while pies and pastries lay towards the corner of another. Above it a two-page calendar was pinned against the off-white wall; its image of a West Highland Terrier that stood proudly in front of a brown fence, framed in stillness above the twelve small boxes below.

Ellis stood outside and waited for the doors to open. As he stood, he remembered that once he had been told that nomadic foragers several hundred years ago had had a comparatively good diet. Before the industrial revolution came and bread or rice became part of every meal depending on which side of the world you were in when the sun set. A diet of snails, mushrooms and edible roots offered far greater sustenance and variety than two bowls of rice each day, he recalled.

In his sleep-deprived state he romanticised the notion. How easy it must be to eat well with the offering of each passing season. To not get drawn in with the ease of supermarkets and their bright lights, ready to eat products and plentiful offering. Perhaps he could leave it all behind, he told himself. Take what money he had and go and live in the woods, away from all of the things that he no longer cared for in his current set-up. Run away from the pressure to do something with his life, whatever do something meant. To no longer have to make decisions about which bills to pay, or which streaming service film to choose on yet another lonely evening. Yes, he decided. That would be the life for him. Scavenging amongst the flora and fauna and eating whatever he could find among the fields and hedgerows. Catching wild game and fish and living as his ancestors had done, and their ancestors before them. He looked up into the trees and the mountain peaks far off in the distance and decided that he was going to do it. Then he caught his reflection in the bakery window and came to his senses.

Within minutes he found himself slumped against the paint-flaked windowsill as he greedily bit into then swallowed a cold pie. The salt, grease and pastry satiated his appetite but did little to avail a growing hangover. He had come home after the park, drank one bottle of red wine, then gone out and bought another. None remained.

It was not yet five fifteen a.m. and the sun was yet to rise in the east. His sluggish mind was overcome by a steady throbbing that grew as each minute passed. Walking back into the shop, he bought another pie and a soft drink and took his place once again on the window ledge. He would have to go back home and sleep for an hour or two, he told himself. After waiting some months, today was the day he and Andy had planned to once again look for the treasure, but a couple of hours of sleep would not be any cause for concern. The silver and gold had been in the mud for several years and some more hours would do it little harm, he reasoned. Swallowing the last of his drink, he wiped the flakes of pastry that had fallen across his chest and walked the two hundred metres to his home and what he knew was a warm, welcoming bed.

The lock on the outside door of his building was regularly stiff. In rainy or humid weather there were occasions where occupants would have to take their time in the process of opening it, gently forcing the key and increasing the pressure bit-by-bit so as not to snap the thin metal. This morning was one such occasion. It sent Ellis' tired brain into a state of anxiety and his own calming hand placed behind the small of his back was met with cold sweat. He slowly took the key out the door, blew on it gently, for reasons known only to him, then placed it back in the lock and slowly rocked it back and forth. He heard a telltale click and rhythmically edged the key to the left, whereupon the bolt slipped into its place and away from the door. He stepped inside with relief.

Dust had started to gather in the corners and skirting boards of his flat, but Ellis gave it little notice. He thought that he could still sleep for an hour or so and still have time to meet Andy. There would be little harm if he just rested for a moment. In fact, he told himself, he would be all the better for it. A renewed sense of vigour; more stamina for the trail and a keener eye to spot signs of treasure, whatever those signs may be.

Stepping into his bedroom he pulled off his clothes and cast them into the corner of his room, scattering dust as they fell upon the floor. The button on the fly of his jeans gave a sharp cracking sound as it hit the wooden floorboards. The light from the street below crept in the room through a gap in the curtain and illuminated a steady stream of dust. Ellis watched as it warped, dropped, fell and rose, moved by the hidden currents of air that crept in through gaps in the roof and under skirting boards.

He realised that the pace of his breathing had increased, and his heart pounded heavily. An acidic taste rose within his chest and into his throat, and he swallowed hard against the burning sensation. In and out, over and over, went his breathing, as it had done since the day he was born. And it was now this breath that gained his focus as he stood naked in the bedroom. An irregular breath - fast, shallow and growing in intensity. He tried to calm himself down by consciously taking in a deep breath whenever he could muster one, but he sensed his face growing redder with each inhalation.

He ran to his bed and pulled his bedsheets to one side. He quickly made his way onto the soft mattress, doing all that he could think of to calm down. He squeezed his thumb and forefinger against a soft spot in his hand, then gently rubbed his weary temples with both hands. He focused on a spot in the wall and tried to temper his racing thoughts, then once more swallowed hard against the acid that rose from his stomach in anger.

The worry gained speed, and it felt to him as if all his failings in life had been brought to the forefront of his memory. He could see the many conversations and the tears, the backs that were turned and the questions that were left unanswered. He turned in bed, his thoughts causing his body to jerk erratically. He stood and scraped his fingers against his scalp, feeling the pain that seared through his head as he did so. He paced the floor and kicked out at things that were not there. The bedroom window was opened to its fullest and his flushed and sweating face was cast out with force, the calming and sedate scene below doing little to allay his growing fear.

Five pigeons paced with authority on the dirty pavement below. Ellis watched each one scatter and fly upwards as an early morning bus pulled around the corner, its doors opening for non-existent passengers. He kept his focus on the bus stop and tried to slow his breathing down. He felt his heart settle and soon his mind filled with a dullness that he welcomed. Making his way back into bed, his eyes closed to a swirl of ideas and memories that ebbed and flowed like the tides of the coastline. Some stayed longer than others and crashed against the rocks with greater severity than those that drifted and dropped as he was lulled into a broken sleep.

The growing dampness from his sweat stained pillow woke him some time around noon. His immediate thought was that it was now too late to meet Andy, but he did not have a contact number to let him know he would not be coming. He was sure Andy would not mind, or that even if he did, he would not say anything to unsettle the mood. That thought in itself saddened Ellis and he was filled with a moroseness that grew as the clock on the sideboard clicked and ticked away the passing minutes.

He stood from the bed, the sweet smell of fresh sweat filling his nostrils. The air that circulated from the various draughts that swirled around his room caught his naked skin and it cooled the sweat that had gathered on him. Taking out a battered old shoebox from underneath his bed, he ran his finger in a line across the dust then wiped it away with his hand so that it came off in great sheets of dirt. It lay lifeless in clumps in piles on the floor, fetid and damp. He told himself that he should try to find the time to hoover under the bed, even to take some minutes each week to actually clean his flat. Properly clean it, not just move some dishes around and dust the top of some books. The shoebox housed white and black electrical wires, chargers and headphones, all in various states of functionality. There was a paper weight from a trip his parents had taken to Canada, while used ticket stubs from music festivals and film nights were bent, folded, and pressed against the remaining space.

    The faint smell of cigarette smoke in the box had already reignited the memory before the picture was found. The corner had been ripped off some years ago and remained that way, a sight that gave Ellis a calming sensation despite his otherwise spiralling downward mood. In the picture he sat at the table of a restaurant, one arm obscured by a plastic wrapped menu, his chest hidden by her hair and face. One of his arms was wrapped around her shoulder while a hand sat on her waist. She lay against Ellis, smiling at the camera. Behind the couple two waiters, blurred with movement, hurried from table to table with black trays of glasses and steaming plates of food. It was Italian or Spanish fusion, something like that, recalled Ellis, as he rubbed a thumb over the photograph. He could still smell the perfume that so faultlessly met with the smell of the cigarette smoke that clung to her blonde hair. To the left of the table sat two glasses, half full of vodka and cola. Ellis could still taste the stale, artificial plastic that had seeped into and flavoured the steadily cracking and melting ice cubes.

    It was Italian, he told himself; they ate spaghetti. And he thought back to the shared £5 notes and accumulated loose change cast into a small side plate by way of a tip. And of the taxi home that weaved between the streets, the face of the driver heading into the darkness. The clunk clicks of the internal locking system as it stopped at red and drove on green, as its sound merged with the late-night radio. And of the kiss, then the night, and into the morning.

He remembered how scared he had felt when their eyes had met under the semi-enclosed safety of the duvet. How all that his mind could focus on was not the warmth of her body, or of the alcohol-tinged sweat that clung to the warmth of the room, but of fear for the moment before him.

Looking at the picture, he knew that in the morning his thoughts had raced with the idea and questions as to whether or not this was his moment. One of the incidents experienced in life that spark something, whatever that something is, so that everything thereafter comes from a place of security.

Still sitting on his bedroom floor, he thought how daunting it was to be younger, going to school, meeting friends, studying, then onto university. All the while waiting for something to happen to signal the change that he so craved. That moment where what was is no longer and all that comes next will be seen with new eyes. He still believed the lie that everything will be different from what came before. Because at any age life happens elsewhere, he reminded himself. It happens in the plans for the year ahead, or in the weekends to follow. It happens in the career path that will open itself up with all-encompassing arms stretched wide, guiding one away from the past and the monotony. Come, yes come, come straight away, for there is no time to spare, they beckon, for life is elsewhere.

The sound of the flat's buzzer took his attention away from the contemplation. The tinny, invasive drone hummed again as he made his way into the hall, lifting the handset to his ear.

'Post,' said a gravelly voice from below.

Pushing the lock symbol, he waited for the telltale creaking sound of the door as it opened, then waited in the hall. The footsteps from below grew louder as they approached his floor, then continued upwards to the flats above.

He knew that he would have to make his way to Andy's house soon and so forced himself into the shower. He turned the shower intermittently from cold to hot, hot to cold, hoping that the change in temperature would invigorate him, or at the very least offset some of the fatigue that now clung to his limbs. His head felt dull and heavy, almost as if in a dream, as he watched the lathered soap fall from his body and gather in swirling pools at the bottom of the shower.

A damp-smelling towel dried what it could as his aching body dripped now tepid water across the hallway and into his bedroom.

Soon, he turned his attention to Andy. He dressed quickly, gave his teeth a cursory brush and grabbing his flat keys from their hook in the hallway, made his way into a world that felt so distant.

At roughly the same time as Ellis' door had shuddered closed, another swung open. Jordan walked along the street carrying six plastic carrier bags between both hands. He gently nudged open a grey coloured door with his knee to stop it closing again, then held it open with his back as he lay the bags down on Kirsty's newly laid vinyl flooring.

'It's just me with the shopping, love,' called Jordan, aiming his voice in the direction of the upstairs bathroom having heard the tap running.

'Thanks, I'll be with you in a minute,' shouted Kirsty from above.

Jordan took the bags into the kitchen and emptied them methodically. Outside he could see his daughter playing on her new plastic slide, the bright red and yellow contrasting with the freshly trimmed grass that he had cut earlier that morning. From this distance he could see some patches, but he gave it no further thought. He tapped a knuckle on the kitchen windowpane and a head moved up in response. Two bright eyes met his own and he was greeted by a smile.

She ran into the house shouting, 'Daddy! Daddy's back from the shops!' before cuddling Jordan's leg. She smelled of shampoo and grass as he bent down to hold her, lifting her into the air with his arms and spinning her around the kitchen.

Kirsty walked in with a towel wrapped around her hair. Without asking if he wanted one, she took two cups down from the cupboard and removed an unopened box of teabags from the supplies that Jordan had just brought in.

'Thanks again for going,' she said. 'I thought we could go to the park today, if that's alright with you two. Maybe even have a picnic?'

Jordan welcomed the warmth in her voice. 'Yeah!' shouted Kate, the couple's daughter.

'That sounds good to me,' said Jordan. 'I just need to make a quick call first then I'll get started on the sandwiches,' he added.

Kirsty brought him the cup of tea and placed it down on the kitchen table. Kate, opened the back door and went out into the sunshine and the fun of her slide. Kirsty waited until she was completely out of earshot before speaking.

'Look, I've been thinking about what you said last night, about,' but she had no time to finish before Jordan cut in.

'About the holiday?' he asked, meeting Kirsty's grin with a smile.

'Yes, about the holiday,' she said. 'I mean, I can't think of anything better at the moment and Kate would love to get away as a family, but do you really think we can afford it? These things aren't cheap these days, you know? More than that and I don't want to upset you when I say this, but are you sure we're ready? Ready to go somewhere as a family I mean?' She looked at Jordan pleadingly, who took her hands in his own before speaking.

'We can afford it,' he said, in as reassuring a tone as he could muster. 'I mean that. We can afford it.' He broke the clasp of hands briefly to take a sip of tea, then stroked the back of Kirsty's hand with his thumb.

'I do mean it,' he said. 'I've missed out on so much with you two, and it's through no fault but my own. This is something I've been thinking about for longer than you'll ever realise and because of that, I've been putting money aside here and there whenever I can. We have a good little pot stuck away for a rainy day but look outside, Kirsty, the sun is shining! It's shining now so let's spend it on a holiday! You know I wouldn't lie to you again, not after what I put you both through,' said Jordan. 'I think we're ready but as with everything here, I don't want to put any pressure on you or Kate. You two are the most important people in my life and I don't want to do anything to hurt either of you again. Even if it's not two weeks in the sun, even a small weekend trip away might be nice, but as I say, Kirsty, it's your call,' he said.

Kirsty smiled. 'Well,' she said, getting up from the table to kiss Jordan on the forehead, before sitting on his knee. 'I want you to know I trust you. I'll be honest with you here and it's not something you don't already know, but I haven't always trusted you. But I see the work and effort you're putting in each day and I'm proud of you. Your flat is spotless and well, the changes that I see in you every day makes me see the man that I fell in love with at the very beginning. That man was lost for a few years, but I can see him coming back now, Jordan. I can see it,' said Kirsty. 'If you're sure about it, then, I'm sure. Let's do it. We'll speak more tonight about destination, but for now, you've got sandwiches to make!'

She kissed his head again and smiled. Jordan wiped a tear from his eye and looked out again at his daughter playing in the garden.

'By the way, who is it that you need to phone?' asked Kirsty.

'Just a friend I've been thinking about a lot over the last few weeks. Do you remember Andy?'

Kirsty nodded and went out into the hall. 'I'll give you some space then,' she said. 'I'm going upstairs to sort out the laundry so take your time,' she added.

Jordan took his mobile from his pocket, placed

his thumb on the side to unlock it, and scrolled to Andy's name in his phonebook. Taking a big sip of tea, he placed the phone to his ear and listened to it ring. He had no idea what he was going to say, but he knew that he wanted to say something. How are you? What have you been doing? He listened to it ring once more before a generic voicemail message sounded. Without thinking he closed the screen, then pressed redial on the handset. Again, he pressed the handset to his ear and again it rang until the voicemail kicked in.

Not to worry, thought Jordan, I'll try again tomorrow. Taking a fresh loaf out from the bread bin, he reached into the drawer and took out the serrated breadknife. Jordan felt the weight of it in his hand as it cut easily through the brown crusty loaf, scattering crumbs across the work surface. He swept them into his hand and dumped them into the food bin that lay under the sink.

Jordan saw faint wisps of blue-grey smoke rising from behind the garden fence. It was too early in the year for Mr and Mrs Ramsey to be burning leaves, so Jordan wondered what it could be and went outside to investigate. While he had no dislike for the elderly couple, there was something about their behaviour, tone and mannerisms that he found frustrating. A frustration that once felt, would only grow and fester until he voiced his feelings to Kirsty. They were too loud; too nosy; too involved in the lives of others. The thoughts came to him as he walked across the fresh grass, the smell of which reminded him of playing football in his youth.

Peering over the fence, he watched as the pair emptied all manner of paper from torn, yellowing cardboard boxes. On closer inspection he could see it was a collection of old newspapers. Why the collection was now being cast onto smouldering flames in the middle of a residential garden was another point entirely, and one which Jordan had every intention of discovering the answer to. He watched as the paper that failed to ignite fully was cast into the air, only to fall gently back down into the flames as if it were grey or black fluttering leaves. Mrs Ramsey gave the pile a good poke with what looked to be an old medical crutch, a remnant from after her knee operation. The smoke grew and blew in all directions. Some heads peered out from the houses that lined the street as a variety of bedroom, kitchen and living room windows were closed in unison.

'You're busy,' Jordan shouted, forcing a smile as the couple raised their head in his direction. Mrs Ramsey smiled, then walked back to the direction of the house. With what looked like a significant degree of difficulty, she strained to lift one of the boxes of newspapers and took it into the direction of her husband. Now quite short of breath, she rubbed her hands on a red-woollen cardigan and took what Jordan thought to be a theatrical inhalation through her mouth. Barely fifteen metres from where he stood, Jordan could smell her perfume that drifted over in the breeze along with the ever-growing smoke and ash.

'We're having a little clear out,' she said.

She gave a languid smile and bent down to cast more of the papers on the flame. Her hands were black and mottled from the newsprint.

'Do you know you can recycle your paper these days?' asked Jordan. 'The council provides you with a box for it. All you need to do is fill it up and stick it out on the pavement every second week. Milk cartons, cardboard, and definitely newspapers. It's probably a lot better than burning them in the middle of your garden!' he added, in a jovial tone that he knew sounded forced.

There was no response and Mr Ramsey took his turn to reach into the box, picking up what must have been years' worth of newspapers. Each one was filled with long forgotten headlines, and he took no time to read over or remind himself as to what they were. Each bundle was picked up in the same rigid yet methodical way, crumpled slightly, then thrown on the flames. The fire was long since choked and the smoke continued to billow and rise. Jordan wanted to tell him that it needed air for the flames to get going again, and that there was now too much fuel to support the fire, but he thought better of it. Instead, his mind drifted to the thought of

Mr Ramsey's trouser leg catching one of the sparks or large pieces of ash, and bursting into flames.

He turned to see Kirsty looking at him through the window, a concerned look across her face. Jordan did not know whether the feeling came from the growing smoke that was now undoubtedly drifting into her house, or about the last time Jordan had peered over the fence as part of a brief – yet anger filled tirade – against Kirsty's elderly neighbours. Whisky would play no part in this encounter, so he guessed it was to do with the smoke.

'So that's you back in the house then, is it?' asked Mr Ramsey, a sneer across his face.

Jordan felt a blistering heat fill his body. His hands shook and his mouth went instantly dry. At that exact moment, he wanted nothing more than to deftly jump over the fence, pick up the loose fence post that sat across the Ramsey's shed door, and deliver it with such a degree of force across his skull that he would never pollute his garden with acrid newspaper smoke again. Instead, he looked across at his daughter behind him and forced a smile.

'I don't think that's any of your business now is it, Mr Ramsey?' said Jordan. 'What goes on in my family should be no concern of yours,' he added for effect.

'Well...' said Mr Ramsey pausing, before looking across to his wife with a wry smile across his face, 'whatever is going on then let's just hope for all of our sakes that it's a lot quieter this time. It's an awful business having to get the police involved, particularly when there are little ones involved, wouldn't you say dear?'

Mrs Ramsey nodded before quickly speaking. 'But look, we're sure that's all in the past now so let's not say anything more about it. We have work to be getting on with, so we'll let you get on with your day.' She almost spat the words at Jordan before turning quickly in the direction of yet another box. Mr Ramsey took an apple from his pocket and bit it noisily. Some of the juice spilled on his chin and he wiped it with a dirty hand. Jordan watched him closely. Mr Ramsey smiled, gave an imaginary doff of a non-existent cap, then turned his attention to the steadily growing pile of ash and cinder.

Back in the kitchen, Jordan took out his feelings on the small cupboard door that lay under the sink. The tap still leaked despite his best efforts, but that was the least of his worries at that moment.

Kirsty popped her head around the doorframe from inside the hall, her arm strewn with tea towels and various items of underwear.

'Is there anything you want to talk about?' she asked calmly.

Jordan flicked some remaining crumbs from the countertop into his hands. 'No, it's nothing,' he whispered.

'You sure?' asked Kirsty, placing one of her

hands on his back. 'You know it's important for us to speak, don't you? No secrets, remember?' she added.

Jordan felt his jaw tighten and his teeth pull towards each other in an involuntary clench. He tapped his index finger on the rim of the sink, the dull beat filling what was an otherwise pregnant silence.

'It's just that lot next door,' he said, nodding in the direction of the smoke. 'They just always have to say something, and I'm fed up with it. There's never any chance to forget and move on with those two peering over at us daily, getting involved in our business, and thinking they are better than we are. Did you see they were burning newspapers? Huge piles of them too. I've got no idea what they were doing but it's just got to me, that's all. I don't like Kate playing in the garden when they are around, because do you know why? Do you want to know? Because I don't trust what they are going to say to her,' he cried. 'I don't know, Kirsty. There's something about them and I can feel myself feeling lost within myself whenever I see them. The way their fence creaks and the way the radio is always just that little bit too loud. I hear him clearing his throat each morning and I can't stand it,' he said breathlessly. Kirsty beckoned for him to sit down at the kitchen table.

'I know you don't want to hear this, but they've,' she stopped as she saw Jordan sit upright in his chair. She noticed his eyes looked glassy. 'Well look, I just want you to know that they've been good to us in the times that...well, those times you weren't here,' she said quietly.

Jordan looked out the kitchen window at the ever-rising smoke. 'I'm sorry,' he said. 'I've said it before, I'll say it again, and I'll continue to say it. I'm sorry.'

'It's not about sorry, Jordan, not anymore,' said Kirsty, taking his hands in her own and giving them a delicate squeeze. 'I don't want you to think that this is a criticism of you, but you need to understand that they're not out to get us. Both of them are who they are, and I appreciate that there's a lot they do as neighbours which can be a bit, well, a bit, tiresome, I suppose? But be that as it is, they were good to us. I think they have our best interests at heart, and I know that in time you'll see that,' she added.

Jordan stood up from the table and kissed the crown of her head. It smelt of coconut shampoo.

'You're right,' he said. 'Just give me five minutes, I'm just going to try and give Andy a quick call again. It's good that we can talk like this now, you and me, I mean,' he said, feeling a growing sadness and embarrassment at his earlier anger. An anger that when honest with himself, persisted and grew, as his nostrils once again recognised the damp, cloying smell of a choked fire.

He dialled Andy's number, and as before, the phone call went to voicemail. Outside Kate raised her arms upwards to the sky. She called out to the space outside and laughed. Jordan watched as the ends of her hair rose and fell with the gentle wind. Pulling herself forward on the slide, she lifted both arms skywards and hurtled around the lawn with laughter that could be heard through the double-glazed kitchen window.

Chapter twenty-four

On the upper floor of the number five bus, towards the back and close to where a red poster advertised home insurance, a couple sat in front of Ellis, kissing passionately. A shadow from one of the embossed letters had cast the man's blonde hair in shade that moved and swayed with each slight turn of his head. Ellis stared, unthinking and numb for several seconds, then turned his gaze towards the windows to watch the passing houses. Even before he had looked at the spare change in his pocket and the bus had pulled into sight after its ten-minute delay, he had realised that the newly purchased metal detector had been left in his flat. The consequences of a hungover and tired brain, he thought, and he fretfully chastised himself as the bus drove on.

He told himself that it would not matter now given it was unlikely that they would have the time to continue the search that afternoon. He questioned why he was even going to see Andy at this stage of the day. Guilt arose from the fact he had gone back on the plan, however loose, and the foolishness in himself that he had no way of getting in touch with Andy.

He pictured that he would get off the bus, look at the weeds and wildflowers, kick loose stones across the pavement, and find the shape of Andy's bungalow on the horizon. The white framed windows would welcome him in, and he would accept a cup of whatever was offered. He practiced the apology he would deliver while stood on the porch over and over in his head: I'm sorry... time got away from me... I've not been feeling very well... you'll never guess what I've bought for us... what are you doing next weekend?

He nodded to himself involuntarily and hoped that Andy would accept what he had to say. Ellis had little understanding why he had felt so unsure about coming, and who knows, he pondered, perhaps Andy had also shown some similar wariness; perhaps even a similar degree of scepticism for what if anything lay ahead of them?

The bus slowed to a stop and the amorous couple stood up and walked off, their hands clasped tightly together. Their arms swung in unison before the pair turned up a side street and on to wherever it was they were going. A man sat down in their place. His nose bristled at the smell of the girl's perfume that lingered in the air, and he sneezed into the crook of his elbow in response.

On his lower back, Ellis could make out a growing sweat stain that contrasted against his slightly too tight sky-blue shirt. He could smell the scent of warm body odour as it mixed with the man's aftershave. It made Ellis feel sick and he suddenly felt overwhelmed by the warmth of the bus and its constant, shuddering movement. He tried slowing his breathing to regain his already frayed, questionable composure.

In front of him, the male passenger rifled through his bag and took out a tattered looking book. He pulled a blank scrap of black paper from within its pages by way of a makeshift bookmark. Ellis felt the need to close his eyes and did so without obstruction. He thought back to the months before where he had looked for whatever he could find within the pages of books. A search for guidance, or hope; a thing, *the* thing, anything, to take him out from within himself. He had discovered that he wanted to break free of his enforced confines but had not reached the place he wanted to find. Nor did he know or could he even picture what it looked like in his turbulent thoughts. But he was sure that he wanted something different. How comforting to do that which you have always known and done, he thought. But how little was to be achieved by those actions and how small the reward, if any reward was derived at all.

The bus snaked its way through narrow streets and stopped sporadically at the various traffic lights that lined the route. The mechanisms of its engine sent vibrations through the window where Ellis' head now rested. While only minutes before he felt that his heart would burst from his chest, he now harboured a sense of clarity that he had not felt for some days, and he enjoyed the sensation of the steady hum as it ebbed deeper and deeper into what he imagined was the centre of his brain.

He thought of the arguments at work. Arguments that he would routinely back down from, only to run what he should have said over and over until he understood that he could no longer go back to work. When he closed his eyes at nights the various scenes would replay in his head. Then the desire came. The desire and drive to show them, whoever they were, that he was worthy of something. That he was competent and that he could, no, indeed that he would achieve! Was this achieving, he wondered? His mind skipped to another memory. The days of the loud music; of inextricable banging on the roof and walls, and of the water that had steadily formed in an opaque pool outside the front door of his flat.

As before, he had done and said nothing. The music blared and the tears rose, tears of anger and of frustration. A frustration borne of his inability to get dressed, walk into the hallway and out of the front door, and hammer loudly on the flat above with all his might. He would kick and bang, shout and swear, and engulf the letter box with a fury unseen. The noise would cease never to return. But he did not. And it did not.

For a while, on each and every Sunday, he would wake with a renewed sense of confidence in both himself and his predicament. He knew that what he lived in those moments was merely a staging post to something better and that life, real life, his life, lay elsewhere. To look forward is to live, he told himself. So perhaps things had not worked out up until now, but just look what lies around the corner! He imagined himself in a year, working in a job he enjoyed, while perhaps in even a year or two from now he would be painting the walls of his new home, a welcoming and congenial song playing from the radio. Those daydreams and fantasies remained but as the years progressed, the outcomes failed to come to fruition, and so they too diminished. But still he knew, or at least could tell himself, that his life was elsewhere, and far from the loneliness and emptiness that were his daily companions, whether he believed it to be true or not.

Slowly opening his eyes, he watched as two girls in the seat beside him giggled and ate, passing a bag of salt and vinegar crisps between them. The man in front circled pages of the book in black ink, an action that Ellis found to be deeply unsettling. His stomach fell away and dropped once more, as if as that very moment he was going to have to vomit on the bus. The dampness on his skin had grown. He thought the girls would be judging him in his anxious state, sweating and red-cheeked, as he had judged the reader with the ever-moving black biro pen. He decided that the next stop would be close enough to walk to Andy's house, so he pushed the stop button and felt his muscles loosen as the bus slowed down. Once outside, he placed both hands behind his head and breathed heartily. The air met his lungs with a speed and ferocity that soon produced a strong sensation of dizziness, and all of his extremities tingled.

His mercurial thoughts spun and made him unsteady on his feet. To want to do something is never the same as actually doing it, but he had once had plans, he reminded himself, holding his head in his hands and swaying on the pavement. Plans to travel and to swim in seas unknown; to see the world with a never-ending supply of funds from a never quite imagined business idea. The Italian course was short-lived, but he had battled through for several weeks before appreciating that when it came to it, the thought of doing something was greater than any desire to actually see it through to completion. The woodwork course held a greater place in his psyche in what was an otherwise blank schedule, but this soon too was added to the list of steadily growing former pastimes.

It was the desire to achieve that he found so difficult, and which led to his inability to do anything. It is better to sit and wait, than move and fail, he told himself, though even he had begun to doubt it. He wondered if this was still what he believed, more so since the discovery of Andy's treasure map, or if he was honest with himself for one of the very rarest of times; of Andy himself.

'Do you know if this is the stop for Royston Place?' came a voice from behind him. He turned to see an elderly woman sitting down at the bus stop. He attempted to regain his senses and hesitated for a moment. Not answering the question in a time that was acceptable saw it asked once more.

'Royston Place, I said. Is this the stop for Royston Place?'

'Yes,' said Ellis, though he felt as if the words were coming from someone else. As if this conversation was like he was watching a dream and not one where he was a participant. 'This is the stop,' he added quietly. 'I think the next bus should be along quite soon. It's the number eight you're looking for,' said Ellis, still feeling groggy and distant.

'Well then,' came the reply. 'I suppose I'd better wait here. Only, may I ask a favour from you? Could I perhaps ask you to sit with me until the bus comes? You see they drive so fast, and my eyes aren't what they once used to be. Do you know what? It wouldn't surprise me if it's already driven past, and I've just been sitting here. Not to worry,' continued the voice, in a softly spoken accent that Ellis recognised but could not place, 'I'm sure the next one will be along any minute. Only if you could wait, I would be ever so grateful,' she said beseechingly.

Ellis sat down beside her on the bench.

'I can wait,' he said.

'Oh, you've no idea how joyful that's made me. Thank you, oh thank you very much,' said the woman gratefully.

'So where are you going on such a lovely sunny day? Off to see your girlfriend no doubt?' she asked with a smile.

'No, nothing like that, I don't have a...' said Ellis, before trailing off and starting the sentence again. 'I'm going to visit a friend today, but what about you? Where are you going?' he asked quickly in an attempt the change the conversation's course.

'A friend? Oh, how lovely, that's very nice to hear. Friends are oh so very important, so I hope you two look after each other. Keep each other right, I mean,' she stated.

Ellis had not anticipated this response and being unsure of what else to say, he simply nodded meekly.

'When you get to my age you begin to look at friends as your family and they become more so with each passing year, you mark my words,' mused the old woman. 'A good friend will be there to share your highs and your lows and unfortunately, many of us experience more of the latter than the former. You won't know Eadie, or Rose for that matter, but they certainly did. I've had my own low points over the years, but haven't we all? The important thing is to keep on moving. Movement is progress, just you remember that. Movement, a strong sense of faith and a knowledge that our Lord God Almighty, has a path set out for each of us. Do you believe in God? Do you have faith?' she asked.

'Here comes the eight now,' said Ellis forcibly, cutting her off before she could finish the sentence. 'I hope you have a lovely afternoon,' he added, receiving a smile by way of thanks.

'I wish you and your friend a good afternoon as well and remember what I said!' she shouted over the growing traffic noise, with a sternness not in keeping with the earlier conversation.

Taking her seat by a window, she watched Ellis intently until the bus pulled away and onto the main road. Ellis would have seen her staring at him before the bus took a right turn on Runcorn Street, had he not quickly turned his head to walk with purpose in the opposite direction.

The quick movement invigorated him. Each stride closer to Andy's saw the noise of car engines reduce and soon the sounds that filled his ears were that of faint birdcall and the leaves above as they rustled gently in the late spring breeze. The weeds and wildflowers looked different in the afternoon sunshine and Ellis watched as bees and hoverflies bobbed and wove their way between the petals. The air smelled sweet and perfumed, not at all unpleasant, and he bent down to tie a loose shoelace.

At ground level he saw that the roots of the plants were hidden not only by their foliage but by bits of assorted plastic and rubbish. Crisp bags in all manner of semi-composition, yoghurt pots, and beer and soft drink cans, some with holes of rust in their sides, tops and bottoms.

Walking on, he spotted Andy's bungalow as he came towards the narrow lane. Its smokeless chimney stood out against a clear blue sky and Ellis could see that the curtains were closed, giving the house a strange, almost claustrophobic sensation at that time of the day.

He put what thoughts he did have to the back of his mind, but there was a strong sensation to urinate while his stomach churned and rumbled. His pace had dropped as he got closer, and the house seemed to shun him with its abject lifelessness. The white paint that had so beautifully framed the window was now patchy and flaked. Ellis saw that some of it looked to have been sanded off, but in a pattern that pointed to a lack of any plan about what would be done next. Resisting the urge to take a closer look, Ellis stood on the doorstep, held the heavy brass door knocker in his left hand, and lifted it heavily against the door in three solid, slow, thuds.

Chapter twenty-five

If one were to ask him now, Ellis would not have been able to recall how long it took him to look through the letterbox. What felt like an hour of waiting would have only been, at least he thought this now, around five minutes. That in itself is a long time to be standing alone outside a home, its curtains drawn to enclose whatever was inside. A lot can happen in five minutes. Many things can be imagined, but often the outcome is better than the thoughts racing through a mind clouded by the darkness of the unknown. Often, yet not always.

When Ellis finally did give a gentle push on the creaky letterbox, his gaze met a scene he would never have thought possible. The hallway was strewn with bits of paper and the various pieces of artwork that had adorned the walls on the last visit had been cast away on the floor. Smashed shards of glass glistened from the sun that came in from cracks in the curtains near the back of the house. A stale smell seeped out from within and hit Ellis full on, causing him to retch and lose his balance on the front steps. The shock and severity of the assault on his senses was total and his brain struggled to process all that lay before him.

The house was in chaos. Yet despite it being full

of every imaginable item; clothes strewn across the floor and empty bottles, it remained motionless and still. Not a sound could be heard, and it felt deathly. Ellis sensed that he was intruding on a scene that he had no right to see, and a chill shot sharply down his spine at the thought.

His myopic gaze still centred on the hallway yet something within Ellis told him, almost threateningly so, to look right towards the back of the living room. Still in a state of worry and shock, he slowly moved his eyes upwards inch by inch, on and on until they reached the very back of the hallway. There was nothing there when his eyes ascended, all except a bare, off-white patch on the wall where a print had been pulled off in haste. It was a picture for Caledonian Railways, the corner of which he could now see ripped and crumpled near the shower room entrance.

The view from within the rectangle made Ellis wobble and bob, disgusted at what he saw, and fearful that he would soon see more. His heart pounded and his pulse throbbed in every limb, threatening to topple him. His jaw clenched so that he could hear his teeth scrape against each other. Towards the end of the hallway, close to the back of the house, there was a right turn that led to Andy's bedroom. At the level of the skirting board, two sock-clad feet lay pointing upwards, motionless and cast in a shadow that gave the sight a degree of calming beauty that was incongruous with the scene.

Ellis banged on the door again, harder than before, over and over, until his knuckles became scuffed, and patches of blood formed between his torn white skin. 'Andy!' he shouted, over and over, made louder by an otherwise total silence. For it seemed to Ellis that even the leaves of the trees now ceased to rustle, nor did the bees buzz around the flowers that looked dry, scorched and dead.

'Andy! Andy please, it's Ellis!' he screamed. He took one step back then another, before running at the door, screaming and kicking at it, spitting and pushing. Every muscle in his body strained as he shouted out into nothingness. He moved towards the back of the house, searching for something to smash a window with. Towards the door sat a terracotta pot, devoid of life inside. Some painted stones and a children's windmill, itself spinning slowly in the breeze, were all it housed. Ellis lifted it with ease and put it above his head ready to smash it against the frosted glass. As he lifted it behind his head, he spotted a small brass key that was partly covered in soil, some wood slaters and a centipede crawling beside and away from it, towards the dampness and darkness of whatever safety they could find.

Ellis' hands shook as he slowly got the key into the lock. It was stiff and he tried to push the door to ease the mechanism. It clicked open, sending the same odious smell into the freshness of the warm day. Ellis retched and spat in the hope of forcing the acrid, rotten taste from his mouth. He pulled a sweat-soaked shirt over his nose in a futile attempt to avoid the growing stench. What became hidden from his nose was impossible to avoid for his eyes. The contents of Andy's life were cast aside, senselessly and in places none belonged. A navy-blue suit jacket lay loosely inside the kitchen sink, both arms dark with water. Some photographs had been scattered on the kitchen table, scorch marks on some of them, the ink from a black pen scrawled tightly in circular patterns across others. It was on this table that Andy had shown Ellis the treasure map. There was no treasure to be found in any of what Ellis saw.

Soon, he found himself in the hallway, for it was there Andy lay. Shaking, he went to take a mobile phone from his pocket, but did not know if he was required to phone the police or ambulance first. Andy lay on his back. He wore tan corduroy trousers and a loose-fitting black shirt with no collar. His eyes were motionless and unblinking. Ellis saw something that he found unsettling: the steady rise and fall of Andy's stomach. He was breathing.

'Andy!' he shouted, crouching down to place a hand on his stomach. Ellis looked at Andy's face, still radiant and pink. He could see that his nostrils flared and that the skin around his mouth and cheeks twitched involuntarily. He was alive.

'Andy?' whispered Ellis, fearful that all of this was a horrible dream. That he would soon awaken in his own bedroom, gasping for air and clutching at sweat-soaked sheets.

'Andy, what are you doing? What is this? Do you need an ambulance?' he asked again, grasping at the curtains and opening windows to let some air and light into what felt like a cave; deep underground, damp and cold. Ellis felt his mouth dry from fear and smelled the staleness of his own breath. Andy turned his head slowly and looked deeply into Ellis' eyes. Ellis could see they were bloodshot, framed with large, painful looking bruises. His pupils narrowed as he blinked in the light, the space of the home seeming to grow with the air that now cast out the stagnant dampness of days if not weeks of decay.

'Help me,' he whispered, holding an unsteady arm upwards, his open palm pointing towards Ellis. Reaching out for his hand, Ellis felt the dryness of skin that had known the toil of manual labour. While he had never looked at Andy as a strong man, his pitiful look as he lay on the floor made Ellis think of a sick child or lame animal.

'What have you done, Andy? What is this?' he asked. Andy turned his body so that his back was now raised from the floor. He reached for Ellis' forearm and attempted to pull himself up using what strength he had.

'Have you eaten something, Andy? Have you drunk anything?' asked Ellis hastily. 'Have you hurt yourself?'

'No,' said Andy, though it was barely audible. 'I have not, but...' he said, trailing off as he struggled to find the words.

'How long have you been here? On the floor, I mean?' asked Ellis.

Andy ignored the question as tears began to stream from his eyes. Ellis pushed his forehead onto Andy's chest.

'Andy, Andy,' he called, as Andy's body shuddered and convulsed. 'I'm here, Andy, I'm here. Whatever this is it's okay. I'm here, and I'm sorry, Andy, and I'm here. Please, please Andy, please, know that I am here.' He pulled Andy's body further into him and was shocked at how weightless it felt. A fly on the wall remained where it was, unmoved by the drama unfolding below.

'Let me call someone, please,' pleaded Ellis. 'We can fix this, I promise you.'

'I'm lost,' wailed Andy, beating a fist across the back of his head. Over and over, he pounded, the strength of the blows scattering tears and saliva in the direction of the wall.

'Stop! Stop! Andy, stop this, you're hurting yourself, just stop! Please!' screamed Ellis, pinning Andy's arms back to the floor. Andy's breathing slowed and he mouthed something to himself, softly and gently under his breath. The words spoken were said with no intention of reaching Ellis.

'It's important you're honest with me now,' Ellis said, sternly, his face hot and red from the restraint. 'Have you taken anything? Have you hurt yourself in any way? Let me know, Andy, just let me know one way or another,' he said, his voice shaking with adrenaline.

'I've not, I promise you that,' whispered Andy. 'That's the one thing I can promise. I've not taken anything and this, whatever this is, isn't me, and I'm scared.' Andy rubbed his rough hands over his forehead, wiping away some of the accumulated sweat. He sat up gently, holding his hands against his hips for support, and rocked backwards and forwards, like driftwood on the waves. Neither it nor Andy had control of where the motion sent them.

'I'm not myself,' he said.

Ellis sat down beside him and put his back against the wall. He moved his neck to stretch it, a practice he had long done when nervous, and felt a reassuring crack. Andy looked at the floor, his senses dulled, and his eyes numb to the carnage that surrounded them.

'We can speak to someone about this, Andy,' Ellis said warmly. 'We can get you the help you need, whatever that looks like. You can't live like this, nobody can. Look around you, this isn't right,' said Ellis, motioning around the house. He instantly felt that this was the wrong thing to say in such a situation, but there were now greater worries ahead of him.

All was silent for what felt like an eternity, except for the heavy breathing of each man. For a brief moment, some clouds covered the sun, and the room took on a gloomy, overwhelming, and constrictive feeling once more. Ellis watched the shadow grow across the hallway then drift away until the room was once again lit.

'Tell me what's happened? I mean, only if you want to,' said Ellis, in what he hoped was a reassuring and empathetic tone. 'Only if you can, I mean,' he added.

Andy looked back at him. Ellis did not recognise the face, bereft of any joy, ashen and as fragile as brittle clay.

'How can you explain darkness within?' Andy asked, rubbing a finger over his upper shirt button. 'A few days ago, I woke up and heard something. I don't know what it was, or is, but I heard it. It's probably still here. Can you hear it now? Do you hear it?' he asked, standing up quickly and peering behind his bedroom door.

Ellis felt shivers go up his spine and felt as if his body had been cloaked in ice, but still he listened intently, pushing hard against the rising fear.

'It said things to me. Told me to do things. Things that no person should do to themselves. But I didn't do it, did I? I didn't do it, Ellis, oh no, oh no,' he said, his voice rising in confusion. 'So, I hid from it. I took down the things that the voice spoke to me from, and I hid. I burned and ripped and tore and ripped and burned and fucking hell, they still spoke to me!' Andy roared as he spat out the last of the words. 'So, I hid once more, down low, you see. Right here,' he said, pointing to the space around him. 'And the voices went away, and when they did, I was scared to move. Scared they would come back, you see. But you can't hear them now so they must be gone. They must be gone,' he trailed off, nodding his head by way of reassurance.

'I'm going to make a phone call, Andy,' said Ellis. As he held his mobile phone, Ellis looked down at Andy as he shook in the corner of the hallway.

'There will be no more voices. There's nothing to be frightened of anymore,' he said softly, before he heard someone on the other end of the line pick up.

'Ambulance! I need an ambulance now,' called Ellis down the line.

Chapter twenty-six

The wheel of the year is always turning. The warmth of summer gave way to a coolness in the air. The winds grew, blowing brown leaves down to gather in beds, as if hopeful that clumping together as one would provide safe haven from the autumnal storms. Soon, however, an endless rain had turned them into rotting piles on the street.

Ellis looked through his kitchen window at the scene below. Condensation had pooled on the bottom lip of the window, and he soaked the water up with some toilet roll. He tossed the dirt black and sodden paper into the bin under the sink. Outside people rushed home from work or from school, moving with pace and purpose, with jumpers and jackets pulled tight around their necks to keep out the cold.

Ellis knew that he too would have to leave the warmth of his flat to visit Andy that evening. It would be his first time back at the house since the events of the spring and he could not place how that made him feel. He was 'doing better,' the specialists had said, but Ellis knew that better from a point of absolute darkness and loss was still a low place to be. While it would be the first time he would go to the house, it would not be the first time he had seen Andy since the incident in the shadowy hallway. Over three hospital visits, the last two in a former country house, nestled towards the hillside; secluded and isolated in equal measure, Ellis had spoken and met with the man who was now his friend.

The psychiatric hospital's inpatient ward saw Andy lose his freedom and autonomy for fifty-six and a half days. Where at first the poet, collector, painter, writer, cook, man and son had become a patient, then a service user. The psychotic episode, diagnosed as brief reactive psychosis, and thought to have been brought on by post-traumatic stress disorder, had seen him cease to exist in the life he knew before it. When something like that takes place, the only thing that can logically follow is change, for good or for bad. Things do not remain the same once you hear an inner voice.

With no immediate family, Ellis had been named as his close contact and had told the various psychiatrists and nurses all that he had known of Andy's past, which he soon realised was little. As Ellis looked out from the window of his flat, he could still smell the strong scent of disinfectant that crept into each corner of the hospital, and he could picture the chairs in his memory; their plastic blue contrasting with the small, austere, white snow drop patterns. The wood reminded him of those he sat in while at school. The words stuck with him too: referral, Mental Health Act, seclusion, therapy, struggling, crisis, breaking point, sedative, detained, liberty, sectioned.

On the third visit, Andy had been clear that he had been treated with nothing but respect, but Ellis wondered if it was like that across the rest of the country.

'It's a waiting game for us all, Ellis,' Andy had told him one day, as they walked in the stately gardens, with only the smallest degree of scrutiny and observation. 'A waiting game and I waited too long,' he said.

That was three weeks ago, and Ellis had since been in touch with Andy, arranging a visit for the last Sunday of the month.

The bus that morning brought back memories which he had tried to push back from his mind since the summer. The bus stop and the pathway, the flowerpot and Andy, sprawled in the hallway, tears streaming down his face. The words help me, help me, repeated over and over. He would not yet admit it to himself, but the incident had sparked something in him that made him realise that it was not only Andy who needed help, but himself. The thought grew as he made his way closer in the direction of the house. The wildflowers were gone yet the rubbish remained.

Ellis was relieved to see Andy sitting on a bench in the front garden, steam rising from a cup of milky tea. He had not wanted to knock the heavy brass knocker again, through a growing, if not irrational fear, of it being left unanswered.

'Hello, my friend,' called Andy, rising from the bench to stand. Ellis noted that he looked taller than when he had seen him in the hospital ward, and his skin looked fresher and vibrant. The stubble had now grown into a short beard, and Ellis remarked that it suited him. Andy nodded in recognition, pulling his fingers through the hair and rubbing his chin.

'Come inside,' said Andy. 'The kettle has only just boiled.'

Ellis could not help but think back to the scene of destruction and despair that had met him the last time he stood in the hallway. While still not back to a level he would have described as normal, it was now in a condition that was very much liveable, if empty of the pieces, things and loose bits that give a home its own personal, living touch. In the corner of the hallway there was a small table, the size of which could carry little more than an old landline telephone. Instead, Andy had placed a pot of pens upon it and a small sketchbook.

'Are you drawing, Andy?' asked Ellis.

'Oh, drawing,' Andy said, looking startled at the question. 'Yes, something I spoke about with my social worker so I'm trying to draw. I can't say it works, but it's important to try,' he said, smiling at Ellis. 'Did I ever tell you the story of the flower collector?' he asked.

Ellis shook his head.

'I met her through a friend, oh what would it be... perhaps twenty years ago or more now?' Andy asked rhetorically, exhaling slowly at the memory. 'She lived on an island, an island far off the coast, and had done since she was a child. She told me that from a young age she had fallen in love with flowers. Of a daffodil in spring, or the flowering poppy in its August bloom. The only thing was, Ellis, and this was the strange thing, but she had never actually seen a flower. Nothing grew on the island apart from reeds and grass. Can you imagine that? Nothing to look at but bog and moss, and not even a tree to walk under? She had seen the flowers in books, you see, and she knew what they were supposed to be. What they were supposed to look and smell like, I mean. As she got older, she would leave the island each spring and summer and collect what she could find, but never too much, of course. Delicate wood anemone wrapped between tissue paper, or purple columbine taken home safely in Tupperware boxes. Each and every stem and petal she brought back was pressed between the pages of a heavy book. So, there were no flowers that grew on the island, but she had her own little garden library known only to her.' Andy's gaze was distant. 'Sorry, I don't know why I'm telling you all this,' he said, motioning for Ellis to move into the kitchen. 'Please, take a seat,' said Andy.

Ellis pulled a chair out from under the bare table, lifting it slightly as he did so to avoid making a noise. The hum of the refrigerator was the only sound that filled the room. Sensing the void of silence was making Ellis unsettled, Andy moved towards a kitchen drawer and took out an old radio.

'I just need to find...' muttered Andy, 'ah yeah, here we are,' he said, taking a handful of batteries and forcing them into a slot at the back. The static of dead air hissed and crackled but soon the duo were listening, whether either wanted to or not, to a lively radio phone in.

'I'm due you some thanks,' said Andy. 'For what you've done for me these last few months. I mean, I don't...'

Ellis interrupted him, an unwelcome habit of his when he was uncomfortable with the topic of conversation.

'You don't need to say anything, and look, I'm not here for that, am I?' he asked. It was now Andy who was silent. 'I'm sorry,' said Ellis. 'I don't know what to say to you.'

Andy sighed and took a napkin out of his pocket. He opened it to reveal four small pieces of metal.

'Is that?' asked Ellis. Andy forced a smile then placed his head in his hands.

'You know, don't you?' asked Andy. 'Know that I did all this to... well, I did all this. I can't explain why I did it. I thought it would be fun, something to do together as friends, you understand? We do the same job, and you know how tiresome that becomes, but you can never become or be just a title. I'm not just a binman, and nor are you,' said Andy. 'It was all a lie. There was never any treasure map,' he whispered.'

'You don't need to do this,' said Ellis, 'not now, not ever.'

'When did you know?' asked Andy. 'You did know, didn't you?'

'I didn't,' said Ellis. 'I didn't know.' Ellis walked to the sink and poured himself a glass of water. The glass looked dirty, but he drank the cold water down in one. 'This is selfish of me but even now, as you and I stand in this room, and we avoid speaking about things that should be left unsaid, I still want you to tell me that it is real. That we will find something, that there's...' He poured himself another glass and sipped it this time.

A bird landed on a tree and hopped from branch to branch, seemingly confused about which spot suited its needs best. After thirty seconds it gave up and flew away.

'I want there to be something. Coming here today I wanted you to show me more, tell me more, let me know that for once, something that I wanted, I mean something I really, truly wanted was there for me. That for once, it would all fall into place. How selfish is that? You've just had a fucking mental breakdown, and that's all I'm thinking about!' Ellis threw the glass down in the sink, but not hard enough for it to smash. 'I'm sorry,' he said. 'You lied, but I let myself be led through nothing more than blind faith. I don't resent you, Andy, not one bit. This, all of this, is the strangest and most unnerving experience of my life, but I'm here. I'm here for news that I knew would never come.'

'When I was a child...' said Andy. Ellis cut him off.

'Andy, not now, I don't need a story, please...' he said.

'Listen,' said Andy. 'Listen.' He paused to ground himself then spoke.

'When I was a child, things weren't easy for me. Things were hell, as I've told you before. An absolute living hell, where all I wanted to do was escape from the life that was going on around me. I've told you parts before, but I had nothing to do but hide away within myself. It's not about pretending, how can you pretend that someone hasn't, hasn't...' he let the sentence trail off. 'I just want you to know that things were difficult for me. I'm speaking about the things that happened to me with people who can help me. A large part of that comes from you, Ellis. You saved me,' he said.

'The things we experienced were real, Ellis,' he said. 'The excitement and the desire to move forward and work towards something was real. None of that was imagined or untrue, none of it. The only lie was that there was something at the end of it; something more than hope,' he said. 'But that's what life is, Ellis. Nothing is certain. Nothing. But you need to keep moving forward and striving to do something, anything at all, just do something. Life isn't something we can always plan for, it's what's happening now, with each and every breath we take. But we all waste huge parts of it, we all do. You and I know we do. There's rarely a realisation that what's being lived, done, and felt today, felt in this very moment, is life,' said Andy, finding a fluidity and clarity at odds with his otherwise fragile looking appearance.

'This is life, not the plans you make for next weekend, next month, or the year after, yet rarely fulfil. This. This is life,' said Andy, standing up from the table and joining Ellis where he stood at the kitchen sink. 'Thank you, Ellis. Thank you for helping me feel again.'

Some thirty minutes later, Ellis found himself walking down the path that led onto the main road. He would soon be home; the same empty space where he had spent too many of his evenings doing too little of what he wanted. On the left-hand side there was a small house, and, in its garden, a woman stood working, forcing a spade into the ground before throwing the soil she gathered into a mound. Ellis looked down at his own hands, feeling the callouses on his left that remained from when he last held a shovel. A growing breeze brought dark clouds that sat far out to sea, soon to be blown inland to soak the ground. He rubbed his hands together and moved a finger over the dry, hard nub of calloused skin. He decided at that moment that he would not go directly to the bus stop and when he had come to the decision, he paused, deciding which path was the best one to take.

As he walked, the steady buzz of energy gathered speed, ebbing and flowing from limb to limb, as quick and powerful as electricity. His footsteps now matched the growing speed of the charge within, and he realised that he was smiling.

The sun had set by the time he reached the harbour. Finding a bench, he opened up a damp, hot package of chips in newspaper. The chip shop had been busy with weekend trade, but he had been served quickly and had managed some small talk with the girl behind the counter, someone he had known since his school days. He balanced the chips on his thigh and felt the warmth of the fat and potatoes against his skin. The boats bobbed calmly in the harbour, sheltered from the breakwater and from the growing waves beyond. Ellis placed another chip into his mouth, the pile fast losing their heat in the autumn night, and chewed readily. He thought of the flower collector and her dried blossom, an image that gave him such a sense of comfort, that he wanted to lie down where he was on the bench, call out with joy, and close his eyes to be rewarded with the warming embrace of sleep.

Chapter twenty-seven

The site's cafeteria was busy that morning. Men sat blurry eyed, watching the rain falling steadily, and making idle Monday morning small talk about weekends spent far away from where they found themselves in that moment.

In a separate room, its desk full of papers and bric-a-brac, a gruff-looking man sat. The smell of coffee and cigarettes already permeated the small room, and it was not yet seven a.m. Ellis stood, his body erect and proud, both hands placed behind his back in anticipation at what was to come.

'So where are you going now then?' came the voice behind the desk. Mr Gallacher was the depot's foreman, at least that's what he liked to refer to himself as. In reality nobody really knew what he did, but once a man or woman had their own desk and office space, it proves very difficult to prise it away from them.

Earlier that morning, his wife had burnt two slices of his wholegrain toast, and it had put him in a foul mood, that only seemed to increase with each passing minute. He had cursed the toaster and the unopened marmalade, but most of all, he had cursed his wife. The image of the burnt toast, lying without purpose in the bottom of the sink filled his mind as he cast one eye over Ellis that morning.

'Has another job come along with better money, as I'll tell you now, these agencies say they will match our wages but it's all overtime based. Are you happy with overtime, Elliot?' he asked.

'It's Ellis,' said Ellis, 'and no, I'm not going anywhere to be honest with you. I just wanted a change so that's what I'm going to do.'

'Hmm,' said Mr Gallacher with a suspicion in his voice that Ellis ignored. 'Well, we have a lot of people looking to come on, so I won't beat around the bush here. You've got two weeks' worth of holiday to take so I'm happy for today to be your last day and we'll end things cleanly at the end of the month. HR will sort the details, but that's what works best for us if it works for you?' he asked.

'That sounds good to me,' said Ellis. Avoiding the platitudes he felt obliged to say in such circumstances, he turned on his heels and went to his locker. It was full of damp-smelling waterproofs, a sepia-tinged plastic lunch box, various pay slips, and a black biro pen.

Ellis felt movement behind him and turned. It was Jordan.

'I don't want you to think I was listening in, but I was,' he laughed, smiling at Ellis. 'So, you're leaving then?'

'Jordan!' said Ellis, shocked at the visitor. 'What the hell are you doing here?' he asked, still startled at the vision of the man stood in front of him.

'There's a few things I have to organise with HR, to be honest with you. Some taxation issues and the like, but look, don't worry about all that,' said Jordan. 'Like I say, where are you off to now?' he asked.

'I'm leaving,' said Ellis. 'No idea what I'll do now, but you know how it is, don't you? We had spoken about it a few times when we worked together and you knew I just wasn't happy here,' said Ellis. 'It's not even that I wasn't happy, it's more than I wasn't anything, just a thing that was going through the motions of it all,' he added. Jordan smiled then looked over his shoulder, lowering his voice.

'I'm happy for you but there's also something I wanted to ask you. Have you heard about Andy? There are some people here saying that he's had a nervous breakdown? Have you heard anything, as I know you and him spent some weekends together this year?' asked Jordan, his voice reduced to a whisper.

'I know,' said Ellis, before Jordan spoke again, this time with greater animation in his voice.

'Come to think of it, mate, what were the pair of you doing?' he asked.

At that moment all Ellis could think about was the first day he met Jordan. Of the plastic tinged sandwiches and the deathly silence. The unsavoriness of the mid-morning swaying, pissing behind street corners and in bushes, and of gratitude at the help in lowering and holding a branch to pick some of the summer cherries.

'It's good to see you like this,' said Ellis. 'I mean that, and you don't need me to tell you, but it's great actually,' he added, smiling at Jordan.

Jordan looked embarrassed but thanked him regardless. 'It's like I've got my life back, Ellis. There's a cure for alcoholism and it's called alcohol,' he said, looking at Ellis straight in the eye, 'but you can only treat the symptoms for so long. It's the cause that you need to address.' He looked around making sure there was nobody listening. 'When you feel like I felt, it's still living, but there's more to life than just waking each morning and breathing. There's got to be more to it than that,' he said.

'Do you ever wonder what someone's thinking about when you look at them?' Jordan asked.

'You wanted to know about Andy?' said Ellis in reply, politely avoiding a question that he hoped Jordan did not anticipate an answer to.

'Yeah, yeah, sorry, I was in my own world there,' said Jordan.

'He's okay,' said Ellis, that's the main thing. 'I'm not telling you anything that he wouldn't tell you himself, but he's been under a lot of pressure recently. I don't know how else to say it, and you know what? I think it just got too much for him in the end. He's okay now, or he will be, that's the main thing,' added Ellis.

'It's good you're there for him. I tried to give him a call a while back now but there was no answer, so I thought I should leave him alone. You never know when someone wants, no, needs would be a better way of putting it actually, their own space. I for one know that,' said Jordan.

'He burned his phone,' said Ellis, in as matter-of-fact a way as one can when speaking about such matters.

'What?!' barked Jordan, sounding shocked.

'In the back garden,' replied Ellis. 'There was actually a lot of things that he burned, but like I said, he was under a lot of pressure. He's getting better now,' he said.

'Christ,' said Jordan. 'If you see him again, tell him I'm asking for him, will you?'

'Of course I will. He'll want to see you as well, I'm sure of it,' said Ellis.

Jordan tapped his finger against the locker door, a sign Ellis took to mean that he had no more to say on the matter.

'Jordan...' said Ellis, unsure even then if he would ask what he wanted to say. 'When I first met Andy, he told me something, and I wanted to check,' he paused, not knowing how Jordan would react at what was to come. 'To check if it was something you knew of,' he finished.

'Go on,' said Jordan.

It was a story that Ellis had not looked forward to telling, embarrassed by his inability to spot an old tale when he heard one. No doubt told by Andy over the years between pub companions and anyone who would listen, each drink leading to more lurid add-ons, even if the libation only came from sparkling water, or when he permitted himself, the odd glass of rum.

'When I first met Andy, he spoke about something that even saying it out loud sounds funny now, but I'll just say it,' said Ellis, wishing beyond all else that at that moment some distraction would take place and would save him from his embarrassment. 'He spoke about treasure. He spoke about a sunken ship, about loot and plunder, and about a map that leads to it all,' Ellis forced himself to laugh, mocking himself as well as the story. Jordan blinked, then burst into laughter at what he had heard. Then as quickly as the laughter had come, his facial expression changed to one of great solemnity.

'All of it true,' he said. 'All of it,' said Jordan, his voice again lowered to a whisper.

Ellis was shocked, unsure why a second person would now seek to humiliate him and take advantage of blind trust. What benefit did they get from his gullible nature?

'Yeah, yeah,' said Ellis, scoffing at Jordan. 'Are you in on the joke too then?' he asked.

'Ellis,' he said, leaning in. 'Listen when I say this. All of it is true. Andy and I heard about it when we were much younger. I can't remember his name, but there was an older man who used to come into the pub, a right academic sort if you catch my drift. Tweed suits and ruddy cheeks. We overheard him outside one day telling someone about it and the next time we saw him, some flattery loosened his tongue. He told us all we needed to know. There were four or five summers spent on the hunt before either of us got bored, or at least I did, and at that age you want to be getting on with your life don't you, not off looking for treasure,' he smiled. 'Come to think of it, it's funny how neither of us did get on with living life, but you know what they say, there's a second chance for everyone,' said Jordan, pouring with pride and hopefulness.

'Andy said he had a map. Well, he said he did, then apologised for making it up,' said Ellis.

'A map? Well, that's the first I've heard of it if so,' he laughed. 'He has made that up, so no, let me tell you there's no map, but I've no doubt that the rest of what he's told you is true. Is that what the pair of you have been off doing all this time? Hunting for treasure? Let me give you some advice, Ellis, it's there, but you'll never find it. Get on with something you can control and don't let it swallow you whole, as you're looking for something that you'll never find. At your age you don't get these years back, none of us do,' said Jordan.

'Right, lads, come on. Everyone out for the shift,' called a voice from down the hall.

Ellis felt his head spin at what he heard and felt a high pitched and shrill buzzing in his ears. Jordan placed his hand out and the two joined palms, shaking hands purposefully.

'It's been good working with you. Keep in touch and remember what I said about Andy. I'd say we could all meet up for a pint one day, but you know,' laughed Jordan.

'I'm sure we'll all catch up soon,' said Ellis, unsure whether he would ever see Jordan again beyond today. 'All the best now,' he added.

Ellis' last day of work was filled with the nothingness he expected. At the end of it there was no magical moment where Ellis felt free; where he saw his options line out in front of him, ready to be readily picked off with fervour and delight. There was no card, no cake and no gift, nor had he expected there to be. Jordan was long gone by the time he returned to base and after a brief goodbye with Archie, he was out, on his way and unemployed.

The bus was the same as it had always been: people leaving work, their heads turned towards the floor gazing at books, phones, or at rest. The lock to the flat's entrance creaked open, and the stairwell gave off the faint smell of soap and cigarette smoke, that made Ellis feel that home and solitude were just around the corner. But as he took the steps in leaps of two, it was increasingly becoming a solitude that he no longer craved.

As he opened the door of his flat, a warm rush of air welcomed him home. As was often the case, the letters scattered across his hallway floor were bills, advertisements and take away menus, but on this occasion, Ellis read each in detail. He looked at the words and use of language. The irregular capitalisation and adverbs; oxblood read font and analogy. He placed each pamphlet, envelope and leaflet with care on his kitchen worktop.

At that moment a glimpse of a memory passed through him that had long been forgotten. The lady he met at the book fair, Emma, he recalled, had given him a book to read. He remembered that he had taken it home and placed it into the drawer of a long unused desk that sat in the corner of his bedroom. How strange he thought, to have that memory now, but with a growing desire to read something new, he made his way into the bedroom and opened the desk drawer. The book was where he had left it, wrapped in its wrinkled casing. Ellis tore at the paper, excited at the chance to read a paperback that Emma had given such credence to. Open it when you need it most, he remembered her saying. Whether he needed it now was not something he could answer, but he was intrigued by what she had given him and tore off the last sheet to reveal nothing. Not nothing exactly. The book was there, held in his hand and passed back and forth, but the cover was bare. On opening its pages, they too carried nothing, not even uniform lines. It was a blank notebook. He turned it over once more, running a finger over the dry cover. He held it to his nose and smelled the faint scent of almonds. The notebook was for writing, he thought, so that is what he did.

With a blue pen, its ink first dry then flowing, he wrote until the muscles in his hand and arm ached with strain. He wrote of fear and of failure and of worry and hope. The letters turned to words and soon filled the pages, and with each stroke, he found himself writing faster and faster, moving towards a place that he had no idea where it led. He rubbed his aching hand and closed the book, placing the pen horizontally across the front cover. It was at that moment that a great weight shifted, like a blockage that had kept him rooted to where he stood. It was still there, but it was lighter, and no longer hidden within. He sensed a feeling of hope and expectation, emotions which had long abandoned him.

And soon he found himself running; running out the door, down the stairwell and along the street. Once more onto the bus, this time smiling at those he passed. The bus drove through the streets and the great mountain range loomed far above, this time hidden by the darkness of night. But he knew it was there that evening, as it would be tomorrow. It had been there before Ellis had come onto the earth and would remain long before he would leave.

People got off as others got on, and soon Ellis was one of those to depart, walking with purpose. His hands soon felt numb from the cold of the night, and he inhaled deeply, breathing in the smell of wood smoke and thinking back to family camping trips, the memory bringing a feeling of joy and contentment. Still he walked, a clear goal and destination in mind, and he would not stop until he got there.

Up ahead he could see the streetlamps shining down on a small house, faint smoke drifting upwards into the crisp air from its chimney. When he got closer, he could see that its window frames had been painted white again, and he gazed at them as clouds moved to show the moon, illuminating all that lay below it.

A brass door knocker was lifted and all but crashed down on the wooden panel. Boom, boom, boom, it sounded, keeping pace with Ellis' rising heartrate.

Music could be heard from within and the smell of cooking only intensified as the door was opened, the warmth and light from the hallway rushing onto the porch.

'Shall we go?' asked Ellis quickly. 'Shall we?'

Andy stood in the doorway and stared down at the visitor. A dish towel was placed over his shoulder, with what looked like flour cast across his jumper. He blinked as the cold air met the warmth of his home, before a smile grew on the corners of his mouth.

On the street, a car reversed slowly onto the road. The driver waved to an unseen figure in the window of the house they had just left, then drove off into the night.

Printed in Dunstable, United Kingdom